'It s w,' he murmured. That muc ld the reassurance came out so much easier than the lies.

"Are we getting married tonight?"

He jerked back. "No!"

She stared at him, going even paler, and her green eyes were wide. He had the ridiculous notion to kiss her freckled nose. What was wrong with freckles anyway?

Her eyes narrowed as color flooded back into her cheeks. "When, then?"

Hell's bells, she thought he was Rafael.

"I'm Daniel. I'm going to be your brother. Rafael—"

He stared at her as the color drained from her face again. Her mouth flattened and her eyes shot shards of bottle glass in his direction. Then she shoved him away.

Katy Madison invites you to her

# WILD WEST WEDDINGS

*Mail-order brides for three hard-working,
hard-living men!*

Three penniless East Coast ladies are prepared to
give up everything they know for the lure of the West.
Will they find new beginnings, new families and
eventual happiness as mail-order brides?

Their advertisements answered,
three rugged frontiersmen await their new brides—
with eagerness and not a little trepidation!

What have they all let themselves in for?

Read Olivia's story in
*Bride by Mail*
already available

and

Anna's story in
*Promised by Post*

Look for Selina's story,
coming soon!

# PROMISED BY POST

Katy Madison

Published in Great Britain 2015
by Mills & Boon, an imprint of Harlequin (UK) Limited,
Eton House, 18-24 Paradise Road, Richmond, Surrey, TW9 1SR

© 2015 Karen L. King

ISBN: 978-0-263-24776-3

Printed and bound in Spain
by CPI, Barcelona

Award-winning **Katy Madison** loves stories. At the age of eight Katy went to her mother and begged for a new book to read. Her frustrated mother handed her a romance novel and Katy fell in love with the genre. Now she gets to live the glamorous life of a romance writer, which mostly means she stays in her pyjamas all day and never uses an alarm clock. Visit her at www.katymadison.com

**Books by Katy Madison**

**Mills & Boon® Historical Romance**

*Wild West Weddings*

*Bride by Mail*
*Promised by Post*

**Visit the author profile page at millsandboon.co.uk**

# *Chapter One*

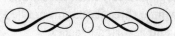

*California rancher, in good health, age 26, dark hair and eyes, seeks agreeable woman for purposes of matrimony. Interested parties send photograph.*

*San Joaquin Valley, California, August 1862*

Today was the day. Anna O'Malley slid her damp palm over the silk of her skirt and darted a furtive glance at her good friend Selina's pinched face. They would meet their future husbands in just hours, perhaps be married by nightfall.

The stagecoach rolled over a rut, and all the passengers swayed. "Are you nervous?" Anna whispered.

Selina pressed her lips together, looked at the other occupants of the coach, all men, and then gave a quick nod.

After traveling with the others night and day for twenty-one days straight on this last leg of their journey, they all knew as much about each other as they were willing to share. Across from Anna sat a California miner returning from a trip back east to settle his recently deceased mother's affairs. Opposite Selina was a one-armed soldier, mustered out of the army and hoping for a better life out west. Seated beside the soldier, a slender man wearing a threadbare suit cradled a case of paint jars and assorted brushes.

On the far side of Selina, a preacher dressed soberly in black bent over his worn Bible and mouthed the scriptures as they rumbled along. He was headed to a new flock in San Francisco. Three farm boys from Illinois riding on the back-seat preferred California over getting conscripted. The youngest brother looked as if he should still be in school instead of worrying about fighting in Mr. Lincoln's war.

Anna and Selina had reluctantly shared with the other passengers that they'd worked in a mill until the cotton shipments dried up over a year ago. The lack of work had forced them and their roommate, Olivia, to answer advertisements for brides. Knowing all they wanted to know about each other, the passengers' conversations had de-scended into banalities about the ever-changing landscape, the weather and the monotonous beans and bread offered at the eating stations.

Most of the trip Anna had been concerned that Selina's secret would be found out. But Anna could scarcely contain her own worries anymore. With each passing mile, her misrepresentations to her future husband had grown into massive cankers. She leaned close and cupped her hand around Selina's ear. "I didn't tell Rafael that I worked in a mill."

Selina's gaze flicked to hers. "Why? You had nothing to hide."

Who would want to marry a dirty Irish immigrant? Anna whispered, "I told him my family was well-to-do."

"Oh, Anna." Selina put her hand over hers and squeezed. "Anyone who knows the real you will love you."

Anna shook her head. She didn't believe that. She was nothing special. Not beautiful like her friends Olivia and Selina. Not American born as they had been. They hadn't been spit on for merely being Irish.

Anna's friends had at least come from respectable families with property before the deaths of their fathers had drastically changed their circumstances. Certainly no stranger with a spread would want a freckled working-class girl like her. She'd written that her father was a successful businessman and she was one of only four children instead of one of more than a dozen.

In reality, her four older brothers built railroads, dug canals or laid road, and they lived in shantytowns. Two sisters and her mother worked as maids for the kind of families she'd told her fiancé she came from. Her father had died of cholera barely five years after leaving their farm in Ireland. After his passing, they'd been evicted from their tenement apartment. She and the rest of her siblings had scattered to the mills and factories that would hire them.

Her parents had endlessly debated leaving Ireland for the land of opportunity. But that drawn-out decision had been one of the worst of their lives.

No Irish Need Apply signs had turned them away from the best jobs. Without their own land, they were powerless to gain stability. She was determined to marry a landholder. Selina might have found a store owner acceptable, and Olivia had wanted to be certain her future husband owned a real house, but Anna had quickly weeded through the newspaper until she found advertisers who owned land. With land came the power to live independently. She'd fired off responses pretending to be worthy of a good marriage before she'd thought about the dozens of ways her husband could eventually learn the truth.

The seemingly endless journey across the country had given her too much time to fret. She was better off when she just acted and didn't have a chance to worry about making the right choice.

Outside, the coachman cracked his whip, and the stagecoach jerked forward as the horses broke into a gallop. They bounced on their bench seats and grabbed for the leather straps. Anna cast a glance out the window, wondering if hostile Indians had been sighted. Maybe they had hit a patch where the driver felt vulnerable, or they had fallen behind schedule.

A rocky hill rose up beside the stagecoach until she could no longer see the horizon through the small opening. She leaned forward to look out the opposite window. The ground sloped up slightly less steeply, a fringe of the grassy meadow still visible beyond the rise, but they were in a gully or tight valley nonetheless. The stagecoach drivers didn't like these narrow spots and ran the horses through them. Her breath caught as she waited for the pace to ease when they reached safety.

"Ya, ya—get!" shouted the driver.

A shout in what Anna suspected was Spanish rang out. A shiver ran through her. Her husband-to-be was of Spanish descent, even though he wrote in flawless English and his surname was northern European.

Of course, there were a lot of Spanish-speaking people in California. Other than the Indians, the long-standing residents had arrived when Spain owned the land.

The brake was applied with a loud thump, and the thunder of the horses' hooves ceased with a jangle of the traces. The stagecoach screeched and jerked as the horses neighed. Wheels slid, no longer rolling. The occupants bounced around like beads in a baby's rattle.

As the skinny artist slid off the center bench with a thud, his bottles clanking, Anna leaned toward the window. Dust clouded the air, obscuring the road.

Selina grabbed her and tugged her back.

"We're being robbed," the miner said tightly.

They all sat still as stones as the driver replied in that same foreign tongue. They'd very nearly made it to Stockton without any of the incidents they'd been warned about: no scalping by marauding Indians, no breaking a wheel and being stranded dying of thirst in the desert, no toppling over and floating downstream in one of the many waterways they'd forded.

The preacher began a prayer, but the soldier shushed him.

The miner held up a hand. "He says he has accomplices in the rocks. If we don't get out, they'll shoot, but if we cooperate, no one will get hurt."

He squinted and tilted his head as he strained to listen to the exchange. "He says he's looking for a man who cheated him in Santa Fe, but if he's not on the stage, he has no affair with the rest of us."

Anna looked at the men one by one. The wide-eyed farm boys gripped each other's hands, and the soldier glowered at the silently praying preacher, while the artist carefully moved off the floor. None of them lowered their eyes or reddened with shame, nor were any of them likely to have been in Santa Fe lately, except the miner.

"Did you?" Anna asked their translator.

He shook his head. "I didn't cheat no one. Not in Santa Fe, not anywhere."

"Ain't me," said the oldest farm boy. "I ain't been to Santa Fe ever."

"I was fighting until three months ago," the soldier said. The pinned empty sleeve of his shirt moved as if to point out he'd been in a hospital until coming on this trip.

"He wants the passengers to get out," the miner said.

Anna got up from her seat and opened the door. "Soon as he sees the man he's looking for isn't here—"

Selina grabbed a fistful of her skirt and yanked, and Anna landed back on the seat. She couldn't risk ripping her only good dress, a dress Olivia had painstakingly made over from the stash of her mother's old gowns. It wasn't as if Olivia were there to sew the green silk back together again with her perfect tiny stitches. No, she was in Colorado with her mail-order suitor—likely her husband by now.

"It's just a ruse to get us out so he can take our valuables." The artist pressed his case of paints to his chest.

The driver shouted back.

"What did he say?" demanded Selina.

The miner held up his hand again. "He asked for the name of the man who cheated him."

There was a pause, and the robber yelled.

"He says the name doesn't matter. It was like as not false."

The sound of scrabbling above her head had Anna looking up as if a skylight might materialize to allow her a view through the roof panel. She hated not being able to see what was going on.

"The coachman told him if he put his weapons down on the ground, he'd let the male passengers disembark to be inspected," said their translator.

"I wish he would speak in English," muttered the preacher.

"Filthy Mexicans," the one-armed soldier mumbled.

Anna flinched. It was too close to the "dirty Irish" or "white Negro" epithets hurled at poor immigrant families like hers. Were those of Spanish descent looked down upon, too? Did they have to deal with the equivalent of NINA attitudes?

"We should just get out and get this over with," blustered the oldest farm boy. He put his hand under his coat and swung out the door. Gunmetal glinted under the edge of his jacket.

Her throat tightened.

"Hands up!" came the shout. This time in perfect English.

"Well, if he knows English, why isn't he using it?" the preacher asked.

"Don't do anything stupid," hissed the miner. "No one's been hurt yet."

The farm boy slowly raised his hands. His two brothers followed him outside, then the preacher with his Bible. The artist clinked his way out the door.

The miner and the soldier exchanged looks, then checked their revolvers. With their weapons tucked in the back of their pants, they climbed out. Unable to stand not seeing what was going on, Anna followed. Selina was half dragged, since she'd never let go of Anna's skirts. The preacher reached to hand them down.

There was a low call from above. "Ladies, get behind the stage and get down."

Anna looked up the road where the robber's voice had come from. A large boulder shielded him, but the bandit focused on her.

A cold chill ran down her spine, and her hands tingled.

Perhaps he wasn't looking for a man who'd cheated him, after all.

A shot blasted from the roof. A mule kick to the center of her chest wouldn't have jolted her more. She'd heard guns fired plenty of times, even fired them herself, but never at a man.

The robber raised his rifle and aimed. Passengers dived for the dirt. Pistols came out. The preacher knocked off her picture hat as he pushed her toward the rear of the stage.

The artist covered his head and hit the ground as the miner, the one-armed soldier and the two oldest farm boys fired.

The robber wheeled his horse all the way behind the massive boulder. Bullets pelted the stone and dirt where he'd been. Selina jerked Anna down to her knees.

A *pfft* overhead made Anna duck; then she twisted to look up.

A lasso swung through the air. The loop swirled around the outrider's shoulders. The rope tightened, and the rifle flipped out of his hands. The line snapped taut, toppling the man backward off the stagecoach.

The outrider hung in the air for the longest time. His hands wagged like flippers, the rope restraining his flails.

His gun thudded in the dirt, and the lassoed guard thumped down with a grunt. The panicked horses dragged the stagecoach forward, the locked wheels scoring the earth.

The rope from the fallen outrider led behind the stage to a man on a horse. A multicolored cape hid his lower face, and he was working swiftly to uncoil the line from his saddle horn.

"Anna." Selina tugged her.

The man looked directly at Anna.

It felt as if time had slowed to a trickle as she met his dark eyes. He stared back at her, and his hands stopped moving. Anna's heart turned over, and she couldn't look away. He briefly closed his eyes as if he needed a physical action to sever their locked gazes.

The rope dropped, and he spurred his mount away. Horse and rider raced up the incline beside the road. Leaning close to the horse, he moved with the animal's sleek muscular lines almost as if they were one melded beast. Then he was out of sight behind the grassy hill.

The breath whooshed from her lungs.

"The gun. Under my skirt," Selina hissed.

The spell broke. Anna sprawled in the dirt and grabbed the wooden stock. With Selina between her and the first bandit, she pulled out the rifle and positioned it against her shoulder. Anna checked her aim over Selina's shoulder. A thousand thoughts rolled through her head. That she hadn't fired this gun and didn't know if it would pull left or right. No wind to speak of. Roughly thirty yards' distance.

The mad firing around her stopped as the men's guns emptied. Her fellow passengers scrambled to reload. The bandit came out from behind his cover and took deliberate aim with his rifle. Methodically he shot. A crack. The hiss of a bullet. The miner spun. Another crack. The oldest of the farm boys yelped.

"On three, roll away," Anna said.

Selina's eyes met hers, and she gave a grim nod.

"One, two, three."

Selina rolled. Anna sighted down the barrel.

The terrified horses reared and stomped, neighing wildly. The driver fought for control. She was in the open, but so was the robber. She squeezed the trigger.

Daniel galloped his horse behind the large boulder where Rafael half sheltered. He reined in. "*Vamonos*, you *loco* idiot!"

"She shot me," said Rafael with such a mixture of shock and horror that something broke loose in Daniel.

He laughed. "Good for her."

"It's not funny. That *puta* shot me."

"You deserved it. What were you thinking?" Daniel grabbed the bridle of his brother's horse and spurred his own mount. If they decided to give chase, he wanted to be well away. But Rafael was right; it wasn't the least bit funny. "You shouldn't call her that. She was just defending herself."

"I wanted to see—" Rafael took his reins, yanked his poncho down to his shoulders and spurred his horse alongside Daniel's "—what my bride looked like."

"*La Madre de Dios*, you have a photograph," hissed Daniel. A photograph that showed her trim figure and her hair as light in color, but it failed to do justice to her.

"I've never seen a photo…graph…of her." Rafael pressed the heel of his hand against his chest.

*Ah, hell.* He'd never seen the photograph because Daniel had tucked it in his saddlebag for safekeeping and never turned it over to his brother. He'd handed over the rest that had come, but that one he'd held on to for just one more good look at the girl.

Heaviness pushed at Daniel as he tried to assess his brother's injury. Not that he'd ever expected Rafe to hold up a stage, but if handing over the picture might have prevented his brother from his foolhardy attempt to see what his bride looked like…

"We're going the wrong way," said Rafael.

"Because leading a tracker straight to the ranch is such a good idea." Daniel risked a look back. No signs of pursuit yet. The enormity of what they'd done slammed into Daniel like a bull at full charge. He'd just participated in a stagecoach— well, not a robbery, because Rafael hadn't planned to take anything—not that the law would be inclined to see it as anything less. A stagecoach holdup, then.

"Right," answered Rafael.

Why had his brother thought stopping the stage to get a look at his bride was a good idea? Daniel's stomach burned, and his head buzzed. "I can't believe you did that. Why would you shoot at them?"

"They shot at me first. I was only defending

myself," Rafael said. Grimacing, he pressed his palm against his upper chest.

"If you weren't shot, I'd shoot you myself," muttered Daniel. He jerked down the poncho he'd pulled over his face.

When Rafael had taken his new rifle, Daniel had followed him to get it back. Only he'd had to saddle a horse and then chase after Rafe for miles. He'd nearly caught up to his brother when they'd both seen the stagecoach rolling toward Stockton. Rafe had shouted back he was going to stop it, then spurred his horse toward a ravine the road ran through. Daniel hadn't wanted any part of stopping the stage, but his protests had been ignored.

"I knew you'd help." Rafael managed a smile despite the blood dripping down his poncho.

"I was just trying to keep you from being killed." Daniel jerked back on his horse's reins and caught the other horse's bridle, pulling it to a walk.

Daniel's head spun. He had to get Rafael away from the scene and back home before a posse was sent after them. "They could have recognized us or our horses, or, damn it, you could have killed someone."

A vee appeared between Rafael's eyebrows, and his eyes narrowed. The look of pain cut short the berating Daniel wanted to give him.

The enormity of what he'd done—*they'd*

done—poured over him in a cold wave, worse than the time they'd gone to the ocean and Rafael had pushed him into the frigid surf and left him gasping for air. Not for the first time he felt old, much older than his twenty-two years. Older than the hills, older than his reckless brother.

There were times Rafael didn't make sense. Over the past year, he'd been almost totally disengaged from the process of getting an Anglo bride, but he'd said he needed one to help their land case in the district court. Now he was acting ridiculously anxious. Daniel hoped a wife would temper Rafael's drinking, disappearing for weeks on end and gambling in the raucous San Francisco farther west. Holding up a stagecoach was far worse than anything Rafael had done before.

"Don't think I killed anyone," Rafael observed as calmly as if he were talking about shooting bottles.

"Did you hit any of them? And where is my rifle?"

"Dropped it when I got hit. I can't believe my bride shot me."

The moment Daniel had stared at his brother's fiancée he'd felt a punch to his gut. For a second it was as if time had stopped and he couldn't look away. They'd been too far apart for him to see the color of her eyes, but the way the sunlight caught in her hair, lighting gold and copper strands, had caused a shift inside him, almost as if the ground shook underneath him. "Well, at least she's pretty."

Rafael coughed and slumped in his saddle. "Not so much. Probably freckled."

"You'd better hope she doesn't recognize us."

Rafael's mouth tightened, and pale lines bracketed it. He coughed again.

As if Daniel had been lassoed the same way he'd roped the outrider, his chest squeezed tight. "How badly are you hurt?"

"Through and through." He spit. "Might have nicked a lung."

"I should have left you to die."

"You should have," said Rafael before he slumped forward.

# *Chapter Two*

*My father wants me to marry one of the respectable bankers or businessmen he has presented to me, but I find them all boring. I dream of living in the land of milk and honey, but I am accustomed to certain standards. Please tell me the size of your home and how many servants you retain.*

"Hey, he dropped that rifle," shouted the artist from behind the boulder where the first robber had taken cover. The artist had run up the road as the two robbers galloped away. "I think you hit him, Miss O'Malley. There's a bit of that cape here with blood on it."

The sunshine dimmed, and the ground tilted. Selina grabbed her. "Don't faint now."

She'd shot a man. Goodness, what if she'd killed him? No, he'd been shooting at them. She'd done what she had to do. But there was a world of difference between shooting rabbits or squirrels on the outskirts of the city to supplement her family's meager diet and shooting a human being.

"That was a great shot, ma'am," the outrider remarked, awkwardly bending to pick up his rifle. "Where'd you learn to shoot?"

"My brothers taught me," Anna managed. A lady never would have shot at anyone. Likely a gently bred lady never would have come close to a gun. Back in Ireland, her brothers had insisted she learn because they'd believed America was still beset by wild savages and knowing how to shoot would save her. They hadn't encountered any wild Indians in New York. But when her next-in-age brother couldn't see well enough to shoot the small game she pointed out, she had been able to take the shots for him.

"Right fine shooting, ma'am." The oldest farm boy had his hand clamped over his right arm. "You saved us. Thought we were goners when all of us had to reload at the same time."

Anna shook her head. How likely was it that a young woman of breeding would know how to shoot a gun? But then the green silk dress didn't cover a lady, just another poor immigrant whose family had fled Ireland after the potato famine ruined them. "I just got off a lucky shot when the robber left his cover."

The soldier stared at his bleeding forearm, probably hoping he wasn't about to lose his remaining arm. That wasn't right. A fiery ball fisted in her stomach. Selina turned toward him. The miner leaned against the stage and cussed a blue streak.

"Sirruh," objected the preacher.

If she were really a lady, she likely would have fainted dead away at his language.

"Damn," Anna muttered. And she certainly wouldn't have known any swear words, either. Dropping to her knees beside the shot farm boy, she lifted her dirtied skirt, ripped off a clean petticoat ruffle and wrapped it around the young man's injury.

How was it all the men bore wounds in their right arms? Their shooting arms. And only the men who'd had guns. The artist, the preacher and the youngest farm boy had not been wounded. The middle farm boy picked up the bent gun from where it had been shot out of his hand.

She twisted, taking in details. How could the man's shots have been so accurate? *Dear Lord.* Her heart pounded and her hands shook as she secured the makeshift bandage around the young man's arm.

"There were at least three of them," said his middle brother.

Her dry mouth tasted like copper and dirt.

"Or four," added the youngest farm boy, bouncing on his toes, his eyes bright.

His excitement sickened her. Lives had been on the line or at least the life of the man she'd shot. She'd aimed for his chest, but it looked like he'd intended to just disarm the men shooting at him. Which was pure foolishness. Any gunshot could prove fatal. Including the one that had come from her.

Nausea churned in her stomach while hot shards throbbed in her veins. She shook her head. "No. There weren't. There were two."

One hadn't fired a single shot. No, he'd roped the outrider and yanked him from the roof before he could shoot a second time.

She fumbled with the makeshift bandage. Her hands wouldn't hold steady. She couldn't have hit the side of a building if she tried to shoot the rifle now. She could barely tie a knot.

"She's right. There was the one behind and the one in front," confirmed the guard, who couldn't seem to straighten all the way. His face twisted as he braced his palms on his thighs.

Anna scrambled over to the miner while Selina bandaged the soldier. Whatever injuries the outrider had sustained in his long fall, the men with bullet wounds needed attention first.

Trying to keep her face composed, she urged the miner to sit and lean against the wheel as she ripped open his sleeve. A deep gash ran across his upper arm. Blood welled in the wound. Her stomach turned again, and she swallowed hard. She bunched another strip of petticoat ruffle and pressed it against his arm.

The miner sucked air between his teeth.

"Sorry," she muttered.

"No. Thank you," he said. "Much as I hate to think a girl saved us, you did. Wait'll they hear about your shooting in town."

"Oh, no." The last thing she needed was being made into a heroine. "I just was lucky enough to have the rifle fall beside me. Over that distance, it's hard to be accurate with a pistol."

"Reckon so," said the soldier. "But most folks ain't got the gumption to shoot a man when they've never done it before."

"Well, I didn't have time to think about it." Sour acid burned her mouth, and her eyes watered. She'd shot a man. She pressed the back of her hand against her mouth for fear she was going to be sick. Oh, goodness, she'd shot a man—a robber for certain—but she'd never wanted to shoot a man.

The driver finally calmed the horses, and he climbed down from his perch. "We need to get to Stockton as quick as we can. There's a doctor there."

He drew to a halt and gaped at her dress. "Are you injured, miss?"

She followed his gaze to a smear of blood on her sleeve and another on her skirt. "It's not mine."

Her bodice was filthy; the dust of the road was streaked all down her front. Oh, no, this was her best dress. Her only good dress, really. The dress she planned to wear while being married. She brushed at the dirt and added a new blood smear. A lock of hair slipped from her head and in front of her eyes. She reached up to feel the whole mass of the once-neat bun hanging lop-sided on her head.

She must look a fright. What would Rafael think when he saw her? He'd never think her a lady. A real lady wouldn't have jumped out of the stagecoach, shot a robber or looked like a raga-muffin. No, a lady was always clean and properly coiffed and didn't sweat as if she'd been digging ditches. Her hat lay in the dust of the road, and surely her fair skin was freckling under the harsh midday sun.

If they pulled into town and he saw her like this, he'd likely put her on the next stage back.

Anna tried to think what her friend Olivia would have done in this situation, but the truth was Olivia would never have been in this situa-tion. Olivia had probably never touched a gun in her life, let alone known how to fire a one. Anna hadn't even made it to Stockton and already it was clear she wasn't genteel in any sense of the word.

Daniel had to get his brother home fast, but he couldn't lead a posse directly to their ranch or they'd be dead men. Plenty of the newcomers to California didn't trust Mexicans and would be glad enough of an excuse to hang Rafael and himself, even though Daniel was only half-Mexican.

"Are you going to fall off?"

"I'll try not to," answered Rafael. He coughed up a frothy pink spittle.

"Damn." Daniel's insides went watery. A lung shot meant the wound could prove fatal. "I need to get you to a doctor."

"Can't. Home." Rafael straightened in the saddle. "Doctor won't do anything Ma can't do."

If he took Rafael to the doctor in Stockton—likely the same doctor the men his brother had shot would see—the jig would be up. Everyone would know Rafe was the man who held up the stagecoach.

Besides, until recently there hadn't been any doctors around. Men healed or they didn't. A few years back when one of their vaqueros had been thrown from his horse, he'd broken ribs and been spitting blood the way Rafael was. Madre had wrapped his ribs and kept him in his bed. He'd been as good as new in a month. A doctor couldn't do any more. Trying to get Rafael to San Francisco and a doctor who didn't know him would likely aggravate the injury Rafael had.

Glancing over his shoulder, Daniel didn't see any sign of pursuit, but they couldn't wait around. He would have to patch Rafe up enough that he could make it home—fast.

He drew up alongside his brother. "Is anything broken?"

Rafael moved his shoulder in a small circle. "Doesn't…seem so."

Daniel tugged off the stupid poncho Rafael had thrown at him just before stealing his rifle and galloping off this morning. He wished he hadn't followed or that he'd turned back sooner.

He should have lassoed him, would have, if he'd had any idea that Rafe would stop the stage as if he were robbing it. When Rafael had tugged his poncho over his face, he should have realized.

Using his bowie knife, Daniel hacked the bright material into strips and knotted a make-shift bandage around his brother's shoulder. Then he tied Rafe to the saddle, just in case he passed out. That his brother didn't protest knotted Daniel's neck.

"We have to go," said Daniel. He scanned the horizon, looking for a dip or a cluster of trees and shrubs that would indicate a waterway. They were at least twenty miles from the edge of their ranch. Making sure they didn't leave tracks leading straight back would make it thirty, but the detour had to be taken.

He took the other horse's bridle, headed toward what looked like the best possibility and prayed that no one would come across them.

Hours later, they finally drew their horses to a

halt in front of the house, and Daniel dismounted. Fortunately, their hands were all out on the north range with the cattle.

Rafael was trying to untie himself, coughing. He'd said next to nothing for the past hour they'd run the horses toward the ranch. His face was chalky, but he'd held his own for miles and miles of hard riding.

"Madre!" Daniel shouted.

He untied Rafael. Dismounting, Rafael collapsed. Daniel staggered under his brother's solid weight.

"Madre!" Daniel shouted again. "I need your help."

Rafael opened his mouth, but ended up coughing again. He gestured and they turned to step onto the long wooden deck.

"I am cooking. Do not shout at me," their mother retorted.

Rafael pointed at his chest and then raised his hand toward their house. "Tell...her."

Daniel steered his brother, who was now weaving like a drunk. "Ma, Rafael's hurt."

Their mother appeared in the open doorway, her dark eyes open wide. She took one look at her older son and ran forward to help. Her footsteps shook the planks under their feet. "What happened?"

"He's been shot," said Daniel.

"What did you do, Daniel Werner?"

"I kept him from being killed," Daniel told her, not that he expected his mother to appreciate that fact.

"How could you let him get shot? On the day his bride comes?" demanded Madre.

"Leave him 'lone, Ma," said Rafael. "Not his fault."

Their mother narrowed her eyes and glared at Daniel. In his younger days, he would have expected the paddle when she looked at him like that. Now he was just tired of everything being his fault. Defending himself to his mother was just wasted breath. He'd stopped trying years ago.

"Let's just get him inside. You'll need to plug the hole in him and get him bandaged up."

"You'll have to get Anna." Rafael panted.

"No." He couldn't go get Anna. The moment when they had locked eyes crowded out his other thoughts. For that one minute all the rest of the world had melted away, and he could see nothing but her. Her image was seared into his brain.

Daniel shivered.

His brother's bride had gotten a good look at him, too, the best look at him of anyone on the stage. Granted, he'd pulled the poncho up to his eyes, but if anyone would recognize him, it would be her.

"She can't know," Rafael groaned.

"Why not? Daniel, what is going on?" Madre

likely would have put her hands on her ample hips if she weren't helping to support Rafael.

"Tried to stop stage," said Rafael.

"Why would you do that?" She lapsed into Spanish, calling on the saints and muttering indignations.

"He wanted to see Miss O'Malley. But people who stop stages are generally robbers." Daniel glared at his brother.

"Did you do nothing to stop them, Daniel?"

"He…tried," huffed Rafael.

His brother's shortness of breath worried Daniel.

Madre shot him a dark look as they maneuvered Rafael through the doorway. "It was just a misunderstanding."

"There was a gunfight," Daniel said. "I don't think anyone is going to call it a misunderstanding."

"You shot at people?" screeched Madre, but she was looking at Daniel.

Rafael met his eyes, and Daniel closed his.

"No, Ma. Daniel didn't shoot at all," Rafael said and then stopped to pull in some breaths. "I did."

"You would not defend your brother?" she demanded of Daniel.

"God, Ma." Daniel tensed and then lowered his voice. He had no idea where the girl who helped Madre about the house was. She might be in earshot, although he hadn't seen her. "It wasn't my intention to help him stop a stagecoach. Now we can't let Miss O'Malley know, or who knows what she'll do."

"Listen to him, Ma." Rafael heaved in a whistling breath. "'S right. Anna can't find out."

"Oh, my poor angel." Madre stroked Rafael's hair.

All the way home, Daniel had just been thinking he had to get Rafael home before he collapsed, but now a hell of a lot more problems had to be dealt with.

"No one can know that it was Rafael, Ma. Otherwise they might arrest him." Of course, he'd be arrested, too. And they'd both be hanged. Daniel's throat tightened as if a noose were already strangling him.

"Go…get her…late," mumbled Rafael. "If no one…"

If no one picked her up, people might wonder what was amiss. If even a whiff of suspicion came their way, they might suspect Rafael had something to do with the gunfight. It wasn't fair that a lot of the new white settlers looked down on people of Spanish descent, but they did. He would have to go get Miss O'Malley. And Rafe was right; it had taken them so long to get back, he'd be late.

"Did they see your horses?" asked Madre. "You will have to get rid of them. Shoot them."

A shudder ran down Daniel's back.

He looked out at the winded animals that had galloped their hearts out getting them home. His mount bore a white blaze on its forehead and the single stocking on its back leg made it identifiable, and even though Rafael's horse was a solid dun, the color was unusual enough to stand out. "I'm not shooting the horses."

"Then you will get your brother hanged over a misunderstanding." Madre glared at him. "You will shoot the horses."

"Because that wouldn't be a dead giveaway that we were involved," muttered Daniel. She couldn't be serious.

"You will do as I say," Madre hissed.

"Ma," Rafael protested on a puff of air. His voice was too faint. Madre turned her attention back to her favorite son.

"We just need to take care of Rafe." Daniel steered his brother through the door, bearing most of Rafael's weight.

"You still have to get rid of the horses," she said.

Madre was right. The horses had to go, but he wasn't shooting the poor animals.

"I'll set them loose in the hills. I'll tell the sheriff and your—" Daniel found himself unable to say *bride* for some strange reason "—your Miss O'Malley that the horses were stolen overnight, and you're out tracking the horse thieves. That'll explain why I'm picking her up and provide cover if anyone recognized our horses."

"Good thinking," Rafael murmured.

They passed through the long front section of the house into the open courtyard. "Get him patched up enough to hide his injury. Plus Miss O'Malley will need her own room."

"But you were to go to the priest and marry her before leaving town," said Madre.

"Can't hide…gunshot from…a wife," huffed Rafael.

Madre opened her mouth to say something.

"Open his door and get his bed ready, Madre," Daniel said.

She threw back her shoulders and glared at him. She would hate that he was ordering her around, but he didn't have time to coax cooperation out of her. Instead, he poked Rafael, so he'd prod her. Rafe had much better luck getting their mother to do things.

"Please, Ma." Rafe slumped against his brother.

They staggered across the courtyard toward Rafe's room.

Pressing her lips together, she hurried ahead to open Rafael's door and yanked down the covers on the freshly made bed.

"Damn, this messes…up…every…thing."

Daniel leaned close to his brother. "You'll just have to wait until you're healed to marry her. Tell her you're giving her a chance to get to know you before…" Daniel's ears heated as he thought of his brother bedding the pretty redhead. Not that women ever seemed to require a long acquaintance with Rafael before they were willing to share intimacies with him. In fact, they rarely even noticed anyone else in the room once Rafael flashed his smile at them. Although, neither of them had a lot of experience with respectable women. "After all, she's been raised to expect courting."

Anna wasn't the kind of fancy piece men traveled to San Francisco or into Mexico to find. She was a rarity in California: a respectable unmarried woman. Even back when the rancheros had gotten together for regular fiestas and the daughters of the other ranch owners were there, they'd gravitated toward Rafael and all but ignored Daniel.

"But…" Rafael frowned.

"With Madre in the house, there is no impropriety."

Rafael lowered his eyelids in an almost sleepy look.

Daniel wanted to kick him for even thinking about seducing his future wife. He shook his head at the odd spurt of jealousy.

Daniel got Rafael on the bed and backed toward the door. "You got this, Ma?"

"Daniel, you stay here and help," ordered Madre.

"He needs t' go." Rafael insisted. "Can't let it get any later."

* * *

The light grew murky as Daniel neared the edge of town. He'd run the horses as much as he could but had had to slow them to a walk rather than look as if he was in a crazed hurry.

First he'd pick up Anna, then head to the sheriff's, report the horses stolen and determine what the sheriff knew. Really, though, the idea of a rancher with one of the biggest spreads around stopping a stagecoach was ludicrous and the best protection they had against the law putting two and two together.

He tried to slow his breathing. If she recognized him from that moment when they'd looked at each other, he didn't know what he'd do.

He turned onto the street with the stage office. In the gloom, a woman in white instead of green sat on the bench. A broad-brimmed hat with flowers covered her hair so he couldn't see if it was red. Still his heart thundered in his chest. He just knew. It was Anna.

He drew closer and pulled the horses to a stop in front of her. The minute he saw her face, he couldn't look away. His muscles tense, he waited for a glimmer of recognition.

She stood up, her gloved hands twisting in front of her. "Mr. Werner?"

"Yes." Belatedly, he realized he couldn't know her beyond her photograph. "You're prettier than your picture." *What a stupid thing to say.* "Miss O'Malley."

She inclined her head, blocking his view with the wide straw brim of her hat. Then she met his eyes.

He tightened his hold on the reins, waiting for her to recognize him. Her head tilted.

She heaved a deep breath that made her chest rise and fall under her white gown. "I was beginning to think you'd never come."

He dragged his eyes away from the lace over the material that covered her chest, but in reality added an extra layer. Forming words with his suddenly too thick tongue he said, "There was a bit of trouble back on the ranch."

His throat clogged, and he had to clear it. He had to get down out of the wagon before she started to wonder what was wrong with him. Forcing his rigid body to move normally, he set the brake and wrapped the reins around the handle.

"It has been a trying day," she said in a small voice. "When are we going to the ranch?"

She couldn't be the one who shot Rafael. She'd have trouble swatting a fly. He swallowed a deep breath. The lies he'd rehearsed on the way into town threatened to choke him. "I'm afraid I need to speak with the sheriff before we leave."

"Do you know, then?" Her face paled, and even in the dim light it made the scattering of freckles across her nose stand out. "About the robbery?"

Alarm jolted through his chest. Daniel tried to sound casual. "What robbery?"

In the normal course of events, he wouldn't know about the stagecoach shooting yet. Attempting to smooth out the jerkiness his body seemed intent on imposing on him, he lowered the tailgate and waited for lightning to strike him dead. Damn Rafael for putting him in a position where he had to layer falsehood upon falsehood.

"There was a stagecoach robbery," she said.

Daniel missed a beat as he tried to figure out how to respond as if he didn't know. He stared at her and had to take a deep breath to force out what was likely the appropriate response. His hand fisted so hard his fingers cramped. "Are you all right?"

"I'm fine." The waver in her voice suggested she wasn't.

He wanted to kick his brother for terrorizing an innocent woman. But Rafael must have it wrong. It must have been the other one who'd shot him. Anna's friend, Selina, the one coming to marry the store owner.

Daniel stepped toward her. The urge to comfort her pulled at him.

The questions he should be asking jumbled in his brain. He knew she hadn't had anything stolen, but a man in his position would ask. "If anything of yours was taken, we can buy new. Send back east."

She hurtled forward and tossed her arms around his neck. "I was so scared."

The contact of her body set him on fire. His breath whooshed out. *Hell and heaven.*

He hesitated. He hadn't the right to hold her. She was his brother's intended, but she trembled. She drew him like a lost calf would. Wrapping his arms around her, he pulled her against him.

"It's all right. You're safe now," he murmured. That much was true, and the reassurance came out so much easier than the lies.

Damn, she felt delicious. Her breasts were against his chest, and her nose was tucked into his shoulder. Her scent—sweet, spicy—fogged his brain. He wanted to hold her forever.

"Are we getting married tonight?"

He jerked back. "No!"

She stared at him, going even paler, her green eyes wide. He had the ridiculous notion to kiss her freckled nose. What was wrong with freckles, anyway?

Her eyes narrowed as color flooded back into her cheeks. "When then?"

Hells bells, she thought he was Rafael.

"I'm Daniel. I'm going to be your brother. Rafael—"

He stared at her as the color drained from her face again. Her mouth flattened, and her eyes shot shards of bottle glass in his direction. She shoved him away.

Damn. He'd never let her loose.

"What was that?" she demanded.

Now she seemed like a woman not afraid to turn a gun on a man instead of the waiflike thing she'd seemed when he had driven up. Thank the Lord she'd be Rafe's problem, because the last thing Daniel ever wanted was a strong-willed woman, no matter how good she felt curled against him.

# *Chapter Three*

*We have six hands that work the spread and you'll have my mother and a girl to help you with the house. A neighbor comes in twice a month to do laundry. Life is probably simpler out here than you are used to. The hands all live in the house with us and we share meals like one big family.*

"Comfort?" *Daniel* Werner said.

Anna searched the dark eyes of the man before her. His hug had felt nothing like what one of her brothers might have given her, and it had set off a riot of sensation deep inside her. But he was to be her brother-in-law, not her husband.

She wanted to drop through the boards under her feet or to smack him. But she'd thrown herself at him, not the other way around.

"You went through a lot with a stagecoach robbery." He screwed up his nose and had the grace to look slightly sheepish. He reached for his forehead as if to adjust a hat, but then ran his fingers through his uncovered dark hair. "You have a trunk?"

Grateful for the reprieve, she turned around and pointed to the lone bags left on the walkway. There was nothing to do but march to the wagon and climb onto the seat. Then, of course, she realized a gently bred lady would have waited for assistance. She tried to gather herself together and ignore that the past few minutes in Daniel's arms had been like a homecoming.

The minute she'd seen him, a sense of familiarity had come over her like a soothing bath, but he was the wrong man. She'd gone easily into his arms and felt welcomed and wanted by a man who would be her *brother-in-law*. Could the day go any more wrong?

Then again, as she watched her soon-to-be brother-in-law lift her trunk as if it weighed nothing, her stomach did somersaults. She tried to draw her eyes away from his broad shoulders, his easy stride. For heaven's sake, she couldn't dwell on the solid breadth of his chest against hers, but the thoughts and prickly sensations wouldn't leave her.

God help her, his brother had better be an older version of him. Surely he was. Surely it was just a brotherly familiarity that had her heart galloping. Or the relief of knowing she had a home to go to after thinking she might have been abandoned. Or rejected outright for shooting a man.

She tried to shift through a thousand different thoughts. "Why is Rafael not here?"

"He's tracking horse thieves." Daniel thumped the trunk down into the bed of the wagon, set her carpetbag beside it and scowled. "We had some stolen last night."

Horse thieves and stagecoach robberies. A shudder passed through her. "Are we going to the hotel, then?"

"No. To the ranch. It's only a little over three hours' drive. We'll be home by midnight. But first I have to tell the sheriff."

"But there's been an armed stagecoach robbery and horses stolen from your ranch. I don't think it is safe to travel after dark." Not for three hours. Maybe fifteen minutes. She looked into the dark hills beyond the town. Going out there with criminals roaming around didn't seem like the smartest idea.

"It's perfectly safe," said Daniel as he threw a leather strap over her bags and secured it to the wagon's sides.

"Did you know about the attempted stagecoach robbery?"

His hands stilled. He had lovely hands, the fingers long and strong with a scattering of dark hairs across the tanned backs. "We don't get the latest news until we or our hands come to town."

He finished tying the strap, walked around and swung up beside her with a lithe grace.

"Is California so lawless? Is it normal for criminals to be running around?"

"No, it's not normal." He sounded terse as if her question bothered him.

"Then how can you think it is safe? The robber shot several men." And she'd shot him. If he was the vengeful sort, she could be in deep trouble. Bad enough she had to wear her old Sunday best dress to greet Rafael—dressed all in white she was an easy target in the dark.

She didn't want to tell Daniel that she'd shot the robber, because he would tell his brother and then she'd be exposed for the fraud she was. She just needed to convince him to stay in town and she wouldn't have to reveal why she feared being targeted by the robber.

Daniel turned and looked at her. "My rif—my shotgun is just behind the seat." He pulled back a leather flap and showed her. "Right here. I'll protect you, but really no robber will be out in unfamiliar territory after dark."

"How do you know it is unfamiliar territory? Do you know who stopped the stagecoach?"

Daniel's gaze shot away. "We have to go."

Anna stiffened and gathered her resolve. "I want to stay in town overnight. There is a hotel."

"No."

Anna scrambled for the edge of the seat to jump

down. She wasn't comfortable with the idea of going off alone with a man she didn't know, a man who had hugged her intimately with one arm curling around her, fingers almost brushing her breast, and the other pressing her to him. "How do I know you are who you say you are?"

He caught her arm. His grip was sure and firm. "If you want out that bad, I'll help you down, but we're going to the sheriff's first. He'll identify me. Besides with the stage coming in today and the packet ship leaving tomorrow, the hotel is bound to be full."

Anna settled back on the seat. His words and low, measured tone made her want to trust him, but she didn't want to go to the sheriff. That she'd shot one of the robbers would come out. She'd just have to keep the sheriff from revealing her role and have him tell Daniel how bloodthirsty the bandit was—the one who had done the shooting—and convince him it was unsafe to travel with that man out there.

"He's just a couple of blocks over," Daniel said.

She knew that to be true. After the sheriff had allowed her to change and clean up in his quarters, she'd spent an hour sitting in a hard chair explaining what she'd seen, because she'd been the only one who'd gotten a good look at the second horseman. But when she'd tried to reveal details, she had been unable to tell them anything, beyond that his hat was low and his multicolored cape was pulled up below his dark eyes. At least she thought they were dark. She couldn't exactly remember if she could see the color from as far away as she was. That she'd felt mesmerized by his gaze she had kept to herself.

"Why couldn't Rafael come for me tomorrow?" She'd had to fight through her disappointment that he wasn't there earlier to shield her from the barrage of questions the way Selina's beau had shielded her friend. Of course, the stage had been early after they had galloped into town to get the shot men to the doctor.

"I'm here now, and we can't travel to town at the drop of a hat. We have work to do. Besides, he'll be worried if you don't get in tonight."

Not so worried that he'd come after her himself. She pressed her lips together. Surely the sheriff would be on her side when it came to traveling out of town in the dark.

In front of the sheriff's office, Daniel set the brake and climbed down. He walked around and offered his hand to Anna. He had to convince her to leave with him tonight. He had to get back and set the horses free in the hills, then make his way to where he and Rafael had climbed out of the creek bed and obliterate their tracks before a tracker could find the spot. He hoped the false trail he set would lead a posse in the opposite direction. Hiding the truth was against his nature, but he couldn't let them arrest Rafael. The very idea of losing his brother drove a spike through his chest and ripped it straight down, cleaving him in two.

His brother might have behaved like an idiot, but Rafe had been there for him when his father had died, stepping up and teaching Daniel how to ride, how to shoot, how to ranch, even though he'd barely been old enough to know how himself. They'd grieved together, gone everywhere together and grown up together. Rafael was his brother and best friend; he couldn't risk the truth as much as lying pained him.

Anna slipped her hand in his with an odd demureness that seemed out of keeping with her argument to stay in town.

Daniel had to pound on the door to get the sheriff out of the back, where he lived.

The paunchy middle-aged man opened the door, and a triangle of light spilled out. "What is it, Danny?"

Daniel wished people wouldn't call him that anymore. He'd turned twenty-two some time ago. Folks should recognize he could be addressed by his regular name now. "We had horses stolen last night."

The sheriff looked at him for a full second. Daniel's stomach turned over. Did the man have any idea he was staring at one of the men who'd held up the stage? Damn, Daniel hated lying to people who trusted him. Using the currency of his reputation for being honest and fair dealing made something inside him shrivel and wither. How would he ever face the townspeople again if they learned he had lied?

The man mopped a kerchief across his brow and looked pained. "Never rains, but it pours. Come on in."

Daniel reached for Anna's elbow and guided her in front of him. Somehow touching her calmed the stew of dismay churning in his stomach.

She crossed the room and sat in the chair by the desk. He started to cross to the other chair when he spotted his rifle leaning against the wall. For a second he froze, his foot in the air. Damn Rafael for dropping the rifle he'd taken from him.

The condemnation of his brother shamed him. Rafael wouldn't have dropped the rifle if he hadn't been shot. Blowing out a long breath, he turned to the woman who'd pulled the trigger. Her gaze darted away. She dropped her head, leaving him looking at that monstrosity of a hat. Not that it was her fault for shooting Rafael, either. He blamed his brother, but he couldn't let Rafael hang or go to jail for a misguided attempt to see his bride.

The sheriff tucked in behind his desk. "Now, what did these horses look like, and what would you say their value was?"

The sheriff held a pencil poised above a blank piece of paper. Daniel described his horse first, the blaze and the one sock, then Rafael's. Then because the sheriff seemed to be waiting and perhaps the two horses matched too exactly, he described his brother's favorite piebald stallion.

He bit his tongue hard before suggesting the horses had been stolen by the men in order to rob the stagecoach. He wanted the sheriff to reach that conclusion, but forcing it upon him would be to paint the lily. During his hurried journey into town, the story had seemed to make sense, the inferences obvious, but now the wild concoction seemed to have more holes than the grounds basket for a coffeepot. A drop of sweat itched down his spine as he waited for the sheriff to reject his story.

The sheriff frowned. Was he now thinking that it could have been the Werner brothers who stopped the stage? "Where is your brother?"

"He went out to track the horse thieves. He wasn't back when I left." Daniel's stomach knotted tighter and tighter as he made up excuses. "He told me to come get Miss O'Malley if he hadn't returned in time."

The sheriff glanced toward Anna, then back at Daniel. Heck, he wished the man wouldn't do that. The silences were like the screech of splitting wood, and Daniel fought to keep his shoulders level instead of up around his ears.

"Sound like the horses you saw?" the sheriff asked Anna.

"It could be." She leaned toward the desk. "There are some very bad men out there."

Daniel tensed. Even though the sheriff was drawing the conclusion Daniel wanted him to draw, it only served to darken and twist his insides. He wanted to scream out he was lying. Instead, he recited an Ave Maria in his head—the first of the ten thousand or more he would be required to recite when he confessed his lies—unless God struck him dead first.

"Think it might be a couple of renegade banditos—Mexicans. They spoke in Spanish." The sheriff set his pencil down and leaned back in his chair. "Do you agree, Miss O'Malley?"

"I wouldn't know, sir." She shifted in the chair as if it had suddenly grown uncomfortable. "I just know they are very dangerous. Murderous men."

That wasn't fair. He hadn't fired a shot and Rafael had only winged the armed men to halt the shooting, not to kill, but he couldn't make that argument. Daniel wanted nothing more than to run a finger under his collar, but he tucked his hand in his belt, willing it to stay still. Certain his every expression gave away the deception, he watched the sheriff.

"Any chance your brother could help track tomorrow?" asked the sheriff. "Sent one posse out, but they lost the trail. Going back out in the morning. Reckon Rafe'd be an asset with his skills."

"I don't know that he will want to, with his

bride here and all." Daniel cast his eyes toward Anna. If he helped track, he could steer them away from the real trail. More lies, but Daniel couldn't let them know Rafael was injured. For years his brother had protected him, and if this was what it took to repay that, he had to get past his misgivings. "I could do it. He's taught me what he knows."

"Which is why we should stay in town tonight," Anna said brightly. Then, as if she was afraid he might get a word in edgewise, she continued rapidly. "Tell him, Sheriff, how dangerous those men are and we should not be out on the road after dark. Why, we'd never see them approaching. And if we stay here, then Mr. Werner can be part of the posse in the morning."

*No.* Daniel tightened all over. "I— We have to get you back to the ranch tonight. Madre—my mother will worry. Rafael will worry. Besides, the thieves are probably already in Mexico." He tore his gaze away from Anna and cast a quick glance at the sheriff. "I'll come back at first light."

Anna shook her head. "It's too dangerous, isn't it?" She looked from the sheriff to him.

*Damn.* Her mouth looked adorably kissable, pink lips slightly open as if she was breathless. Daniel's head spun. He tried to remember the reasons it was so urgent to get home.

"Danny's right. They're probably halfway to Mexico by now." The sheriff leaned his chair back farther and nodded toward the gun in the corner. "And they lost their rifle."

"I have a gun in the wagon," Daniel said belatedly. Then it seemed like the wrong thing to have said, even if it was the truth.

"If you were to encounter any thieves, I reckon the two of you could take care of yourselves. The Werner boys are both great shots and you're not so—"

"Fine, I'll go." Anna popped out of her seat so abruptly, Daniel stepped back.

The sheriff nearly fell backward off his chair before he managed to stand.

"But it is the height of absurdity. If I'm killed, I'll hold you personally responsible."

She flounced toward the door.

"Well, here, you might as well take this with you." The sheriff leaned over and scooped up the rifle. "Don't expect the owners are going to be back for it."

Daniel was almost afraid to reach out and take his gun. A cold sweat broke out all over his skin. It was too easy.

"Reckon Miss O'Malley has a better right to this than most, seeing as how she managed to shoot one of them robbers and made 'em give up and run off."

Her back went rigid, but she continued out the door. What had changed her mind all of a sudden?

Daniel reached out to take his rifle. All right,

the thing belonged to his brother's bride, and he'd probably be able to use it, even if he couldn't claim ownership. As he went to pull it back, the sheriff didn't let go.

Oh, hell, did he know? Chills snaked through Daniel's veins. Had the sheriff just been toying with him to trick a confession out of him?

"You remember, son, that's your brother's bride." The sheriff let go of the rifle.

Daniel stared at him. His brain was moving awfully slow because he'd expected a warning or an accusation, but not one about Anna. "I know that."

The sheriff nodded. "I'll see you at dawn, Daniel."

Anna clasped her hands tightly in her lap. She wanted to keep swiveling around, checking for men following them. Except a lady of breeding and refinement would rely on a male escort to protect her.

Besides, genteel ladies didn't fidget. The almost preternatural calm that Olivia always managed was not normal. Still, Anna hoped she could salvage her image as a pampered rich girl seeking adventure, not a desperate Irish immigrant who'd spent five years working in a mill, because her only choices were marriage to another poor immigrant or working her fingers to the bone.

They'd been driving for some time, and Daniel had said little since leaving the sheriff's office. The bench seat was hard, unlike the padded seats of the stagecoach, and every bump jarred her teeth. If she relaxed, it wouldn't be so bad, but her thoughts kept scouring the same ground. No man wanted to marry a woman who'd shot a man. No rancher would see her as a fitting bride if she didn't know her place as a woman. Other women might see her as a heroine, but most men would see her as a freak.

"So you shot one of the banditos," said Daniel.

"I'd rather not talk about it," she said tightly. "And I would appreciate it if you wouldn't tell your brother."

Daniel leaned forward and twisted to look at her. "Don't think it is the kind of thing I could keep from him."

"I should hate for his first impression of me to be that I go around shooting people. It's not very ladylike."

Daniel's mouth twitched. "Shot anyone else?"

Her jaw dropped. "No! Of course not. I haven't even handled a gun in years."

"Then I think we can count it as an aberration," he said.

"It makes me sick just thinking I shot a man today, even if he was trying to kill us."

"I would think if he was trying to kill you, some of you would be dead," said Daniel tersely. He leaned back against the board that served as a backrest.

"That's an odd thing to say." She bit her lip. Though the fact that every wound was to the shooting arm of a man who'd pulled a gun had not been lost on her. Her brother once told her that the eye was drawn to muzzle fire and consequently so was the aim. That was just as likely an explanation for the similarity in wounds as thinking he just meant to disarm the men shooting at him. She certainly didn't want to risk depending on the imagined benevolence of a renegade who'd shot four men.

"Did you get a good look at them?" Daniel asked, his voice less smooth.

"Not really. They had their faces covered."

Daniel blew out. "Chances are we'll never catch them."

"You will try."

"Huh?"

"Tomorrow when you try to track them. You will do your best to find them, right?"

"'Course. They took one of my favorite horses." He slowly smiled, his teeth shining white in the moonlight.

Her breath disappeared in a whoosh, and a tickle wiggled through her belly and lower. No, this was not good. "Does your brother look like you?"

His expression went flat. "Yes. We're 'bout the same height, same hair, same eyes."

Same breathtaking smile? "What's he like?"

Daniel's jaw ticked. He took a second before answering. "He's a good rancher."

Which told her nothing. She sighed. "So will you tell him about the shooting?"

She gave up the pretense of being a perfect lady and folded her arms.

"Doubt if I'll have to." Daniel twisted the ends of the reins around his hand as if he felt the urge to fidget as strongly as she did. "Not much farther now. We're on Werner land."

If they were growing close, the time she would meet her affianced husband was drawing near. Her arms prickled with gooseflesh and a shudder ran through her.

"If you're cold, there's a blanket behind the seat," said Daniel.

Would Rafael be so aware of her every move, too? If he was, she wouldn't have a chance of persuading him she was anything other than what she was: an undeserving Irish immigrant who had lied about everything.

# Chapter Four

*Goodness, only one maid to help. Life must be much simpler. We have a dozen servants and two groomsmen. I can only assume it is because the population is so sparse. I am sure I will learn to make do.*

After miles of nothing but grassy hills, they crested a rise and drove down into an open valley. A long, low and pale building loomed out of the darkness ahead. Anna's heart fluttered with anticipation.

As she leaned forward, Daniel said, "That's the house."

Her future home. She tried to make out details as they approached. It seemed rather large, although only one level. Beyond the house a barn and fenced corral were barely discernible.

They pulled in front of a long wooden porch. Only moments away from meeting her intended, her palms grew damp. She scanned the porch, waiting for him to come out.

The house was nothing like she'd ever seen back east, and its foreignness only contributed to her uneasiness. Surely the creak of the wagon or the jangle of the harnesses would have been heard from inside. Yet no one had come out to greet them.

Her throat went dry. Anticipation at meeting her future husband, surely. "Where is Rafael?"

Daniel looked uneasy as he set the brake. "He might not be back yet."

She had the oddest urge to grab Daniel's arm and hold on. "I've come three thousand miles, and he isn't here to greet me?"

"He planned to pick you up, but with the stolen horses…" Daniel's voice trailed off as he hopped out of the wagon. "You should just come inside, and we'll see what's what."

When she slipped her hand into his, tingles traveled up her arm. She jumped rather than attempt to find footholds in the dark and hold Daniel's hand any longer than necessary. Even though the thought of driving away occurred to her, she didn't intend to do anything so silly. No, this was to be her home, and she'd enter as if she deserved to be here.

He moved to the back of the wagon and shouldered her trunk with ease. She swallowed hard. She could not keep from looking at her future husband's brother as if he were a refuge in this strange and frightening world of horse thieves and stagecoach robbers, where shooting a man seemed all in an ordinary day's events. Plus she didn't have a promise from Daniel that he wouldn't tell his brother. Far from thinking her a refined eastern lady, Rafael's first impression would be of a hellion who had shot a man.

"Through that door there." Daniel nodded toward the dark porch.

So no particular welcome for her, unless Rafael waited inside. Her heart leaped into her throat, and her knees wobbled like jam. She stepped onto the planking, and her boots clunked shockingly loudly against the boards. She was about to tiptoe when the door swung open. *Rafael?* Hot and cold streams rushed through her.

"You are finally home," said a short, round woman with dark hair sparsely threaded with silver.

Her hopes dropped like stones through her insides. Still, Anna tried to draw on the mask of a lady and not let her disappointment show.

"Madre, this is Miss O'Malley. Miss O'Malley, our mother, Consuelo Valquez Werner." Daniel thumped up onto the low porch, her trunk hoisted on his shoulder.

Anna jerked to a halt and debated protocol. Should she extend her hand to her future mother-in-law? Press her cheek to hers? But she'd been too busy contemplating meeting her intended to think about proper greetings for his family members. "Pleased to meet you, Mrs. Werner. I'm glad to finally be here."

"Come in, come in," said the woman warmly. "Oh, I am so happy to see you. Welcome to our hacienda." The woman enfolded her in a hug. "I have tamales for you."

Well, that took care of that. Perhaps Rafael would hug her next. Perhaps the family hugged everyone, and she'd overreacted to Daniel's embrace. Anxious to get inside and see if Rafael was waiting for her there, she peered through the open door. The angle was too much to see inside. Perhaps he was waiting with flowers or candy. That would be exciting and, she supposed, would render his failure to collect her in person forgivable.

"Is Rafael back?" Daniel asked in a very still voice. A cautious voice.

Why was his tone so careful, like a warning? Confused, Anna turned and looked at him. He ducked away as if her scrutiny made him uncomfortable.

"*Sí, sí*, but he is *mucho* hurt. He fall from his horse and hurt his shoulder. I have put him to bed." Mrs. Werner waved her hands wildly. "I give him medicine to sleep."

"Goodness," said Anna. She should go to him, but if he was in his bed… No, she was to be his wife. "I will go to him."

Mother and son seemed to exchange some silent communication, where Mrs. Werner's brow furrowed, and she gave a tiny shake of her head. "No, no, you must sit. He is sleeping."

Daniel moved through the room around a long table that seemed as if it were cut from one piece of wood, but much bigger than was possible. Anna stared at the table, not knowing what to do and trying hard not to twist her hands. "Is he badly hurt?"

"No, no," answered Mrs. Werner. "Just sleeping."

"Won't you wake him? Wouldn't he want to know I am here?" Anna asked. How could he sleep knowing she was arriving today? Did her fiancé feel none of the strange anticipation that was rattling through her?

"Better to let him sleep," said Daniel.

How would he know that? She looked between Daniel and his mother. "This isn't right. What are you hiding from me?"

Mrs. Werner spoke in Spanish. A chill ran through Anna, spinning her back to the shouts of the robber. She shook off the odd connection. This was California, and it had been part of Mexico until recently. Probably a lot of the locals spoke Spanish. And not that anyone had said, but Daniel, with his near-black hair and coffee-colored eyes, was at least part Mexican. His mother, with her darker skin and round face, looked completely Mexican.

Daniel frowned. "I'll take your trunk to your room and see if Rafael can be woken."

"Thank you," Anna said tightly.

He went out through the open door opposite where they had entered, which seemed to lead outside. How was that possible? The house looked so much bigger from the outside. Either that or she'd lost all sense of space. She felt a little as if she'd entered one of those crazy tilted houses at a fair. The ones where they could make water run uphill.

Mrs. Werner bustled up to her, her dark skirts rustling. She wrapped an arm around Anna's shoulders and steered her toward the table. "You sit here. I will feed you."

Anna fought the urge to fling off the woman's arm. She didn't want to eat or sit. She wanted to meet her future husband. "I'm really not hungry, thank you."

"Sit. Tell me—how was your trip?"

"Long." She stared at the door Daniel had gone through. How could it have led outside?

Her stomach knotted. Well, she wasn't just going to wait around forever. She'd been traveling for months. If Rafael was here, she didn't see any reason she couldn't meet him now. She got up and stalked toward the door.

Mrs. Werner moved in front of her and put her hands on her hips as if Anna were being rude.

"Daniel will tell Rafael to come eat with you, if he is awake. You sit now."

She sat in the chair she was led to because it didn't seem she had much choice in the matter. In the low light of tin lamps, she stared at the unending grain of the table. Even that was impossible and made her feel off-kilter.

Mrs. Werner shouted in Spanish, and Anna nearly jumped out of her skin. A few seconds later a girl on the verge of womanhood entered through the open door. The smell of beef and maize wafted through with her. The girl carried several plates, looking as if she might drop them at any time. "This is Juanita. She helps out."

"How do you do, Juanita?" Anna resisted the urge to spring to her feet and take dishes from the overburdened girl. A genteel lady would be used to being waited upon.

As Juanita moved to set the plates on the table, a big brown glob plopped right on Anna's chest and slid into her lap, ruining her second-best dress.

Back in Connecticut Olivia had helped her turn the seams and they'd boiled it in borax for hours to rejuvenate the white. Still in places the material was damnably thin and the ruffles along the bottom covered hems that had frayed and worn through. Her hopes were wearing just as thin.

Now with it stained and the green silk filthy, she had little left to wear except a few work dresses. Even those weren't clean. She'd worn them over the long stage trip and washdays hadn't been in the schedule.

Mrs. Werner berated the girl in rapid-fire Spanish, while Juanita stared at the floor, her shoulders up around her ears. At least Anna rather suspected she was being berated. Anna just wanted the crazy, disappointing day to end. "That's enough. It was just an accident."

Mrs. Werner started. Her eyes narrowed.

Anna started to shake. She had no idea what a woman of breeding would do in this situation, but she was in no mood for any more ugliness. "It has been a long day. I believe I will retire. Juanita, will you show me my room and help me out of my gown?"

Perhaps if she rinsed out the stain soon enough, it wouldn't set. She had less hope for the green silk. Blood was always difficult to get out.

"She doesn't speak much English," said Mrs. Werner.

Anna was torn. She really didn't want to leave the girl alone with Mrs. Werner.

"Then translate for me." Anna glanced toward the open door, wondering what was keeping Daniel. She had visions of him going through her trunk, unpacking her unmentionables. Heat washed through her. From mortification, she assured herself.

"You need to eat," Mrs. Werner insisted.

The girl lifted her gaze from the floor and stared at Anna with dark accusation as if it were Anna's fault Mrs. Werner was angry with her.

Anna's stomach churned, protesting. She wasn't exactly sure of the food that had been set down before her. Long yellowish things with a sort of brown gravy and a plate stacked with round flat bread. "Excuse me, please."

Really what she wanted was a nice roasted potato dripping with butter or a hot slice of soda bread. Neither of which were likely to appear. Nor apparently was her fiancé.

If neither Mrs. Werner nor Juanita would show her to her room, then she'd find it herself, or find Daniel to guide her. Why had he disappeared for so long? How long did it take to put her trunk and carpetbag in her room and rouse Rafael? Or was Rafael not willing to meet her?

She headed for the door that Daniel had gone through. Juanita darted out ahead of her. For a second, Anna suspected the girl would push her back in to eat whatever it was that had been set down in front of her.

"I show you room."

"Thank you, Juanita." But mostly she was speaking to the girl's back as she darted ahead along the covered walkway that encircled an open center of the building. Anna stared at the stars over the wall ahead of her. Juanita went to the corner, turned right, following the interior of the building, then opened the first door. Beyond the girl, Anna's trunk sat at the foot of a narrow bed.

"You come to marry Rafael, *si*?" asked Juanita.

"Yes."

Juanita glared. "Fool—foolish are you. The ranch belongs not to him."

*What?* "Who does it belong to?"

"Go home."

*Go home?* She didn't have a home to go to.

The girl darted off. Anna stood stock-still for a second. What on earth was Juanita trying to tell her? Rafael didn't own the ranch. She'd pinned everything on coming here to marry a man who would take care of her, make sure she had regular meals, a man who owned his own land. Her legs muscles tightened as her stomach burned.

Her shoulders stiff, she returned to the main room. "Mrs. Werner, Juanita says the ranch doesn't belong to Rafael. Is that so?"

"No, no, she did not say that."

"Yes, she did."

"I tell you her English is very poor. She say it wrong." Mrs. Werner waved her hands wildly and looked away. "Of course the ranch belongs to Rafael. You do not worry. Juanita is a silly child who thinks Rafael will marry her when she grows up. You forget what she say."

The reassurance didn't settle her one bit. This was not how she had expected her arrival to be. No, she needed to meet Rafael and have him straighten this out. The sooner the better. Otherwise she wouldn't be able to sleep a wink.

"I have to get back, or Miss O'Malley will wonder what is taking me so long." Daniel had put Anna's trunk in the room next to his and hurried across the courtyard to Rafael's room. He hadn't been certain from their mother's look how his brother was faring, and he was relieved to discover Rafael in pain but completely lucid. They had to get through the next few days without Anna realizing he'd been shot.

"You need to meet her," Daniel said. "You'll have to pretend you're well long enough to say hello."

The bandage starkly white against his skin, Rafael groaned and rolled to the side. "Can't."

"She is already confused by me fetching her instead of you." Daniel pulled his brother's legs off the side of the bed. He'd get Rafe sitting, then get him dressed and standing.

Rafael grunted a protest.

"Just hold it together long enough to say hello." Daniel tugged on his brother's arm until Rafael was halfway upright.

Rafael ran a hand through hair that was matted and sticking up on one side. Had he been thrashing around?

"You look like hell." Daniel scrutinized his brother. His stomach fell. Rafe wouldn't fool anybody looking like he did. "Do you really think it wise for Ma to give out that you have a shoulder injury?"

The corners of Rafael's mouth turned up for the barest second as if he'd meant to smile. "Got to give a reason…couldn't track…the horse thieves."

Daniel's shoulders slumped. His brother had a reputation as a great tracker to protect. He, on the other hand, was going to have to "fail" to follow the tracks tomorrow to save them from discovery. "Wonderful. I can't fake a fall to explain why I won't be able to track the stagecoach robbers."

"Not a robbery."

"If you didn't want people to think it a robbery, you shouldn't have covered up your face, stopped the stage in a pinch point and pointed my rifle at the driver. If all you really wanted was to see your bride, you could have hailed them in an open spot and asked for her by name. And you dragged me into this mess. We'll be lucky if we aren't hanged."

"Sorry," muttered Rafael, which was unlike the sarcastic "You're welcome" he usually would have shot back.

Daniel snatched a shirt out of Rafe's wardrobe. "Try and get yourself together well enough to greet her. You can pretend to be groggy. Ma said she gave you something to sleep."

"Wish she had." Rafael rolled back onto the

bed. His shoulder hit the pillows behind him, and he groaned. "She took away my whiskey."

But not before he'd indulged, Daniel noted.

If Anna figured out they were the men who'd held up the stagecoach, she might very well go to the sheriff and turn them in. Speaking of her, he should probably go back to the main room, but he needed to tell Rafe that she didn't want him to know she'd shot a man. "Rafe, she—"

A sharp rap on the door raised the hairs on the back of his neck.

"Mr. Werner, are you in there?"

*Damn. Anna.* Sounds didn't carry through the thick adobe walls, but Rafael's window to the courtyard was open to allow a cross breeze. What had she heard?

Rafael shooed him toward the door. "She can't see…this," he hissed, pointing at the bandage.

Daniel tossed the shirt in Rafe's direction as he went to the door.

Anna stood on the other side, a shawl draped over her chest although the evening was warm. "Is your brother in there?" she demanded.

"Yes, I was just checking on him." Daniel reached to take her elbow and guide her back to the main room. "You can't have eaten already."

Anna wrenched her arm away and darted toward the open door. "I want to see him."

Daniel caught her around the waist and pulled her back before she could get past him. Squirming against him, she was like a kitten with claws. Heat, need and want slammed him hard. It had to be the feel of a woman against him, nothing more. He lifted and planted her in the courtyard and pulled the door shut behind him. "He's sleeping."

Anna scrambled away and swung around to face him. "No. He's not. I heard you both talking. Why are you trying to hide him from me?"

"What did you hear?" Daniel asked sharply.

Anna's eyes narrowed, and she stepped closer. "Something about whiskey. Is he some kind of drunkard? Is that why you and your mother won't let me near him?"

Daniel let out a slow breath. If she thought Rafael a drinker, that was far better than thinking he had been the stagecoach shooter. "I'm afraid he's not fit company—"

"I'll have you know I've seen drunk men before." She poked him in the chest. "And I'd like to see him."

Her breasts rose and fell rapidly. Words deserted him with a heavy rush. He stared, knowing he was going to have to say something, but the swirling thoughts in his head were nothing he could have said out loud.

She flipped open the shawl. "Is this what you're looking at? The second dress I've had ruined today."

It took him a second to realize she was talking about the brown blotch in the center of her chest. His gaze was more drawn to her curves. Her breasts would fit perfectly in his hands. His palms even itched. *No, this isn't right.*

"I've come clear across the country. I've had a very bad day. I want to meet your brother. Now."

He dragged his gaze up to her pursed lips, only that was worse. He wanted to claim them and soothe the anger from her. "Anna."

"What?" she retorted, then squinted at him.

He didn't have the right to call her by her first name. "Miss O'Malley, it would be better if you saw him in the morning." Surely Rafael could manage to be up long enough to meet her. "You are tired. He is—" Daniel struggled for the right words "—not up to meeting you tonight. Everything will be better in the morning."

She stared up at him. Her skin glowed under the light of the moon. She was so fair. Her lips parted, and he wanted to close the distance between them, reassure her, distract her, taste her.

No. He didn't. She was completely the wrong sort of woman for him. After dealing with Madre all his life, he wanted a biddable woman, one who wouldn't fight him at every turn.

"Does he drink, then?" she asked in a low voice.

"We all drink," said Daniel, folding his arms. Lying to her made his head hurt, but he hadn't actually lied, and Rafael did occasionally drink more than he ought to.

"He isn't really hurt at all, is he?" Her expression fell. "That was just to keep me from seeing him in the state he's in. That's why you had to get me." She wrapped the shawl tighter around her shoulders. "I knew this was too good to be true."

The urge to hold her, comfort her, returned full force, but comforting her was a dangerous thing. He'd reacted too strongly when she'd thrown herself into his arms in Stockton. And the way he'd been thinking about her made touching her again foolhardy. He tightened his hold across his chest just to be sure he didn't brush the hair back from her temple. Didn't trace a finger along her smooth cheek. Didn't kiss her.

"My brother is a good man, he just…" Daniel floundered. *Occasionally loses himself.* He didn't understand Rafael's recent reckless streak. Ever since he'd returned from a hearing in Sacramento about getting the title issued for his land, he'd been acting odd.

Anna's chin tilted up, and she pinned him with her gaze as if to say she wouldn't tolerate any falsehoods.

"He's a hard worker—the hardest worker I know. And after my father died, he taught me everything."

"Your father?"

Daniel's skin heated. "We had different fathers."

Her fingers twisted the edge of her shawl. "Is he at all like you?"

"I try to be like him," answered Daniel with painful honesty. Except on days like today when Rafael behaved like an idiot.

His *loco* behavior had started about three years ago, around the time of the hearing. Was his foolhardiness just because of that hearing? Granted, he shared Rafael's fear that the request for the land title could be denied. The treaty between Mexico and the United States was supposed to honor the established land grants, but the United States was forcing the rancheros to prove ownership.

Two of their neighbors, men who spoke little English and whose families had been on the land for decades, had lost their claims, while an Anglo man who'd become a Mexican citizen to get his land grant and then switched his allegiance to the United States when California was ceded by Mexico had his title in a matter of months, unlike the years it was taking everyone else. It appeared that whites were much more likely to receive a patent for their land than Spanish were. But Daniel didn't understand why Rafael was acting as though their case was hopeless. Not all the claims were denied. Besides, if it was hopeless, why bother marrying an Anglo bride to improve the odds?

Anna watched him silently for a moment; then her chin firmed and jutted up. "I'd still like to meet him. I'd rather know what I shall have to deal with. And I'd say he's likely to be worse in the morning."

With a small toss of her head, she started to step around him. Daniel caught her shoulders and pinned her against a post to the covered walkway. "You would see him at his worst, yet you don't want him to know that you shot a man?"

The moonlight caressed her face. His breath was sucked from his body. Her eyes glittered. She didn't look down or away as another woman might in her place. He tried to remember he hated such boldness in a woman, but, damn, his blood thickened.

"A thief and would-be murderer," she corrected him firmly.

His brother wasn't a murderer or a thief, but Daniel struggled to keep the objection to himself. So far she hadn't recognized him. Didn't suspect anything beyond Rafael being a drunkard.

"And I just think it best if he hears it from me." Her features had a mulish cast. "When I am ready to tell him."

She had a point. He cocked his head, studying her. "Fair enough, but don't wait too long or he will hear it from someone else."

She shuddered ever so slightly. Perhaps she had been frightened. He lightly massaged her shoulders and cursed himself for an idiot. He told himself to drop his hands, step back, but he couldn't. Wanting to soothe her and reassure her, he stepped closer and lowered his voice. "He's a good man— you'll see. He won't hold it against you that you defended yourself against a man you believed was intent on harm."

"He *was* intent on harm," she insisted. "Someone had to stop him. The rifle fell right by Selina, and she knew that I had fired a gun before." Another tremble ran through her. "I had to shoot."

No, she hadn't needed to shoot, because in another three or four seconds he would have dragged Rafe away, but Daniel couldn't say that.

"He was looking right at Selina and me," she whispered. "There were two of them and—" her pause spoke loudly of fears a lady couldn't voice "—two of us."

*Damn Rafael.* Daniel's stomach turned. She'd likely thought she and her friend were about to be kidnapped and then raped.

"It's all right," he murmured. "Don't think about it. You are safe here."

The less she thought about it, the less likely she would be to connect them to what happened.

"This is a very lawless place," she said.

"No. Not usually. And I promise I will make certain those criminals will never be seen again."

"How?" she demanded.

Because if Rafael had a wild idea like that ever again, Daniel would hog-tie him. But he had to reassure her in a way that made sense. "I'll track them tomorrow. I'll make sure they never come near here again. You're part of our household now, and I always protect my own."

She turned her head sideways, and her chin quivered. *Santa Maria*, she wasn't about to cry, was she? She turned back toward him and placed her hand on his chest. "Thank you, Mr. Werner."

His heart thudded. Could she feel it racing under her palm? His fingers tightened on her shoulders as he looked at her mouth, the slight bow of her upper lip, the cherry pink of her lower.

He should say something, but words flitted out of his brain before they were fully formed. Then he was leaning toward her, knowing he was going to taste those lips, knowing it was wrong yet not knowing how to stop.

"Whash all thish noishe?" slurred Rafael.

Daniel froze. Tension screamed through his muscles as he looked over his shoulder. Rafael leaned against the door frame.

Daniel sucked in a deep breath and then said, "It appears you will meet my brother, after all."

## Chapter Five

*Even with such a large herd the land is often empty, so my brother experiments with grapes and other fruits that grow well in this temperate clime. But I should not bore you with descriptions of our work and will tell you about the mountains and hills.*

Anna stared at the man behind Daniel. Rafael. Her intended. Not even the tiniest flicker in her belly occurred. Nothing like the flutters she had experienced when Daniel pulled up in Stockton.

Daniel stepped to the side. Her husband-to-be lolled against the recessed wall of his doorway as if he wouldn't remain on his feet otherwise. She stared at him feeling as numb and empty as her coin purse.

Well, it wasn't as if she had anywhere else to go. Besides, he owned a great deal of land, the hired girl's cryptic warning aside. She'd just have to make the best of it. She took a step forward. "I'm glad to finally meet you."

He gave a nod that nearly toppled him over.

Giving him an opening to explain or apologize, she said, "I expected you to pick me up in Stockton. I thought that was the plan."

"No," said Rafael.

"I would have thought…" She would have thought he would have wanted to see her, been just a wee bit eager, but, no, he'd stayed home and gotten drunk. Her mouth tightened.

"Thought what?" prompted Daniel.

Some drunks were mean. Would Rafael be one of those? "You're not what I expected from your letters."

Rafael flashed a smile, but it never reached his narrowed eyes before it was gone. "And you're more…spirited than I knew." He pushed away from the wall, then weaved before plunking back against it with a grunt. His brow knit. "Hear you…shot a man."

She gasped. Cold water thrown in her face wouldn't have shocked her more. She turned toward Daniel. He had the grace to look away. He'd not only ignored her request but hadn't warned her he'd already told Rafael first when he'd brought it up.

"Did you even wait five minutes before telling?"

He couldn't have.

"Guess not," Daniel said. He glared at his brother even as he moved closer to him.

Of course his loyalty was to his brother, but after he'd just told her he protected his own and she was part of that circle, his betrayal was a punch to the gut.

Well, that was how it was to be, then. She stiffened her shoulders and looked back at her future husband.

Rafael looked on the verge of being ill.

"I hope you're not a mean drunk."

"Of course he isn't." Daniel leaped to his brother's defense. Like her own brothers, they might be angry with each other, but they would defend each other to the death if any outsider stood against them.

Rafael squinted at her. She supposed he was waiting for some justification from her. If she planned to make this work, she couldn't just smack him for being drunk or making *spirited* sound like a defect.

"The men in the stagecoach were missing their shots," she explained. "I had to do something."

"No need…to shoot…anymore. I'm a crack shot." Rafe puffed as if the words had required a great deal of effort. How much had the man drunk? "And Danny alwaysh hi's his targets, don't you?"

"Usually," muttered Daniel.

"I'll protect…you." Rafael lifted the hand he'd

braced against the wall and waved it expansively. "No one will get…you…here."

His knees buckled, and he scrabbled at the wall.

Scowling, Daniel caught his brother. "I need to put him back to bed."

"Yes, do that," said Anna. "I find I am tired, too."

She spun back and headed to the room with her trunk. Halfway there she pivoted. Both the brothers stared at her, while Daniel appeared to bear Rafael's weight.

As Daniel had said, they were much alike. Same build, similar height, same dark hair and eyes. Daniel's face was squarer and his jaw stronger. Rafael appeared slightly more classically handsome with high cheekbones and a smoother brow. Although anything he gained by reason of his appearance, he lost in her esteem by getting drunk before greeting the woman who'd traveled over the breadth of the country to be his wife. And if he thought she was too *spirited* or she shouldn't shoot, well, he'd just have to learn a thing or two.

"I want my rifle with me." She folded her arms. "Where is it?"

"What rifle?" asked Rafael. "Why's *she* have a rifle?"

"The rifle the robber dropped," Daniel said. "The sheriff gave it to *her*. Some folks appreciate good shooting."

She thought Daniel might have whispered

something more to his brother, but she wasn't certain.

Rafael lurched forward, then stumbled. "*You* don't need a gun."

Daniel steadied him.

"It is mine. You are in no condition to fire a weapon. And you have no right to tell me what to do. Yet." Good grief, if she let him make her angry, he might decide not to marry her at all.

"Hey," protested Rafael.

Daniel shook his brother. "For what it is worth, Rafe is sorry he couldn't pick you up in Stockton. He said as much before you knocked on the door."

The apology—belated as it was—came from the wrong brother. She wasn't certain she believed Daniel, but he was at least aware of her disappointment, whereas Rafael probably wasn't aware of too much. Her betrothed was a drunkard.

Suddenly her body felt made of lead and too heavy to hold upright. After weeks of traveling in a stagecoach night and day, she should be thrilled merely to have a bed to sleep in. But the thought of having shot a man and quite possibly mortally wounding him left her restless.

She told herself it could be worse. She could have killed the robber outright. Or Rafael could be an ugly, mean drunkard and he could have lied to her about owning a ranch.

On the bright side, it did appear that meals were readily had—that was an improvement over her life in Connecticut, even if the food was strange. The house was much larger than she'd expected, big enough to leave open ground in the middle. And there was a lot of land. Daniel must have the right of it. Tomorrow everything was bound to look better, and she'd have the day to get to know her fiancé.

She would marry Rafael. Even if he wasn't what she hoped, life with him would be better than what she'd come from.

"It is my rifle now, and I want it. Is it still in the wagon? I'll go get it."

"I'll bring it to you," said Daniel. "After I get him to bed."

Rafael grunted and wobbled.

Daniel braced a foot and pushed him back upright.

She had seen strong drink affect her father and brothers. More so since life seemed to keep throwing them punches and they couldn't find the security they'd enjoyed back in the old country.

But Rafael owned a large ranch, had a loving and supportive family. What reason had he to drink other than he had had second thoughts about marrying her?

Daniel supposed life had greater ironies than having to hand over your own gun to the woman who'd shot your brother. Or having to steal your own horses so you wouldn't be suspected in a robbery. Or perhaps being responsible for tracking yourself. Then again, nearly kissing your brother's future wife, just because she looked in need of a kiss, might top the list.

Rafael sagged against him. "Hell. Didn't know...be so dizzy."

Daniel pushed him into the room and pulled the door shut. He guided Rafael to the bed. Then, just in case Anna was inclined to eavesdrop, he shut the window to the courtyard. "You rest. You have to get better fast."

Rafael eased back, reclining against the headboard. "Hard to breathe."

A chill ran down Daniel's spine. "I'll go get a doctor."

"No." Rafael glared at him. If Rafe really thought he was dying, he wouldn't turn down a doctor.

"Guess you've made it this long without—a sawbones will only tell you to rest and quit drinking."

Wasn't as if they needed one to dig out a slug; the shot had gone straight through him. He lifted Rafe's feet and put them on the bed. His brother was likely just impatient with his weakened state. He wasn't used to being bed-bound, but an injury like he'd sustained needed time and rest to heal. When the cattle were being branded, gelded or culled for slaughter, Rafe wouldn't sleep more than an hour or two a night until the work was done. Once when he'd been laid out with a bad case of influenza, he'd kept trying to work until Ma dosed him with enough medicine to make a horse sleep.

Rafe heaved a couple of breaths. "'Sides, if I die things will be…right."

His stomach knotting, Daniel stood by the bed. "No, they won't. You'll just mess up everything. So don't."

"Ranch'll be yours." He breathed using all his body. He held out his hand. "Don't let Ma—"

"Stop it. You're not going to die." Daniel took the proffered hand and squeezed. He couldn't face the idea of going forward without Rafael, so he determinedly shoved the possibility away. His brother had managed to get himself out of bed and stood—well, mostly stood—for a good ten minutes. He wasn't on death's doorstep. "Stop being a crybaby."

Rafael gripped his hand hard. "Listen."

Daniel rolled his eyes and tugged his hand free. Much as he adored his brother, he wanted to shake him. Still, he didn't need Rafael getting all riled up. He needed him resting and getting better. "What?"

"Don't let Ma tell you…shouldn't be yours."

"Okay, Rafe." Daniel looked over his brother. Rafael's grip was strong, although his breathing was labored. But surely a man who was going to succumb to a gunshot wound would be worse after twelve hours, not much the same, perhaps even a little better. "You're just being stupid. Again. You're not dying. Although you should be after the stunt you pulled."

"Talk to the lawyer." Rafael coughed weakly. He rubbed a hand across his sternum. "Hell. That hurts."

"If you were going to die, you'd be unconscious by now," Daniel said firmly. He held out the carrot that should make any man look forward to the future. "And you're going to get married soon."

"Fine." Rafael grabbed his sleeve. "You'll have to occupy her…'til this heals."

Thinking of the near kiss, Daniel groaned. "I can't do that."

"You have to."

There were a lot of things Daniel had to do: take the horses into the hills, get their mother on board with the new story that Rafael was a sot, get the rifle out of the wagon before Anna fetched it.

They couldn't take a chance on her looking into the paddock and recognizing the two horses they'd been riding this morning, but spending more time with her was a bad idea. "I'll supposedly be tracking the thieves tomorrow."

"Tell her I'm tracking, too." Rafael rubbed his chest again. "Then I can spend the day…recovering."

Which would make Daniel have to deceive her again. He had done nothing but lie to Anna since he'd first met her. Still, pretending Rafael had gone out to track would buy him time to heal. Daniel ignored the sour taste in his mouth at the thought of more falsehoods. "Fine. I'll get Ma to occupy her."

"Ma's loco. You."

Daniel didn't see the point in arguing any longer. "Right now I have to take her *my* rifle that *you* dropped. You have to get better so you can buy me a new one."

Rafe flashed his teeth in a way that probably would have been an annoying grin if he weren't in pain. "Go. Tell Ma to check on me through there." He pointed to the room's side door.

If Madre was constantly checking on Rafael, nursing him—and she would—he couldn't expect her to distract Anna for long. Daniel blew out an exasperated hiss. "You better heal fast."

After unhitching the team and putting them in the corral for the night, Daniel retrieved his rifle from the wagon.

When he entered the main room, his mother greeted him with a round of complaints about Anna turning up her nose at the food she'd been cooking all day. Hell, if his mother took a disliking to Anna, getting her to keep Anna busy wouldn't work. "I'm sure she's just tired, Madre. I'm hungry. I'll eat it soon."

He spent the next few minutes explaining why Rafael was a drinker.

"No, not ever!" his mother said emphatically.

Which was doing it a little brown, because Rafael did occasionally drink to excess. But Daniel didn't want to spend the night arguing with her. "This is a good thing, Ma. A better pretense than him having a wound in the same place as the robber."

Madre twisted her mouth. "No. I will never say this about my Rafael."

*Of course not.* Daniel added the coup de grâce. "Rafe thinks it's a good idea. Then he can make Anna believe she is saving him from drinking." Or had his mother forgotten why she wanted the marriage in the first place? Their mother hoped settling down would cure Rafe's increasingly dangerous recklessness, and Daniel hoped for that, too. That was why he'd gone along with the scheme to get his brother a bride. And if Rafe thought an Anglo bride sitting next to him in district court would help them get the title to his land affirmed, then that was good enough for him. "You should go around and check on Rafe. He's having trouble breathing."

"He would never drink so much he falls down. He is a good man. You never should have let him behave so foolishly. You should have warned him they will think him a robber instead of stopping the stagecoach for him to see his bride."

Daniel walked out on his mother's rant. He'd probably hear it worse when he returned. But first he needed to get Anna settled in and asleep before he took out the "stolen" horses.

He was tempted to remove the rest of the rounds from the repeating rifle; instead, he carried his gun with the three remaining rounds to Anna. He had to soothe her. The last thing they needed was her looking for excuses to leave. At least if they kept her on the ranch, she couldn't tell anyone if she recognized them.

But the longer Rafe went before showing improvement, the more likely it was that she would put two and two together. Right now Rafe could barely stand—couldn't without something to lean against. He'd never succeed in hiding the gunshot wound from Anna. Preventing her from learning the truth fell squarely on his shoulders.

She sat on her bed, the door open to the night. A nightgown lay on the bed beside her. His heart thumped oddly at the sight. Her hair was down and plaited into a long braid, which she tied with a ribbon as he watched. He wanted to unravel it and let the molten strands slide through his fingers, across his body, splay it out on his pillow.

Her gaze jerked up, and he was caught staring and thinking things he had no business thinking. She stood and crossed the room.

"Sorry it took so long. Had to put the animals in the corral." Not to mention settling Rafe and filling in his mother. He thrust out the sack he held.

Her eyebrows rose; then her gaze lifted to his face and she took the cloth bag, testing the weight. "Ammunition?"

"Almonds." Well, at least she realized the gun was useless without bullets and powder. "In case you're hungry. I grow them," he said lamely.

She scowled and reached out her other hand, but at least she didn't toss the almonds in his face. "The rifle, if you please."

He didn't pass her the rifle. "There are still rounds in it. You will be careful."

She glared at him. "I do know how to handle a firearm, or was that not clear?"

He sighed. "Would it make any difference if I told you that I was going to tell Rafe that you didn't want him to know you shot the robber?" He had intended to tell him that. "I just hadn't gotten to it yet."

Her eyes opened, but then her mouth pursed. "Well, you wasted no time at all in telling him I had shot a man."

He couldn't tell her that Rafael knew from the minute she'd pulled the trigger. "It wouldn't be good for him to be caught unaware, but I'm sure he would have been happy to pretend he didn't know for your sake."

"So you were encouraging him to lie to me." She glared at him.

Daniel looked around for an escape route. Bad enough he had to lie, but to have to lie to make

himself look like a tattletale was just wonderful.
He seemed to be doing the opposite of soothing.
"Not exactly, just not bring it up until you were
ready to talk to him."

"Since he already knows I can shoot, I might as
well keep the rifle." She tugged it away. "Thank
you, Mr. Werner, and good night."

Daniel held back a groan. But for Rafael bring-
ing up the shooting, he might have been able to
reclaim the gun with little problem. Now he was
going to have to make it to San Francisco and
try and buy another one before any of the hands
realized his new rifle was missing and the robbers had left behind one amazingly similar to his.

She reached for the door to shut it.

He put his hand out and stopped it. Then he
wondered what the hell he was doing. He certainly
was not going to kiss her to soothe her ruffled
feathers. "I know you've had a difficult arrival,
and we haven't been as welcoming as we should
have been, but we're glad you're here safe and
sound."

"Really? Because it seems to me that I am
very much an afterthought or perhaps an incon-
venience."

"You are mistaken—"

"Please, don't lie to me. I don't like it."

"I'm not lying to you." But he was, and his
protest sounded insincere. He wished he wasn't
lying to her or could find a better way to dissem-

ble. "Or at least I was not trying to. It has been a bad day for all of us."

"Mr. Werner, I have a gun in my hand, and I'm very short on patience. Now, good night."

He couldn't help it—he laughed. He could have the gun out of her hands before she could get a round chambered. Life with her on the ranch was bound to get interesting. "You are nothing like your letters."

She blanched. "How could you know that?"

He shouldn't have said that, and his ears grew hot. "Rafael read them to us."

After all, there was nothing in them that couldn't have been read out loud. Actually, he'd read the letters to Rafael, but that didn't matter. Once he'd told Rafe she met the requirement of being fair—or more particularly looking distinctly Anglo, Rafael had picked her from the respondents. Why, Daniel didn't know. She'd seemed snobbish and uptight in the letters. He hadn't really understood why she appealed to Rafe, especially since Daniel had never shown him her picture, but she was nothing like he'd expected.

"Well, then, I'm sorry to have disappointed you," she said stiffly and shut the door.

Maybe Rafael was disappointed. Actually, Rafael was probably damn sorry he'd picked a spitfire, but Daniel wasn't disappointed. No, he was rather bemused and thankful she wasn't going to be his. But he'd be glad to see Rafe have to dance to her tune. And maybe she would be the cure his brother needed. Until Rafe was well, he'd have to step lively to keep ahead of her.

Anna stared at the ceiling, then at the interior wall, then the other wall. The minute she closed her eyes, she'd see the man she shot and the shock in his eyes and any hope of sleep died.

Well, there was no point in lying about staring into the darkness. She might as well get up and see if she could locate the kitchen and a washtub. The green silk had to be salvaged. It was the best dress she owned and really the only one that supported her exaggerations about her family's prosperity.

She found the tin lamp with star-shaped holes and lit the candle inside. With a shawl over her nightgown, she opened her door. Light showed from the main room. She looked for another room that perhaps contained the banked glow from a stove, but she found nothing. Perhaps Mrs. Werner was still awake, although it was long past time most people were abed. Carrying the lamp, she crossed the courtyard and opened the door.

Daniel stood on the far side of the room, and his gaze jerked to her. A shiver chased down her back.

She tightened the shawl around her shoulders, firmly holding the ends in front of her chest.

"Is there something I can get for you, Miss O'Malley?"

"I thought your mother might be in here."

"Just me."

He took a step toward her, and her heart skittered. Had to be her anger at him. She hadn't any choice. Unless she wanted to open every door and look in, she had to ask him for help. He was the only one around.

She drew in a deep breath of air that seemed thinner than it ought to be and said, "I'm looking for the kitchen."

"Are you hungry? Madre made plenty of tamales. I can warm them for you." He took another step toward her.

She shook her head. "I was hoping to find a washtub, water and soap."

His eyebrows drew together. "It is after midnight."

"Yes, I know, but I can't sleep. My only two clean dresses were dirtied today, and I would feel better if I could launder them, so that I have something to wear tomorrow." She had been traveling for months and had little that was clean. Yesterday morning she and Selina had managed to get into their trunks so they would arrive wearing their best dresses and clean underthings. Then she remembered she was supposed to have come from a rich family and should act accordingly. A spoiled girl would expect new dresses to replace her soiled ones. "Even the best dressmaker wouldn't be able to finish a dress tomorrow."

"I can send for the wash—"

"If you would point me to the kitchen, I'm sure I can manage."

"Are you in the habit of doing your own washing?"

"If necessary." A warning bell rang in her head. She drew herself up as haughtily as she could. "It is not as if I brought a maid with me on this adventure."

He sighed as if greatly put out.

She took a step toward him. "I am sorry to bother you, Mr. Werner, but I am not in great charity with you, either."

His gaze dropped down to her bare toes. His lips twitched as if he was restraining a laugh.

Curling her toes, she tried to hide her barefoot state. Really, she should have dressed, but she had nothing to wear and putting on shoes when one had on a nightgown and a shawl seemed rather silly. "I shall have to purchase new house shoes. Mine seem to have been misplaced on the trip."

"Of course," he said with just the faintest mocking tone to his words.

She deserved it, because she'd never owned a pair of house shoes in her life. As she narrowed her eyes, she realized Daniel was fully clothed, as if he'd just come in or intended to go out. "Shouldn't you be asleep if you are going back to town at dawn, or was that a lie, too?"

She flushed thinking she was the pot calling the kettle black. Because of her little pretense about coming from a wealthy family, she had to keep twisting the truth.

His face sobered. "I wish I were abed, but I needed to take care of a few things."

"I cannot settle my thoughts, and a labor like laundry does seem to tire a body."

He held out his hand. "This way, then."

She tried to move as if she were dressed like a queen, but she felt as though he could see straight through her.

He went right on the walkway around the interior open area. She followed. The unusual layout of the house would probably make more sense to her in the light of day. Or perhaps it just served the milder weather here. A house where one had to pass through the open air would be the height of absurdity in an eastern winter. "Does it ever snow here?"

"Only high in the mountains," he answered as he opened a door and held it for her.

Tiles were cool under her feet although the room was warm.

There were pans and bowls—clearly it was a kitchen, but where was she to heat water? "Is there no stove?"

Daniel lit a lamp and then moved to the outside wall, where there was a large pale brick fireplace complete with decorative metal doors and a flat shelf on top that likely served as a stovetop. "This brick oven works well enough," Daniel said tightly as if she'd insulted him.

Perhaps she had. Anna couldn't honestly remember Olivia sniffing or turning up her nose at humble things. "I'm just used to stoves is all."

"I'm sure Rafael will be happy to buy you one if you want. Although the cost to ship one out here would raise the price threefold." He placed a couple of logs in the burn chamber, then cast her a wry look. "I hope you do not intend to spend all my brother's money."

She blinked. "Not *all* of it."

He turned toward the wall, but not before she'd seen the edge of his mouth curl.

For heaven's sake, her standard of living would be much improved over the boardinghouse she'd lived in for the past six years, and certainly far better than the New York tenement she'd lived in the five years before. "I'm sure I will get used to the manner of living here. In time. I am not disappointed in the house or its furnishings."

"Just the people, then." He pulled a wooden tub from a hook on the wall. He set it on a large table, then moved to a spigot and started filling a bucket.

"No, that isn't what I meant. You have been kind, and I've barely met Rafael or your mother. I find I am unable to stop thinking about shooting that man today. I know he deserved it, but

I am not accustomed to shooting men. I hope I didn't kill him."

"I'm fairly certain you didn't, or the posse would have found his body," Daniel said. He watched her carefully.

Suddenly, she felt all weepy and in need of a hug. He was the wrong brother. She couldn't throw herself into his arms again. No, she needed to seek comfort in Rafael's arms.

She whirled away. "I will go get my dresses. I'm certain I can manage from here."

But Daniel was still there, watching her, when she returned with an armful of undergarments and the two dresses. She flushed. Now he'd not only seen her in her nightgown; he would get an eyeful of her petticoats and drawers. "Really, Mr. Werner, you can go on about your business."

"I put the tamales in the oven. Thought I might eat some, even if you don't want any." He leaned back against the wall and shaved slivers from a bar of soap.

She stared at him, wondering if she should volunteer to serve the food to him in the main room. While she was pondering her next move, his gaze shifted over her, leaving shivers in its wake.

"You should know that Rafael plans to track with me in the morning."

Her muscles tensed. "But he could barely stand. Surely he will feel too poorly in the morning."

Daniel's dark gaze slid away from hers. "I'm sure he'll manage."

Her stomach fell. Why didn't her future husband want to spend time with her to get to know her?

## Chapter Six

*You say you have a large herd of cattle. My
father tells me I should inquire as to the
numbers and how many acres you own. As
for what I do with my time: I attend a great
many social gatherings. At least once a week
we attend a ball and waltz until dawn.*

Daniel's gut twisted as Anna hugged her clothes
tightly to her. Her eyes went dewy, and she paled
as if he'd kicked her with no warning when he
told her Rafael intended to go out tracking in the
morning. Stifling the urge to soothe her, he forced
himself to stay on the far side of the kitchen table.

He opened his mouth to defend Rafael, then
shut it. It was Rafe's fault he was in this predica-
ment, and she'd very nearly caught him leaving
the house with the remnants of the two ponchos
and the hats they'd worn.

She firmed her chin and stepped toward the
table. "I suppose that will give me time to sur-

vey the house and see what I need to spend your brother's money upon."

He wanted to applaud her pluck and thank her for saving him from the overwhelming urge to gather her in his arms and reassure her everything would be all right.

She put her white clothes in the washtub, laid the green dress she'd been wearing on the stagecoach beside it and reached for the bucket.

It would take a damnably long time to fill the tub with boiling water, and he still needed to get the horses into the hills before anyone realized they hadn't been stolen. He couldn't leave as long as Anna was awake. He set the saucer with the soap shavings on the table. The only thing he could do was help her so the washing went faster. "Every pot we have is heating."

Glancing toward the brick shelf, where he had set filled bowls as well as pots, she put down the bucket.

For a second in profile she looked so forlorn, he leaned toward her. "Rafe is just trying to get our horses back."

"Because that would certainly be more important than tracking down the men who tried to kill me," she muttered.

"Only one of the men fired his weapon."

Her gaze sharpened on him and poked holes in him.

Daniel bit the inside of his mouth. He tried to

remember if she'd said that in his presence. He rushed to move on before she thought about it too long. "Besides, they are probably one and the same. Rafe will just try to pick up the trail from where he lost it yesterday, and I'll be following it from the stagecoach robbery site. With any luck our paths will meet."

Her eyes narrowed.

His spine tightened. He needed to stop talking about the robbery.

"Well, I would feel much better if you did catch them."

He was late in agreeing with her. "I'm sure that would be best."

"But you don't think you will?" She continued to study him.

The weight of her gaze made him want to squirm away like the lowly worm he was becoming. He closed his eyes and drew in a deep breath, then opened them to meet her green ones. "I'll do my best."

But damn it to hell, he would only succeed if he managed to mislead the townsfolk.

He and Rafe were trying to demonstrate they were a cut above other rancheros, hardworking, innovative, willing to learn what the new Californians needed and deliver it, whether it was beef, trained oxen or fruit. Too many of the Mexican landowners were caught in doing what had worked half a century ago instead of recognizing the changes that were coming.

Too many of the Anglos coming in thought the old ways were lazy, instead of realizing the rancheros ran small herds over their big spreads because there hadn't been a big enough local market for beef, and producing more fruits and vegetables than a family could consume hadn't made sense. He and Rafe had spent long hours discussing the future and what would keep the ranch solvent, especially in light of the mounting legal fees. And part of that was welcoming the Anglos and learning their ways instead of becoming more entrenched in old Spanish traditions.

He hated to think how the townsfolk would despise him if they thought he'd become a criminal. All the work he'd done to establish himself as a fair-dealing man would be for naught.

He shifted away from the maudlin thoughts. At least with Rafe pretending to go out tomorrow he could share the blame. "Rafe will find their hiding place if they have one."

"How many horses were stolen?"

"Four," Daniel counted the descriptions he'd given the sheriff in his head. His gut tightened. Keeping his lies straight was difficult. "No, wait, three. We found one of the ones we thought was missing later."

His heart thumped madly. Even though Rafe had told him thousands of times learning to lie to their mother would make life easier, he'd never thought it a useful skill to cultivate. The memory of his father's strictures to be honest rang louder in his head.

"Do you have so many horses you can't keep track of them?" Her face was scrunched with skepticism.

"We have upwards of fifty. When we have to drive the cattle to market, a man will use four or five horses in a day." How the ranch worked was something he could talk about and not have to lie. He breathed out a long breath. "My father always insisted that each man had enough so the horses don't get worn down."

Her head tilted, and he could see the gears turning in her mind. "When did your father die?"

His chest felt cleaved open. Daniel glanced toward the stove, willing the water to boil. He didn't want to talk about his father's death. The grief had never left him, especially since his mother had told him to stop crying about missing his father. He folded his arms. "While back. Rafe had to take on the responsibilities of running the ranch when he was thirteen."

Her brows drew together. "You must have been very young. That must have been awful for you."

Her sympathy was both a balm and an irritant. He tried to fend it off and steer the conversation back to the workings of the ranch. "Rafe increased the herd, and now we not only provide meat but we train oxen to haul cargo wagons. He made the ranch more profitable."

Surely any woman was interested in how much her future husband's holdings were worth.

"Mmm. How did your father die?" she asked.

Daniel rolled his eyes. She was like a dog with a bone, determined to get at the marrow of the thing. He would have to satisfy her curiosity or she'd never leave off. "He was sick one night and just didn't wake up the next morning."

"What did the doctor say was wrong?" Anna's brow furrowed.

"Didn't see one." Daniel walked to the stove and dipped a finger in the smallest pot. Still cool. "Don't know if a doctor would have helped. There weren't any around back then."

"I'm sorry." Her head dipped, and her face screwed up so that he wanted to move around the table and gather her in his arms, which was completely out of place.

"When did Rafael's father die?" Another question.

Why wouldn't that damn water boil?

"I don't know." Actually he wasn't sure that Rafael's father was dead. He wasn't certain Madre had been married to him, but the one time he'd asked his mother, she screamed at him for calling her a whore. He should find out what Rafe intended to tell Anna about his parentage. "You should ask Rafe about that."

She tilted her head again and looked at him askance. "It'll be difficult to ask him anything if I never see him."

"You'll see him." All too soon, probably. And then Rafe would be the one having late-night conversations with her, which was how it should be. No doubt Rafe would be able to charm her once he was well, and Daniel was looking forward to when his brother could take over answering her overly inquisitive barrage of questions.

On her third circuit of the perimeter of the courtyard, Anna peeked in windows, although trying not to be obvious. The Werners were covering up her future husband's behavior, and she deserved to know what she was dealing with. Rafael's room had the curtains drawn so tight, she couldn't see anything at all. She'd tried the door at one point, but found it locked. Odd.

After completing her circuit, she entered the main room of the house and looked for Mrs. Werner. Her questions thus far had been brushed off as well as her offers to help with the housework. But the longer she remained idle, the more restless she became. She was too used to working hard. And her mind was spinning like a whirling dervish.

How bad was a drunk Rafael? She'd seen plenty of men make a habit of hard drinking. Often it seemed to pass from father to son.

Mrs. Werner swept the long porch on the front.

"I could do that," offered Anna.

"No, no, I am done," said her future mother-in-law. "Sit. Sit. You are not to work. You should have let me send for the washerman."

Anna shrugged. Earlier she'd taken her clothes down from the cord Daniel had strung across the courtyard. She'd told him more than once that she could manage without his help, but he'd insisted, even when he was yawning. He seemed easy enough to be with, even if every time he got close to her, her breath caught a little.

He'd been a perfect gentleman, which made her wonder if she was mistaken in thinking he'd been about to kiss her just before Rafael came out of his room. But he'd also been evasive and uncomfortable with her questions about his family, which only fueled her belief they were trying to hide something from her.

She hadn't seen either of the brothers today, and Mrs. Werner insisted they were both out tracking the criminals.

Anna moved forward and sat at the table. "Does Rafael drink often?"

"No, no, just when he have a bad day."

"Did his father drink?"

"Why you ask these questions? His father has been gone a long time. How am I to remember?"

She'd remember if her first husband drank too much. Her lack of an answer was telling enough. How bad was Rafael's father? Had he been a roaring drunk? He must have died young. Could it have been because of drinking? "If you don't mind me asking, how did Rafael's father die?"

"He get sick and go in his sleep." Mrs. Werner put the broom in a corner and brushed her hands.

That sounded a lot like Daniel's description of *his* father's death. "When was that, Mrs. Werner?"

"A year before they found gold at Sutter's Creek."

That would have been almost fifteen years earlier. And fifteen years ago had to have been long after Daniel was born. "Not Mr. Werner, but Rafael's father."

"Mr. Werner is Rafael's father, yes." Mrs. Werner bobbed her head up and down with more emphasis than was needed.

"Not according to your other son," Anna said.

"You wish to eat now. I have beans made. I go get them." Mrs. Werner scuttled toward the inner door.

"No, I don't wish to eat." She wanted to understand the family structure, because the more she learned, the less sense it made.

"But you sit at the table," said Mrs. Werner as she went through the door.

Anna pushed the chair back and followed her into the courtyard. Mrs. Werner entered the kitchen, and, when she saw Anna, she closed the door. The message was clear. She didn't want to talk about Rafael's father.

Anna put her head down and pushed into the kitchen.

"You should not be in here." Mrs. Werner darted around the table and stood between Anna and the room.

Wide-eyed, Juanita looked over her shoulder from the stove where she was ladling out beans into one, two, three—four bowls. Her shoulders rounding, she turned and blocked Anna's view of the bowls.

"Why not?" demanded Anna. "Is this not to be my home? Who is the other bowl for?"

Mrs. Werner paled. "Oh, Juanita—she is a foolish girl and cannot count." She grabbed one of the bowls and put it back on a stack. "It is only us here."

Anna didn't believe her. But she didn't know if Rafael was feeling the effects of last night's drinking or if Daniel had been too tired after staying up half the night helping her do laundry. All she really knew was this family seemed to have a hard time with the truth. A little voice in her head said she'd fit right in with them, given her own massive lie.

Daniel knelt on the creek bank and studied the tracks he'd made yesterday. His eyes were scratchy, and he wanted nothing more than to end this false search and go home, but he had to make certain no one believed the trail led anywhere close to the ranch.

"They headed up towards those rocks, then," said the sheriff.

Daniel shook his head. "I don't think so. Looks like one horse left the creek and then backed up into it."

"How do you know that?" demanded the sheriff.

He knew because that was what he'd done to create a false trail. His neck tightened. Tired and wanting the day to end, he hadn't thought carefully before blurting out the truth. Even if he couldn't disclose how he knew, telling an actual fact was such a relief. But he'd done it before considering the consequences. He needed to focus on what he was doing and what he should reveal. Yet, he couldn't seem to get his mind off Anna.

How was she faring alone in the house with Madre and Juanita? And Rafael, although she wasn't to know that. He wanted to move along so the posse would start thinking about nightfall and turning back before they were caught out in complete darkness. The farther he led them away from town and away from the ranch, the better. "We can look around the perimeter of the rocky section, but I doubt we'll find more tracks."

His brow knit, the sheriff dismounted. "How do you know, Danny?"

Hell. He focused his eyes on the impressions,

looking for differences that a tracker would have used to form his conclusions. "The spacing is different. This set of prints shows a horse coming out at a fast clip, and on this set the weight of impressions is different. The dirt sprays in the opposite direction. The horse was backed into the water. Its hooves were dry, while these impressions were made while the hooves were wet."

The sheriff got on his knees and peered at the tracks, looking back and forth between them. He'd once been a Texas Ranger and probably had good tracking skills, too.

His heart thumping madly, Daniel stood and walked alongside the tracks. He should have been paying better attention. "They appear very much the same size, even this notch in the shoe." The sets made while he was backing up were less distinct and the mark caused by the imperfection was barely distinguishable.

"Don't know as I would've recognized that until we didn't find any more tracks," said the sheriff. "Your father was a good tracker."

His father had been a good observer in a lot of ways. Had to be for his job as a surveyor.

"You remind me of him."

Daniel's gut tightened. The sheriff had been one of the few men who'd been in the area long enough to have known his father. Most Californians had arrived after the discovery of gold, just a little after his father had died. "Thanks."

"Do you think they would have turned their horses and gone upstream from here?" The sheriff turned and looked in exactly the direction that he and Rafael had taken yesterday.

Daniel's heart jolted. He pulled off his hat and wiped his forehead just so he would not look in the sheriff's eyes. "And risk running right back into a possible pursuit? That'd be stupid."

The sheriff pushed to stand and lumbered in front of him. "That way would lead to your ranch, wouldn't it?"

"Eventually," said Daniel. A bead of sweat trickled down his spine.

"Haven't seen any of them cousins of yours lately, have you?"

"I haven't seen my cousins in years. But if we thought they had taken the horses, Rafe and I just would have followed 'em. We know where they live." South of the border. Did the sheriff suspect his cousins might have been involved? That was only marginally better than suspecting he and Rafe were responsible.

"No one came to your house for help?"

"God, no. Could you imagine how that would have gone with Miss O'Malley there?" Daniel blustered. "Don't know who would have been scared worse, her or the man she shot. I'm thinking they took off for Mexico."

The sheriff nodded. "I agree. With one of 'em

wounded and all, wouldn't have risked heading north."

Daniel breathed out a sigh.

"And you said Rafe is hunting for them in the hills. He wouldn't go in after them alone, would he?"

"I doubt if Rafe is that stupid." But, then again, he was stupid enough to think stopping a stagecoach just to get a look at his bride was a good idea. The point was moot since there wasn't any camp and Rafael was safely back home in bed. Again, Daniel wondered what Anna was doing and how Madre was dealing with her determination.

"He needs to come in and tell me what he's found as soon as he gets back."

How the hell was he going to get Rafe to come into town to talk to the sheriff anytime soon?

Anna went outside to wait for the brothers to return. The sun was sinking below the horizon, and she was more confused than ever by Mrs. Werner's nonanswers. Getting information out of her was like trying to get milk out of a cat. Just by her evasive answers, Anna was certain one of the brothers was in the house, but she wasn't certain which one. She was determined to find out.

She hoped it was Daniel because at least that would mean her fiancé wasn't hiding from her.

After a few minutes, a lone horseman rode into

sight. In the dusk she couldn't immediately make out which brother it was. But something about the way he moved easily with the horse's lope convinced her it was Daniel.

Her heart fluttered, which was silliness, and she stood on the edge of the porch as Daniel drew his mount to a halt in front of her and dismounted.

"Enjoying the evening, Miss O'Malley?"

He gathered the reins in his hand, then looked over at her when she hadn't answered.

"I suppose. Rafael is not with you?"

Uneasiness crossed Daniel's face. "He'll be along in a bit."

"I thought you were going to meet up with him," she said. Really, how stupid did they think she was? So it was Rafael hidden in the house. Was he still drunk? Or just avoiding her? Either way, she felt like a loaf of bread someone had sat upon. She had to concentrate to keep her shoulders straight in a ladylike posture.

"We did, but he was going to see if he could catch the sheriff to discuss what he found in the hills." Daniel led the horse toward the open-sided barn. Two fenced areas were near it, a small area with a chicken coop, where Juanita had shooed the roaming chickens and closed the gate on them before the sun fell out of the sky, and a larger area where several horses roamed. "If you'll excuse me, I have to take care of my horse."

"It's all right. I'll just wait here for Rafael to return."

Daniel looked down, then back up. "He might be a while."

He wasn't the best liar. Still, she couldn't work up a great deal of resentment because he was doing it for his brother, and she'd also been less than honest. That didn't mean she would make it easy on him.

She shrugged. "I've nothing better to do. Your mother has made it clear she doesn't want help in the kitchen and wouldn't let me do the milking."

He paused. The horse nudged him. "Do you know how to milk a cow?"

"I've done it a few times." Actually, more than a few times. "Although it's been a while, I can get back into practice. My family owned a cow—" She'd been about to say back in Ireland but stopped herself. She couldn't allow herself to lower her guard so much around Daniel. She'd been careful to scrub the lilt of her native tongue from her voice, emulating Olivia's and Selina's speech patterns. But she didn't need him wondering why she would have milked a cow when she'd claimed her family employed servants for those kinds of tasks. "Did you have success in finding the robbers today?"

"We didn't find the robbers, but we found some tracks." He looked toward the barn as if he was anxious to put up his horse.

"Two sets?" But not a body.

"Well, actually two sets until they went in a creek. Then we found a false trail. We never found where they both left the creek, but it does appear they were headed south." Daniel watched her face. "I think you can rest easy."

"Their getting away doesn't make me feel better," she replied.

"I meant about how badly you wounded the robber. They were taking considerable pains to avoid detection. If your shot had caused a bad wound, the unharmed one would have abandoned the other."

"You think there is never any honor among thieves?"

Daniel smiled slowly. Her heart fluttered. She told it to stop.

"If he was badly wounded and his partner had any honor he would have been scrambling to get to help." Daniel patted his horse. "Looks as though they rode through the night or we would have found signs of a camp. Not so sure a badly injured man could have managed that."

He led his horse toward the outbuilding, and she was off the porch following him before she realized her intent.

"Wouldn't there be three sets of horse tracks or more if the stagecoach robbers were the ones who stole your horses?" she asked.

He jerked, and the horse nickered. "You would

think so," he said in a measured tone. "But we didn't find a third set of tracks. Based on the tracks he found in the hills, Rafael thinks one of the horses might have gotten away from them. Just is odd to have two crimes so close together unless it is one set of criminals." He clamped his mouth shut and tightened his lips as if he suddenly thought he was saying too much.

"This whole thing doesn't make sense to me," she said.

Daniel paused in lifting the saddle from his horse. His dark eyes met hers, then slid away. "What doesn't make sense?"

"If you think the horse thieves and the stagecoach robbers were one and the same, why didn't Rafael just go with you to track them from the stagecoach holdup?"

"We weren't certain until today," muttered Daniel as he disappeared into the darkness with the saddle.

He returned with a blanket and started rubbing the horse.

"So, how far behind you was your brother?" she asked ever so casually.

"Not far, but now that it is dark, he won't run the horse. He might not be home for an hour or more."

He was watching her more than he was watching what he was doing with the horse. Awareness shivered through her.

Heat stole into her face. She told herself it was just nerves at what she was about to ask him. "Are you very certain your brother didn't stay here all day?"

His hands stopped moving and clenched the blanket tightly. His voice was slightly wary as he said, "You don't think that, do you?"

"I don't know what to think, Mr. Werner. Your mother will not answer a straight question."

"I've given up on trying to figure out my mother's secrets," he replied.

"And I know Juanita was dishing up four bowls for lunch, not three."

He frowned and went back to wiping the horse. "Perhaps one of the hands came back early. I can assure you my brother isn't home yet."

She hesitated, almost ready to say she didn't believe him, but she wasn't certain enough. "Then what is it everyone is trying to hide from me?"

His expression went flat; then his eyes narrowed. He watched her so long she wanted to duck.

"The question is, what are you trying to hide, Miss O'Malley?"

# Chapter Seven

*We run a thousand head of cattle over nearly thirteen thousand acres. They often have to be escorted around the land to new grazing spots. They bawl in protest at the change, but we sing to them of highborn Spanish ladies and chivalrous romance until they are soothed. They soon grow content with new pastures.*

"**W**hat are you talking about?" she sputtered. Her breath was gone. She'd been certain she was getting close to the truth, and Daniel had turned the tables on her.

"I mean all your letters said you came from a well-to-do family, but I see no evidence of that. Your petticoats are threadbare, your socks have holes or are darned and you only have two dresses to your name. You can milk, launder your own clothes and shoot. You are the furthest thing from any spoiled rich girl I've ever encountered." He stepped closer to her, his dark eyes narrowed.

"I only have two *good* dresses," she protested, wanting to back away. But the ground under her feet no longer felt solid, and she couldn't look away from him. "I have others."

He arched his brows and looked at her as if he could see straight through her clothes to her skin. The air grew thin.

"I can't believe you inspected my laundry." She lifted her chin, determined to brazen it out.

"I didn't inspect it. I walked through it this morning." His gaze dipped to her chest as if examining the stains she hadn't been able to completely get out of the green silk.

Her heart pounded, and she had only moral mud under her feet if she continued to try and hide the truth about herself. "Very well, my family has fallen on hard times, but we were well-off once," she said with a huff. She folded her arms across her oddly tingling chest.

He blinked a couple of times. "Is that so?"

"I suppose you will run straight to your brother and tell him."

His jaw ticked.

Then he tilted his head to the side. "I should." He sighed heavily as if she were a great bother. "But I don't want to be the one to crush his dreams. And I've done more than enough riding today to go chasing him down."

"Crush his dreams?" she echoed faintly. Oh, no, she couldn't risk losing this marriage. Even if Rafael wasn't everything she hoped for, he was to be her husband. He'd paid for her to travel from Connecticut, had picked her to be his bride. He owned land and a great deal of it. She had to marry him.

What choice did she have really? If she didn't marry him, she wouldn't have a home, a job or even any friends nearby to turn to outside of Selina, who was to be a newlywed herself. She'd likely have to become a housemaid for someone. And that was no kind of life.

"*He* still thinks you are the woman of his dreams, refined and elegant, an English-speaking lady from back east. That you could fire a gun was shocking enough to him. If he wanted a rough-and-tumble girl, he could have married a local one." He glanced toward the house.

Her stomach turned sour. Confessing the truth had seemed like a good thing, but not if she lost Rafael because of it. Anna said faintly, "I didn't think there were that many girls locally."

"You're right—there aren't. But there are women much closer than Connecticut. He owns the largest spread around here." Daniel waved his arms wide. "He could have had his pick from Mexico or from the territories, but he advertised for a wife more suited to what he wants."

He ducked his head, but not before she'd seen the look in his eyes.

She worried her lip. What could she do now to make it better but come all the way clean? "I didn't expect anything to come of my letter. When my friend Olivia first said we should answer advertisements, I just thought I'd write to the richest landowners in California as a lark. I never expected any to answer back." Or pick her, not with her name.

"You sent a picture to Rafael." Daniel winced. "Doesn't seem like a person not serious would go to that expense."

She rolled her shoulders, wanting to crawl out of her skin. "Yes, well, Selina was able to get a photographer to take our pictures very cheaply." Olivia and Selina had assured her the photograph would only help her cause. "So it seemed like the right thing to do. And when Rafael answered…" She pressed a hand against her churning midsection. "I didn't want to marry a poor man. I wanted a man with land for raising animals and crops. I don't want to worry about where my next meal is coming from."

Daniel's gaze softened, and he cleared his throat. Just as she started to relax, he said, "What else did you lie about?"

"I worked in a cotton mill until the shipments dried up because of the war," she said in a hushed whisper.

"So there weren't any parties. Or dancing until

dawn. Have you ever even waltzed?" His expression was inscrutable. He turned toward the horse so she was left with even fewer clues.

She shook her head. She'd put her foot in it now, and she couldn't tell if Daniel was angry or disappointed. She was as much on the outside as she'd been back in Connecticut. Her throat went dry, and her eyes stung. Why had she ever thought she could pretend to be cultured and refined? "I've never actually…waltzed."

"California is getting settled fast, and Rafe wants a wife who will help him fit in with the important people, project the right image. How will you do that?"

Did he now think she was so vulgar she'd repel people? She wasn't that bad. Olivia had never made her feel gauche, even when she explained manners and etiquette rules that Anna never knew existed until she made a mess of them. Nor had Selina or Olivia made fun of her accent the way other people at the mill had. With one question, Daniel had sliced open her fears and reminded her of all the times she'd been told she was nothing, just another worthless Irish immigrant. One that didn't even know her place as a female, let alone as an American.

She'd worked so hard on learning the manners Olivia had said were important and learning to speak like a lifelong resident. If not for the stage being robbed, she never would have been exposed so soon or so thoroughly. That wasn't her fault. And whether Rafael wanted her or not, his neglecting and ignoring her was ill-mannered. "He should mind his own drinking first."

"A man is always allowed a lot more leeway in behavior than a woman is," Daniel countered.

Her outrage simmered. Would he tell his brother, and they'd send her packing because he'd made a snap judgment that she couldn't be the kind of wife he wanted? She fisted her hands to still the tremors. She could and would make him a worthy wife, no matter how hard she had to work at it. Drawing in a deep breath, she tried to hold back her anger before it got her in trouble. She'd come all this way expecting certain things, too, but she wasn't going to ignore her promise to marry Rafael, and he shouldn't, either. "That's hardly fair."

"Not fair, but true. Miss O'Malley, if you want to marry my brother, you'd better be able to convince him you can do him proud as his wife and not embarrass him."

Her thoughts jumped. Did Daniel want her to succeed? "But he has to marry me. He proposed."

"He doesn't have to marry you."

She almost staggered backward. "I could sue him for breach of promise."

Daniel lowered his voice, "Are you very certain he made an unconditional proposal? If he didn't, your case won't have merit. Especially if you deceived him."

Had she come all this way on a whim of Rafael's? She'd staked her entire future on this working out. Her heart was racing, and her ears buzzed. "I will be the best wife I can be. I don't want to disappoint him. Whatever I don't know I will learn."

"I could help you. Teach you to waltz." He ducked his head. "Help you with the things you should know."

"Would you?" she asked, stepping closer. Would Daniel be an ally to her? He was the only one who seemed to at least not dislike her so far. Which must be why she had the urge to burrow into him.

"Of course." His mouth pulled back as if he regretted his offer.

If he had thought she wouldn't accept his help, too bad. She wouldn't turn down help. She needed everything to work out too badly. For a second she wondered if their discussion was meant to distract her from the fact that Rafael hadn't returned home. Probably hadn't left.

"We can start tomorrow," she said. "But tonight I am determined to wait out here until Rafael makes it home safe." She tilted her head and watched him.

"She doesn't believe you went out tracking today," Daniel hissed at his brother. "She's waiting on the front porch for you to come riding up."

"She'll wait…long time." Rafael pressed his hand to the bandage across his chest.

"I'll distract Miss O'Malley while you go around to the paddock and get on a horse. Circle around the back of the house and ride over the hill. It'll look like you've just returned home."

Rafael groaned as he sat. "Can't saddle… horse."

Daniel pressed his hands to his face. "She's going to figure it out. She suspects something already. I had to convince her that you are going to be disappointed in her if she doesn't act like a high-society girl."

"What makes you think I won't be?" Rafael slowly stood. "Hell, I wish…she didn't shoot."

"You can't hold that against her. She had no idea she was shooting you." Daniel's gut burned with the frustration at having to lie to Anna, having to go on the attack because she was getting too close to the truth. It was the kind of tactic his mother would use, and he never wanted to follow Madre's example in that. He hated the twisting accusations and the verbal ambushing.

Anna's background didn't amount to a hill of beans—neither he nor Rafe thought a woman who would choose to be a mail-order bride would come from a perfect life—but if she was embarrassed enough to cover up her past, he figured poking at it would disturb her. And it had—more than he wanted.

The way Anna's eyes had filled with tears gnawed at him. There wasn't much he wouldn't do for his brother, but Rafe was expecting too much. He couldn't keep hurting her to protect Rafael. It made his insides blacken and shrivel. Her eventual anger had been a relief, but he couldn't keep covering for his brother. He was going to have to make an appearance and deal with Anna himself.

Daniel held his brother's shirt open. "Come on, Rafe. She's pretty, she's Anglo like you wanted and she wants to marry you. What more could you want?"

"Wants to marry ranch...owner." Rafe gingerly slid his arms into the sleeves. "Doesn't know me."

A twinge of regret stabbed Daniel between the shoulder blades. Anna's confession led him to believe she saw the land as security against the vicissitudes of fortune. He hadn't the heart to tell her Rafael could lose the ranch altogether if the courts didn't affirm the title.

"Well, she is awful anxious to talk with you," Daniel said. "So you'll have to pretend like you've just arrived home and sit down with her for at least a few minutes." Once Rafe worked his charm on her, she'd be smitten. Then Daniel could worry less about crossing lines with his future sister-in-law. "Better at night when the light isn't so strong."

"You can't be saying...might not be handsome…enough?" demanded Rafael. He slowly fastened his shirt.

Daniel resisted the urge to button his brother's shirt for him. "I'm saying you look like hell, but maybe she won't notice so much in the lamplight."

Rafael swayed on his feet. Daniel grabbed him. This would never work if Rafael couldn't stay upright or say more than three words without gasping for breath.

"Get Juanita," said Rafael. "She can saddle—" he heaved a deep breath "—bring horse around back."

"I hate to involve her."

"She knows." Rafael shrugged, then groaned. "Ma sent her." He gestured to a plate beside his bed. "Anna followed Ma. All day."

"All right. But tell her not to let Anna see or hear."

"Why's she so…curious?"

"She knows something is going on." And she was tenacious and not afraid to ruffle feathers to get answers. Daniel held back a smile at the way she just came straight out and said what she was thinking. "She'll probably calm down once she talks to you."

Rafael coughed weakly and wiped his forehead. "You do the talk…ing."

Didn't Rafe get it? Daniel couldn't keep talking to Anna. "I can't. I'll end up telling her the truth or something."

Actually, he was more worried about the *or something*.

Rafe grabbed his shirt. "What will she…do if… knows the truth?"

"I don't know, but whatever she does, it won't help the title claim."

Rafe sagged, and his expression fell.

Great, now Daniel felt as if he was torturing both of them, Anna with lies and Rafael with the truth. "You made this problem—you need to help clean it up."

"Fine."

"I'll tell Ma to heat up food like she would if you really were returning," said Daniel. And coffee. He needed about a gallon of coffee. Because he was going to have to distract Anna to keep her from seeing Juanita sneak about with the horse and hope like hell Anna didn't hear anything. And then she would be Rafe's problem to fix.

Daniel changed out of the clothes he wore and cast a yearning glance toward his bed. He was so tired his bones ached and his eyes burned as if he'd been trailing a dust-raising herd and the grit churned up by hundreds of hooves had settled under his eyelids.

Hell, this morning he'd been nearly asleep on his feet until a wet black sock had slapped him in the face. Woken him up good and reminded him her laundry was hanging in the courtyard. He'd been dead tired then and he was more tired now, but he couldn't let on. He had to distract Anna long enough so Juanita could get a horse saddled and Rafe could pretend to ride in after a long day out tracking.

A few minutes later, he stepped out on the front porch. Anna continued to gaze off into the night.

"No sign of Rafe yet?" he asked.

She shook her head. "It's pretty dark."

Her forlorn appearance tugged at him. The urge to stroke her hair and tell her none of it mattered tore at him. But he had her on the defensive. He couldn't let up. What he was about to suggest by way of distraction might be a huge mistake, given how much he wanted her in his arms. Hopefully, he could get her to come inside and it would be easier to stage Rafael's arrival.

Daniel leaned and looked out at the starlit sky. "It'll be easier to see when the moon rises."

"I suppose the darkness will slow Rafael down even more," she said tentatively. Her eyes searched his.

His blood heated. No, he couldn't let that happen. "I hope so. Can't afford to lose another horse because he's anxious to get home to you."

"Mmm." She cast an arched look in his direction. "I do hope his horse doesn't go lame, or he doesn't decide to stay the night elsewhere rather than travel after dark."

She was looking for the next lie. His pulse

kicked up a notch. Thank goodness he'd insisted on his brother making an appearance. Otherwise she may have just cut the legs out from underneath any explanation they could come up with for Rafe not showing up.

When he didn't respond, her voice dropped lower and she said, "I don't think he's anxious to be around me at all."

She thought Rafael was rejecting her. He had to convince her that wasn't the case. No man would reject her. "Then he is the biggest fool in all creation."

Her eyes widened, and her lips parted. His gaze dropped to her mouth as unwanted heat thrummed through him. He could so easily show her how desirable she was. She lowered her chin. "Would you tell me if he no longer wants me?"

The spell shattered. What was he thinking? She wanted Rafael to want her, not him. "He wants you, Miss O'Malley. He just has to put the needs of the ranch first. Many people depend on him."

Her brows drew together.

He didn't like her thinking on that too long, because even he couldn't figure out how chasing down two horse thieves and stagecoach robbers was putting the needs of the ranch first. "Madre's making coffee and food. Wouldn't you like to come in and have some?"

She shook her head. "No, I will just wait out here. It is a beautiful evening."

Hell, he couldn't leave her alone or there was too great a chance she'd see Juanita sneaking toward the paddock or leading a horse away. And really he didn't want to leave her. Her scent spiced the air. He wanted to lean in and inhale. Her hair beckoned with the warmth of a thousand fires. Even the dusting of freckles across her nose enchanted him. He reached to put an arm around her shoulders and realized what he was doing just in time.

"It is." Daniel walked to the end of the porch, peered out, then turned and leaned against a post as if he were just enjoying the night. With a few feet of distance, he could breathe normally again.

"Back in Connecticut it would be getting colder at night."

Juanita skittered by the far edge of the porch. Anna looked over her shoulder.

Daniel cleared his tight throat. Had she seen anything? His heart hammered. Surely she would have said if she had, but he had to get her attention on him, away from the horses. "Now would be a good time to teach you how to waltz."

"We haven't any music."

If they went inside, there was much less chance of Juanita being seen. "I can remedy that." He walked across the planks and held the door for her to go inside. "I have a music box we could use."

She shook her head.

"I'd rather not have your mother or Juanita walk in on waltz lessons. Can't we do it out here?"

Damn, she was stubborn, but he couldn't really fault her since she was onto them. "It isn't really wide enough."

Her eyes swept the length of the porch, and she tilted her head. "Seems to me we'd have more open space out here, unless you're planning to move the furniture."

He gave up and fetched the music box. He'd just have to make sure she was facing the wrong way as Juanita saddled the horse and then point her in the other direction in case Rafe didn't ride it completely out of sight before coming back. He hesitated a second, then propped the door open with a chair to hold the music box. "Don't want to miss it when Madre brings the coffee."

That and it would narrow her field of vision. Less chance she'd see the horse being led to the back door.

He turned the box over and wound a small metal key. "My father brought this all the way from Germany."

It was one of the few possessions he had of his father's. He had a hazy memory of his father leading his mother around with it playing. One of the few pleasant memories he had of his parents. Most of his memories of them together weren't so nice.

The only reason the box was still around was because he'd needed it to fall asleep for a long time afterward. The tinny music soothed him when his mother told him he was too old to need a lullaby. But she'd rather he had the music box than have him crying himself to sleep because he missed his poppy.

When he opened the lid, a tinny waltz began to play. He stepped closer. "Ready?"

Her throat closed and all she could do was nod.

"Put this on my shoulder." He lifted her arm and situated her hand. He held out his other hand. "And the other like this."

The minute their palms met, a tingle raced through him. It was just dancing, he told himself sternly. People did it all the time. He put his hand on her back, and he just wanted to pull her close.

He had to pretend this was instruction, not seduction. As adorable as she was, she was off-limits. His body thrummed with disagreement. If he wasn't so blasted tired, he could probably keep a better handle on his base desires, but he was exhausted.

He'd ridden for miles and miles in the past twenty-four hours. Between yesterday's fiasco of a holdup, taking the horses to the hills, coming back to grab a bite to eat before riding all the way into town, then tracking since a little after dawn, he'd been awake and in the saddle far too long. He felt as if his bones were wearing through his skin. He either wanted sleep or her in his bed to rejuvenate him, and neither was going to happen.

He had to keep this light and about learning to waltz. "I'll try not to step on your toes, although I might be a bit rusty."

"I am more likely to step on yours, I think." She looked down at the boards. "I might be better suited for a reel than a waltz."

"Look into my eyes, not at your feet," he instructed. At least if he could make her focus on him, maybe she wouldn't notice the shell game going on around them. "I have to look away occasionally to make sure we're not going to run into other couples." He grinned to let her know he was joshing her.

"Or fall off the porch," she suggested. Her voice sounded high and breathy.

Was she as affected by their proximity as he was? A new layer of heat built on top of the layers that shouldn't be there.

"Or fall off the dance floor. Every time I look down at you, I should see you looking at me."

"All right." She looked up at him.

He was lost in the green pools of her eyes. Only he had to dance. He pulled how to waltz from the dregs of his memories. His father had insisted he and Rafael learn the dance, even though neither of them wanted to. "Do you hear the tempo? One—two—three. One—two—three. Here we go."

He stepped forward, and she stepped back. He continued his instructions, but she needed little guidance. She flowed in his arms as if they were

of one mind. He whirled her around and caught
her again. Then he swept her backward in a slow
circular motion. She felt so right in his arms, and
the way she stared up at him heated him even
more. He swung her closer and caught his breath
as her breasts brushed his chest. A thousand flam-
ing arrows of desire shot to his groin.

He had to stop thinking of her that way.

"The dance floor is quite crowded today," he
said.

"Is it?" she murmured.

"You're doing good," he said in what he hoped
was an encouraging tone.

"And no toes have been trod upon yet," she said
brightly. "I don't think the music box is playing
anymore."

She entranced him. But he had to remember he
was doing this so Rafael could ride up as if he'd
been out all day. "I'd sing, but I don't know the
words," he said.

"Perhaps you should sing of Spanish ladies and
chivalry."

"Do you need soothing, Anna?" He needed
soothing. Perhaps Juanita needed more sound to
cover what she was doing.

"Perhaps, but I should think not exactly like
the cattle do."

He smiled and launched into a song in Spanish. He stopped moving them in a waltz count and

merely swayed back and forth with her. He could barely manage that.

She stared up at him, her eyes liquid and her kissable lips parting. She clung to his shoulders, and he had to keep singing or he'd kiss her or carry her inside and not stop until he had her on his bed.

A horse whinnied, and she jumped.

A much-needed reminder that the world had not gone away. He was distracting her so she wouldn't see the horse being led around back for Rafael. She turned to look.

His throat tightened and his thighs twitched. He couldn't let her catch them.

He caught her face in his palm. "One of the horses must think he will have to work the cattle."

He brushed his thumb against her cheek as he slid his hand to the center of her back and pulled her closer. Her breasts brushed against the hard wall of his chest and he near burst into flames. He wanted her down to his bones, and he had to keep her looking into his eyes. His heart raced. Keeping his voice steady in the song required every faculty he possessed.

They swayed together for an eternity until the song ended and he simply stared down at her. The air seemed thin as she wet her lips. He wanted so badly to kiss her, but he had to remember…something. His brain was muzzy, and she was so perfect. Oh, yes, she was his brother's future wife.

To remind himself and her, he said in a husky half whisper, "My brother is a lucky man, Miss O'Malley."

Her expression fell. She shoved him away and then stepped toward the edge of the porch.

Daniel caught her arm. "I'm sorry."

"We were just dancing. Nothing happened. You have nothing to apologize for." She wrapped her arms around her midsection. "I suppose you will tell me a mannerly woman would never shove a man away."

He didn't say anything. A lot had happened, just none of it spoken. He stared out into the darkness, trying to not want her and failing to rid himself of the need. Could she be meant to be with him and not Rafael?

She peeked a glance toward him. He couldn't look at her or he'd reveal the wayward twist of his thoughts. Even he knew how off they were. He didn't want a wife yet. He wasn't ready. He didn't own his own place. He had nothing to offer a wife, but right now he'd promise the moon if he could have her.

"Is the ranch half yours?" she blurted out.

Was that the only thing that was important to her? How much he was worth, how much land he had? Was she just a fortune seeker like all the rest of the Anglos who'd come to California? "No." The post bit into his hand. "It all belongs to Rafael."

They stood in silence for a while. She looked down, and he tried to still the mad jangle of his blood. She didn't want him so much as she wanted to be the wife of the ranch owner. No surprise in that. Why would any woman ever prefer him over Rafael? If he wasn't so tired, he was certain it wouldn't have even bothered him. He didn't want her as a wife anyway. She was too pushy and confrontational.

When he married, he wanted a meek wife who knew her place. He was certain of that. Anna just stirred his blood as a pretty woman would. His desire for her wasn't so much a surprise as his chest hurting over the idea that she couldn't want him because the ranch wasn't his.

The jingle of a harness reached them. She bounced on her toes and stared off into the darkness. Her eagerness to see Rafe was like a club hitting him in the stomach.

The steady *clop-clop* of an approaching horse grew louder.

The form of rider and horse materialized out of the gloom.

"Hello, my sweet," said Rafael as the horse plodded up to the edge of the porch. He flashed Anna a smile.

She cast a nervous glance over her shoulder and asked in a soft voice, "Has he been drinking?"

"Possibly," whispered Daniel.

"Hope your day—" Rafe shifted out of the

saddle, swinging one leg over and wobbling un-
steadily "—has been better...than mine."

Daniel's stomach rolled. Would Rafael be able
to stand?

"I'll take care of your horse." He leaped off the
porch. He had to make Rafael's arrival look real.
"Miss O'Malley, won't you go inside and see if
Ma has that coffee ready? Rafe looks like he needs
a cup as badly as I do."

Juanita came out and stepped in front of Anna
and pushed at Anna's shoulder.

Anna had said nothing to Rafael, and Daniel
risked a glance at her. He feared seeing the adora-
tion in her eyes that most women had toward his
brother. Instead, her brows had drawn together,
puckering the smooth place between them.

"The food ready. Go inside," Juanita said.

"We'll be right behind you," added Daniel as
he blocked Rafael and grabbed his belt, holding
him up.

They couldn't have gotten this far to have it
fall apart now.

# *Chapter Eight*

*Tell me of your family. I know you spoke of
your brother. Do you have other siblings?
What of your parents? I want to know everything there is to know about you.*

Daniel staggered under Rafael's weight. His
brother's knees buckled the minute he hit the
ground. How in the hell were they going to convince Anna that Rafe was uninjured?

"Surprised her," Rafe muttered.

Yes. Anna's jaw had dropped when Rafael had
appeared. Clearly, they'd shaken her belief that
Rafael had been hiding in his room all day, but
they weren't out of the woods yet.

"You've got to make it in to the table." Daniel
steadied his brother.

"I know." He heaved a couple of deep breaths.
"You have to…keep her occupied."

That was such a bad idea. For the second
time in two days, he'd nearly kissed her. When

he'd looked down into her green eyes, he'd almost leaned in and tasted her pink lips. Only the thought that Rafe could be coming around at any minute had stopped him.

Rafael latched on to his shirt as they walked inside. Juanita was doing everything she could to stand between Anna and them, but Anna was looking around her.

"I am glad you are home safe," she said.

"Me, too," answered Rafael.

Rafe wobbled, and Daniel tensed, ready to catch him. Anna's eyes narrowed, but they were focused on Rafael. A shaft of disappointment cut through him.

"So tired," said Rafe, "falling over…my own feet."

A protest rocked through Daniel. He was the one who had been awake for going on forty hours, but Rafe needed any excuse he could use for his unsteadiness.

Rafael poked him as if to prod words out of Daniel's mouth. He didn't know what else to do, so he called, "Ma, you got that coffee yet? Rafe needs a cup."

Madre came in and beamed at Rafael. "You are back!" She moved forward and gave Rafael a hug.

It gave Rafe another person to lean on and time to catch his breath, but Anna's brow knit. She sent a questing look in Daniel's direction. Daniel's pulse ticked. He told himself it was just fear that she'd figure out that Rafe was injured, but he knew it was more.

He shrugged. "Won't you have a seat, Miss O'Malley?" He pulled out a chair for her. "Even if you are not hungry, I'm sure Rafe would like you to join us."

Juanita brought in the coffeepot and managed to stand between Anna and Rafael as he landed in the chair at the head of the table in a heap.

Anna took the seat Daniel offered her.

"I have to take care of Rafe's horse, but I'll be right back."

"Doesn't he take care of his own?" she asked in a low voice.

"Usually. I thought he might like to sit with you," Daniel answered smoothly. It wasn't even a lie.

He headed back outside, hoping Madre and Juanita could manage to keep Anna's attention occupied until he got back.

As quickly as he could, he took the saddle off the horse and turned it loose in the paddock. It hadn't been ridden long enough to break a sweat. But he was sweating the deception going on inside enough to make up for it.

Anna leaned to see Rafael past the bulk of his mother. She was talking half in Spanish and half in English in a disconcerting way. Just as Anna would open her mouth to say something, Mrs.

Werner would fill the air with babble. Or Juanita would dart in between them. Rafael caught her eye and winked.

Nervously, she attempted to return his smile. Was it too much to hope that she might be able to have a private conversation with her fiancé?

"Excuse me," Anna said. "May we have some time—?"

Mrs. Werner interrupted her. "Do you need coffee, Miss O'Malley?"

"—alone?"

Shaking his head, Rafael put his hand over hers. "Danny needs to…eat."

She jerked her hand back. She wasn't even sure why. Then she felt horrible. He was to be her husband, but she didn't know him yet. Or was she just reacting to his refusal to spend time alone with her? Surely as the owner he could dismiss everyone with a snap of his fingers. But of course Daniel needed nourishment, too, and Rafael's concern for his brother was a good thing. She wanted to marry a man who had regard for his family's well-being. She was counting on his sense of familial obligation.

"Yes, I would like coffee." What she'd really like was a chance to talk to Rafael—alone—or at least with less activity around them. And really get to know him. Perhaps after the late supper for the men, they'd allow them a bit of time to talk.

Pressing her lips together, she felt like an island

in the swirl of activity around Rafael. Mrs. Werner dropped a kiss on her older son's forehead as if her hug had not been enough greeting. Juanita pressed close to Rafael, almost against his side. Her gaze was intent on him, while he seemed oblivious to the young girl's interest. Or was he simply used to being the center of attention?

What drew them to him, she didn't know. Yet. Surely as she got to know him, she would feel it, too. Right now she felt as empty as the grassland around the house. But once Rafael emerged as the man who had written her long letters about the beauty of the valley, the sweet scent of the orange trees in bloom, the warmth of the sun on the earth, then the hollowness in her chest would fill. His lack of attention had confused her, but he was here now.

Rafael squinted and leaned back in his chair, watching her. Mrs. Werner moved the lamp to the far end of the table, leaving his face in shadow. Daniel's warnings about disappointing Rafael rang in her ears. She squirmed on the hard chair, but it wasn't the chair that was uncomfortable; it was her skin.

"Juanita," shouted Mrs. Werner although the girl was right there.

Anna jerked out of the way as Juanita poured. She didn't want to risk more stains to her green silk. The girl shot her a dark look. Then she set down the coffeepot and slapped plates on the table. Juanita stood between her and Rafael as if to keep him from Anna. She wanted to draw the girl aside and warn her Rafael was too old for her. In a few years when Juanita was grown, there would be another man who would see how pretty she was with her long dark hair and sloe eyes. Anna suspected her concern wouldn't be well received, but perhaps she would be able to help when the calf love spell was shattered.

"How do you...like it here?" asked Rafael.

Her gaze shot back toward her fiancé. His brows drew together as he waited for her answer.

"I believe I would like it better if I actually had a moment to get to know you." Her stomach tightened. Her first time to actually talk to Rafael and she'd gotten distracted by Juanita.

He gave her the ghost of a smile, but she didn't believe he was amused. Then again, she had sounded a bit waspish.

She tried again. "When are we getting married?"

That really wasn't any better. She tried to think of what a cultured lady would say in this situation, but nothing came to her. Of course, it always seemed that ladies were very good at saying things without actually saying anything directly, but it wasn't her way to dance around an issue.

Heat cascaded through her as she remembered the dance with Daniel. Her cheeks burned as she tried to dismiss that. It was nothing but a bit of flirtation. She was with the man she intended to marry now, and her focus should be on him.

"Soon." Rafael's smile seemed more genuine this time, but she wondered if she was being laughed at. His attention shifted to Juanita, and he said a word to her that Anna didn't recognize.

Juanita's lips thinned as she cast a glance toward Anna. Maybe he had told the girl to give them space. Anna tried to give her a sympathetic glance, but Juanita whirled away.

"I should…court you." Rafael's gaze landed back on Anna. "First."

Court her? Was that necessary? "Why?"

He tilted his head. "Don't you want…courting?"

Courting was nice and all, but she hadn't expected it. Her face burned, and for the thousandth time in her life she wished her skin revealed less. "I hadn't thought on it. Weren't the letters our courtship?"

He studied her for a minute before he said, "Not at all."

His slow way of talking had her scooting to the edge of her seat, trying to hurry his words. Something was off about him, but as she tried to figure it out, Juanita stepped between them and poured a generous dollop of whiskey into his coffee.

A sick feeling settled in her belly. The way he'd been slumping in the saddle as he rode up might indicate this wasn't his first drink. "Have you been drinking already?"

"A bit."

Her throat tightened. In her family a "wee bit" could translate to a whole lot. She didn't know how much it meant with Rafael. He didn't seem drunk, but his skin glistened in the light that did reach him. Perhaps he was nervous around her and needed the libation to calm him. But in any case it wouldn't be the least bit ladylike if she were to complain about his drinking before they were even man and wife. She desperately wanted to like him, but so far she was more irritated than intrigued. She swallowed hard.

The man of the letters she'd liked. She just had to remember Rafael was the one who had written her—although it appeared Daniel was as familiar with the contents of the letters as she was. She had to put that thought out of her head. The brothers were close. No doubt they shared everything with each other, the same way her brothers Patrick and Sean told each other everything.

Folding her hands in her lap, she searched for a nonthreatening topic. "Your brother tells me horse thieves are a rare thing."

"Never before," said Rafael. Then he coughed weakly.

Perhaps that was nervousness. Lord knew she was nervous, too. Although not as much as she'd expected to be. Instead, she was blank and waiting for an indication that life with Rafael as her husband would be…enjoyable.

With the land he owned, at least there would never be a night sleeping huddled against the bricks of a building because the landlord had forced them to the street. The little ones wouldn't be crying because their bellies were empty. She wouldn't have her lungs ruined by working in a mill. Rafael would give her that. So even if she wasn't particularly enchanted with him, she would be mindful of her gratitude and make the best of marriage and count herself lucky. She knew how much worse her life could be. Her sister Brigit had married at sixteen. After three babies with a husband who couldn't keep food on the table, Brigit was dead before her twenty-first birthday.

Daniel entered the room, his eyes darting between her and Rafael as if he'd expected a brawl to break out. She resisted the urge to look to him for help.

Truth be told, she was not happy with Rafael, not happy that he was drinking again and not happy that he wanted to delay their marriage. Was he having second thoughts? She couldn't ask him with his mother, Juanita and Daniel hovering.

The others could have allowed them time alone for courting if that was what he intended, but this had to be the strangest courtship in God's green creation. "How does one 'court' when one is living under the same roof?"

Rafael blinked, then looked at Daniel.

Daniel sat across from her. When their gazes met, a shiver thrummed through her. For a second, all she could think about was how she had felt when they were waltzing and then when he sang to her. That was courting if anything was. She shook off the sudden heat in her blood. She couldn't think that way about Daniel, certainly not with Rafael sitting right beside her.

But when she looked back at Rafael, his eyes looked glassy and his brow furrowed. He was slumped in his chair as if he were exhausted. Worse than the way he looked was that her heart didn't beat faster, her breath didn't catch, her stomach didn't flutter.

"I expect he means you should take your time getting to know each other. You know, get used to each other before…" Daniel's voice trailed off. "He doesn't want to rush you."

It took her too long to realize they were talking about her impending marriage to Rafael. Well, and likely the relations that were a part of it.

Daniel's face darkened, and he looked down at his plate as he muttered, "He wants you to be comfortable with him before he takes you as his wife."

She turned to Rafael, who added, "Yes."

And he couldn't say that for himself? She supposed a lady might be grateful to not have her sensibilities assaulted by having to share the marriage bed with a husband she didn't know, but Anna wasn't so missish. "I don't mind, really."

"Prefer an eager bride…to one who…doesn't mind." Rafael's nostrils flared. His head rocked back with each breath he took.

Was this supposed to be courting? Although she knew what the brothers were getting at, she couldn't figure out a way she could acknowledge their point and remain in the framework of genteel discourse. She couldn't turn it around and say she was eager to learn the mysteries of the marriage bed. Certainly no well-bred woman would ever even acknowledge that such things occurred, let alone she might enjoy them or hoped to enjoy them.

Mrs. Werner ladled a concoction of shredded beef onto their plates.

Heat flooded her face. That they were even dancing around such issues with Rafael's mother in the room was too much. "If you mean to delay the marriage, I don't know what I can do to persuade you otherwise."

Rafael closed his eyes a second and breathed out heavily. Was the cad relieved? Was she so distasteful to him? Heaviness dropped through her stomach.

"Now that that is settled, we should talk of other things," said Daniel. "What would you like to talk about?"

For one thing, she'd like answers, but she was

reeling from the idea that Rafael was hoping to postpone the marriage; perhaps he hoped to postpone it forever. And then where would she be? But she couldn't press him with everyone around listening. She needed a subject that was safe to talk about.

She stared at her plate. Mundane details clicked off in her head. No one had a fork or a spoon. The dish looked like beef with the peppers Mrs. Werner seemed to favor that made Anna's mouth burn. Other than the same flat bread she'd been served before, there weren't any side dishes. She already knew they used the bread in lieu of utensils. She didn't see any vegetables when this should be the time when gardens were producing string beans and peas by the bushel.

"Do you not have a vegetable patch?"

Mrs. Werner exchanged a look with Rafael.

"Daniel does," Rafael said.

"It is more than a vegetable garden." Daniel's mouth flattened.

"Yes, yes, Daniel is the farmer," Mrs. Werner said. "He thinks we should grow more plants, but the cattle are more important. The fences to keep them out are nuisance."

She looked to Rafael because he'd seemed proud of Daniel's efforts in his letters, but he put a bite of the meat in his mouth.

"Madre has a few peppers, onions and tomatoes off the kitchen," said Daniel.

Too many peppers if Anna was the judge. She turned to Daniel. "I know you are growing grapes and almonds, but what else do you grow?" She hoped for potatoes and string beans.

"I have an orchard with peaches, oranges and lemons. I'm working on the irrigation to put in other produce." Daniel turned over a bit of meat on his plate. "With the right water supply, anything would grow in this valley."

"I tell his father it is a waste of land, but he does not listen," Mrs. Werner said. "He put in all these *estúpido* trees. Then the oranges, they rot on the ground."

Daniel's expression went flat.

Anna's shoulders inched toward her ears. Juanita's dark eyes flitted between the men and then to Mrs. Werner.

"He complain and complain the house is not clean, but he let fruit rot. He was a stupid man."

Rafael hissed, *"Silencio."*

Mrs. Werner pressed her lips together, carried the serving dish to a sideboard and put it down with a bang.

"You should…show her," said Rafael as if his mother hadn't just made her displeasure known.

She turned and wondered if looking at the garden or whatever it was might afford an opportunity to speak privately with Rafael. She could ask him if he didn't want to marry her. She didn't know what she'd do if he said he didn't, but not knowing would be worse. "Perhaps you could show me."

"Can't." He put another bite in his mouth.

Daniel leaned forward. "He has to go check the cattle tomorrow. He'll be gone all day."

"Yes, yes, he will be gone *mucho* hours. Perhaps days." Mrs. Werner returned to the table with her own plate. She sat as if the unpleasantness hadn't occurred.

Rafael grunted.

Anna felt as though she'd swallowed shards of broken glass. The strange friction between the Werner brothers and their mother left her feeling on the outside looking in. They all seemed to understand the reason she and Rafael weren't getting married immediately, but they hadn't told her. And she'd bet money Rafael could have had Daniel go in his place.

"I have to check the vineyards tomorrow. I've been away from them too long," said Daniel as if he'd read her mind.

So neither of them wanted to be with her. Her chest felt ripped open.

How long had Daniel been away from his plants? One day to track the men who'd tried to kill her—or at least had shot several men—she no longer knew what she thought about the stagecoach holdup. But that was neither here nor there. Rafael was doing his best to avoid her. It didn't even seem he wanted to talk to her if the way his mother and brother kept jumping into the conversation meant anything. Even Juanita seemed to be coming between them as often as possible.

"Rafael," she said firmly. "Why are you trying to avoid me?"

There was a beat of silence; then it was as if she'd accused him of murder.

"No, no. He wants to be with you in every way." Mrs. Werner sprang out of her chair.

His mother's reassurance only made Anna more uncomfortable.

Juanita spun and retrieved the coffeepot.

Daniel looked at Rafael, then leaned toward her. "He's not trying to avoid you. It's—it's just that a lot has happened, and he has to take care of the ranch. He has responsibilities. Minding the cattle is no place for a woman."

Her stomach burned. They acted as if he couldn't speak for himself.

"Yes, that." Rafael nodded toward his brother. He reached out and touched her arm.

She waited for the spike of awareness she experienced whenever Daniel touched her, but it never happened.

"Too tired," said Rafael, "to be good...company." He gave her forearm a light caress.

She stared at his hand and fought the urge to yank away from him. Then Juanita shoved between them and poured more coffee into Rafael's cup. He pulled his hand out of the way and stood.

Daniel jerked out of his chair with a clatter. He watched his brother, then eyed her out of the corner of his vision.

Rafael moved behind her chair. She started to twist to see him, but Mrs. Werner grabbed her arm, and Juanita leaned over to pour more coffee in her cup. Anna feared looking away from the girl's serving.

"Sorry, my sweet," Rafael whispered. He leaned down and his breath stirred her hair.

Her skin crawled.

Daniel was practically fighting to get around the table. For a second she thought he would pull Rafael away. It all seemed to be happening fast and slow at the same time. Her gaze kept going to Daniel as if it was pulled there. No, she had to stop that. She was to marry Rafael. Daniel didn't own his own place, and she needed to be married to a man who owned his own land.

"I'll make it...up to you...soon," Rafael said near her ear. He puffed too harshly, almost a gasp, and his breath smelled faintly coppery.

Her head buzzed with the idea that she didn't want his courtship. They should just get married, now, before she lost her nerve.

He straightened and took a few steps toward the courtyard door, and Daniel was right on his heels. Mrs. Werner and Juanita closed in on her. Anna pushed back her chair, determined to follow, but Juanita dumped the dregs of the coffee on her lap.

* * *

Daniel grabbed Rafael under the arms, ignored his low moan and bore half his weight as he got him out to the courtyard. He only hoped that Juanita and his mother were blocking Anna's view sufficiently that she couldn't see Rafe wasn't bearing his own weight as they left. He kicked the door shut behind him.

Rafe took a step forward unaided toward the grassy center of the courtyard. Concerned his brother would fall before he made it to his bed, Daniel followed. Before he made it off the walkway, Rafael grabbed the nearest post and spun as if he couldn't control his movements.

Rafael's eyes went wide. His breath rasped in and out, and his knees buckled. He blindly grabbed as he fell. Daniel caught him, and they latched together in a parody of the way he'd held Anna in his arms earlier. Rafe leaned in, clutching and twisting Daniel's shirt as he struggled to brace his brother. That he shouldn't have made Rafe get out of bed before he was healed enough added to the weight pressing down on Daniel.

Rafael sucked in breaths like a man who'd been running at top speed for the past hour and couldn't catch his breath, and Daniel prayed he hadn't made his brother worse. Rafe had to get better. The idea of life without him was unthinkable.

"Ma's…right," Rafael heaved out. "Got to… be gone…days."

"You can't do that. Anna is already suspicious." Daniel's stomach fell. How in the hell would they hide Rafael for days on end? Anna would be tearing apart the house. Worse than that, he'd seen the hurt pooling in her eyes, the stricken cast of her mouth. She was a vibrant girl, but this pretense and seeming rejection by Rafael was draining the color out of her. "We have to get you to your room before she comes out."

Daniel pushed Rafe backward.

"Diz—" He let go and slid down.

"Rafe," Daniel uttered in a low undertone, catching him.

Rafael's head lolled against Daniel's chest. His brother was as limp as an empty sack. His arms flopped at his sides, and his legs rocked side to side as Daniel shifted him. He still breathed. Holding the dead weight upright was taking everything Daniel had. He was afraid to grab his brother tighter around the chest for fear he'd do damage to the wound.

The door opened. *Hell!* He swung around, wondering how he was going to explain Rafael's faint. Juanita darted through and slammed the door. In rapid-fire Spanish she said Anna was going to kill her.

Dread skittered down his spine like field mice fleeing from a hawk. He twisted Rafe over and told Juanita to grab his legs. They had to get Rafael into his room before Anna saw him like this.

They hadn't gone more the three feet when the door opened again.

# Chapter Nine

*It is my fondest hope that we will marry. If I book your passage, will you come to California?*

Anna woke the same way she'd gone to sleep. Her thoughts spinning, lumps knotted in her belly and throat and the accusing eyes of the man she'd shot haunting her dreams.

Last night had done nothing to settle her turmoil. Even though nothing more than a dance had happened with Daniel, it very well could have. She was so lost and uncertain she would have gladly stayed in his arms and allowed him liberties, but she was here to marry Rafael.

His conversation last night—what little of it there was—would seem to indicate he still planned to marry her after a courtship. If he was avoiding her because he'd changed his mind, that would make sense, but he'd called her "his sweet" and promised to make it up to her. Well, he might as well start now, with answers.

She was done waiting for Rafael to make himself available to her. If they had a private conversation, they could get things settled. She had come out here to marry him, and there was no reason to delay. If he no longer wanted to marry her, she deserved to know now. She didn't need a courtship. She didn't need time. She needed to be settled in as the wife of a man with land.

Nothing was going to stop her from cornering him if she had to. Then she could quit fretting.

She quickly dressed in her old Sunday best, while trying to ignore the green silk hanging from an exposed rafter drying after being rinsed out. Again. Now in addition to the faint yellowish stains, there was a big brown smear where the dregs of the coffee had spilled into her lap. At this rate, she'd have to dye the dress black to be able to wear it.

After opening her door, she stepped onto the walkway. Across the courtyard Rafael's door stood open, and Juanita was sweeping inside. He must already be up.

Quickly, she walked to the main room and found it empty. Rafael's coffee cup from last night was where he'd left it, as well as the empty plates. She frowned at the mess as she opened the front door. The porch and yard between the house and the barn were empty, too. Rafael had to be in the house. Anna went back inside.

Juanita hurried in, her head down. "I tell Mrs. Werner you are here to eat."

She gathered the dishes in a fast rush, the plates clinking together.

"Juanita," Anna began.

Last night after the coffeepot contents were dumped on her, she'd been ready to tear the girl limb from limb, but Mrs. Werner had held her arms back until she wrestled free. By the time she made it into the empty courtyard, she'd realized she couldn't catch up with the young woman. And getting into fisticuffs with the adolescent was about as genteel as shooting a man.

*"Lo siento,"* Juanita said rapidly. "Sorry am I."

"It's all right. I'm not mad." Anna took a step toward the table, which only made Juanita scurry faster. She sorted through how to talk to the girl, who was in that awkward age between childhood and growing up.

Juanita rushed out the door, cold coffee sloshing out of one of the earthenware mugs she carried and the plates looking in danger of toppling to the ground.

Anna sighed. Dealing with her would have to take place eventually but obviously not this morning.

Returning to the courtyard, she looked left and right. Across the way Rafael's door was shut now.

But surely Juanita wouldn't have been sweeping his room while he was still in there. Still, Anna walked across and knocked on his door. When there was no answer, she turned the handle.

The low, wide bed was empty, the blanket neatly covering its expanse. Whenever Rafael got around to marrying her, she would be made a wife on that bed. The thought of that had provided wicked anticipation on the trip west, but now her throat went dry and her stomach lurched. She'd anticipated marrying a man who at least wanted her as a bride. And while she might be an undeserving Irish immigrant, he was a drunkard who ignored her. Seemed like a fair enough exchange to her.

Shaking her head, she returned to her room. Everything was exactly as she'd left it, bed unmade and all, but it was different, small and cold, not the shared bedroom she'd expected when she arrived. Not the welcome she'd anticipated. If Olivia and Selina were with her, they'd help her make sense of what was going on. But they were with the men who had asked them to be their brides in letters just the same as she'd been asked.

She hoped their journeys had met with better welcomes, but of course they would have. Selina and Olivia were beautiful, and they weren't frauds. But Anna had confessed the truth to Daniel. He'd probably already told Rafael—and if he hadn't, she would tell him herself.

Crossing the floor, she pulled the sheets and blanket up. As she made the bed, the oddness of her encounters with Rafael was like a hangnail she couldn't clip.

Really, this was getting ridiculous, but he hadn't breakfasted in the main room, so he was likely still in the house. Fine then, she'd search every room in the house until she found him.

She opened the door next to hers. Sprawled across the bed was Daniel, fully dressed. His only concession to his boots was his feet dangled off the side of the bed. His eyes were closed and his breathing was heavy and slow. Definitely sound asleep in spite of the sunlight filtering in through his window.

Had he been so tired last night he hadn't even undressed? No, his white shirt and brown pants hung over a chair. The plaid shirt stretched across his shoulders and the thick canvas pants molding his legs and backside were different.

She should back away and close his door, but seeing him unguarded and completely relaxed made him seem vulnerable and appealing. The urge to cross the room and pull off his boots for him warred with the idea that she needed to keep her distance from Daniel. No more moonlit dances or private conversations. If she didn't allow herself to be alone with him, there wasn't any danger of allowing their friendship to turn into something it shouldn't.

She shouldn't linger. The room was too small to offer any concealment for Rafael other than under the bed. She leaned over and looked at the open space.

Daniel opened his eyes and jerked his head up.

"Sorry," she muttered and backed up to pull the door shut.

"What?" He swung his feet to the floor and scrubbed his hands across his face. "Wait."

Something inside her went soft. She had to stop that.

"You want to go see the vineyard?" His hair was sleep tousled and his eyelids were inclined to droop.

Heat thrummed through her veins as the memory of their shared dance drowned out all her other thoughts. She wanted to cross the room and lay her hand on his chest, or perhaps smooth his hair—which she should never do. "No. I want to speak to Rafael. I was looking for him. I'll keep looking."

"He's not here."

Her chest squeezed. He couldn't have left already. It was not yet seven according to the clock in the main room. "I'll just be looking around anyway."

She half expected Daniel to spring off the bed and insist they leave before she could search the house—well, not top to bottom. It didn't have an upstairs or a downstairs. But he didn't. He just watched her.

Her suspicions faltered. Yet her feet seemed to have planted themselves in the stones of the walkway. "Where is he?"

"He went out this morning to check the herd." Daniel stood and stretched his arms out in front of him.

She didn't even know if it was a lie, but she wanted to believe him. "So he ate before he rode out, did he?"

"He took food with him," Daniel said flatly, and he turned to look out the far window.

"So a man who was so exhausted he could barely walk last night managed to be up and about before dawn?" She folded her arms.

"Yes. He's up by dawn most days."

Her stomach churned. Her belief that he had been in the house yesterday hadn't been fully eradicated. And it certainly seemed the family was shielding Rafael from her. Was it because he was a drunkard, or was something else going on? She just needed five minutes of conversation alone with him. Or even better fifteen minutes. She couldn't take this uneasy uncertainty any longer. She needed to know where she stood.

"That is the way it is here. The work doesn't wait. Tracking horse thieves and running a ranch leaves little time for courting. I'm sure Rafael would prefer to spend time with you."

If that were true, he could have spent time with her last night. The brothers counting the loss of their horses as more important than the same thieves trying to kill her and her fellow passengers made her throat dry.

Daniel tilted his head and looked at her.

A long breath escaped her. "Are you very certain he's already left?"

"I helped him load the wagon." Daniel's coffee-colored eyes flicked lower, and a rush of heat ran through her veins. She swallowed hard.

She had to banish the idea that she was more fond of her fiancé's brother than she was of her fiancé. It had to be because Daniel spent time with her and Rafael acted as though he couldn't wait to get away from her.

Certainly once she experienced the intimacies of marriage with Rafael—well, then she would surely fall in love with her husband. Then she would be able to put her growing attraction toward Daniel in its proper place. He was to be her brother. But she was in a strange place with strangers. With Daniel being the only one who spent time with her, of course she was growing too fond of him. He wasn't husband material. He didn't have his own home, let alone own any land.

Daniel shrugged with one shoulder. Then looked toward the window. "He'll ask the hands if they saw anything suspicious."

What was outside that kept drawing his attention? He looked back at her, then rubbed the side of his face as his eyes darted away.

Her stomach did a little flip. Was he lying to her about Rafael? Was he looking outside to see if Rafael was getting away? She leaned and peered out at the empty grassland beyond the house.

"What are you looking for?" she asked. If it was Rafael, would Daniel tell her?

"I was trying to determine how long the sun has been up. I didn't mean to go back to sleep this early."

"This early?" she echoed.

"It is early for a siesta. You certain you don't want to go with me?" he asked softly.

She shouldn't spend any more time alone with Daniel, but he knew where to find his brother and she didn't. "Only if you'll take me to where Rafael went."

Daniel looked toward the window. "I have to go divert the water. Check the grapes."

It wasn't an answer. "Then will you take me to where Rafael went?"

"The cattle are miles from here." He rubbed his nose and turned back to look her in the eye.

"Is the ranch so big that we couldn't find a herd of a thousand cattle?" Or was that a lie, too? She no longer knew what to believe.

He blinked a couple of times and ran a hand through his hair. "This time of year when the grass in the valley is drying out, we take them up into the mountains to graze. Off the ranch."

First she would make certain Rafael wasn't hiding in the house. Then she'd decide if the chance of Daniel taking her to meet his brother was worth the risk of spending more time alone with him. "I'm just going to keep looking around."

Half expecting him to stop her, she moved to the next door and opened it. Another bedroom, similar in size to Daniel's. The walls were bare except for a crucifix. A bunk bed was against the far wall. A worn pair of boots were under the bottom bunk. The next room was nearly the same.

Daniel's boots on the flagstones behind her let her know she wouldn't get far without him interfering.

"He's not here," said Daniel.

"Is he not? Then I'm looking at the house." She didn't look back at him. "If—" No, she was going to assume that Rafael would marry her. "As the future wife of the owner, I should have been shown the house," she said breezily. "I might want to sew new curtains."

"Ah," he said. "Better check with Madre first. She might not take it well if you start making changes without consulting her."

Okay, she didn't really want to make curtains, but she was going to check every room. The next open door revealed another small room with a set of bunk beds.

"These are the vaqueros' rooms," Daniel said.

She looked back at him.

"The ranch hands." He reached around her to close the door.

His body brushed hers, and a shiver ran through her. She tried to ignore it.

"Where are they? All the hands?" Was that a lie, too? It did look as though the rooms were being used.

"Rafael had them move the herd the day before you arrived. Since they are only moving them, they won't press them. They should be back in a few days."

Anna moved along the walkway to the next door. She reached for the knob.

"Knock first. That is Juanita's room." Daniel stepped to the edge of the walkway and folded his arms.

She followed his instructions, knocking on the bare wood. When there was no answer, she went in. The room was the same as the hands, except only a single bedstead with a white nightgown draped over it stood against the far wall. The blanket covering the mattress draped to the floor. A dress hung from a hook on the wall.

"I'm tempted to go find coffee to spill on her dress."

"Won't make you feel better," said Daniel with a faint smile. "At least not for long."

"Your mother says Juanita fancies herself in

love with your brother." If the girl had fallen in love with a man almost twice her age, that had to be bad.

A cloud passed over Daniel's face. "Most women do."

Anna crossed the space, lifted the edge of the blanket, bent and peered under the bed. A colorful straw basket held a scruffy rag doll. A wave of unwanted empathy for the girl who had to earn her living at such a young age swept through Anna. "She's hardly a woman."

"She's old enough to think she is." He'd lifted one foot and braced it on the post behind him, and his voice was flat.

Anna returned to the doorway and studied Daniel. Perhaps the relevant part of what he'd said was that women fell for his brother. If that was true, Anna didn't understand it. Rafael was handsome, but so was Daniel.

She closed the door and followed the covered walkway to the corner. The paving stones were slightly different as she turned. Pausing, she looked down at them.

"This part of the house with our rooms was the bunkhouse." Daniel pointed across the courtyard to the section that held the kitchen. "That used to be the main house, but my father decided to join it all together into one big hacienda. He thought if there was going to be war, he wanted a defensible building."

"For the War between the States?" Hadn't his father died long before the conflict seemed inevitable?

"No, war between Mexico and the United States. Didn't end up being a lot of fighting here."

He opened the next door, which contained a desk covered in papers and ledger books. "The office. You wouldn't know it, but ranching requires a lot of paperwork."

Several hand-drawn maps hung on the paneled walls. Noting shelves with books and a safe, she went to the desk. An open ledger showed listings of individual animals. "Who keeps all these records?"

"Rafe mostly keeps track of the cattle. I keep ledgers for the crops," Daniel responded.

Given Daniel was being so helpful, Rafael had to be out of the house. Mrs. Werner and Juanita had spent most of yesterday trying to steer her in different directions, and she'd been certain they had taken turns occupying her. Hell, even the first night, Daniel had practically picked her up to keep her out of Rafael's room.

The office didn't contain a place for a grown man to conceal himself. Her shoulders falling, she sighed. Rafael probably had eluded her again this morning, although she'd been trying to keep one ear open.

Looking for anything to focus on to hide her disappointment, she skimmed down the various columns in the ledger. Birth, sex, disposition of the animal—they kept a lot of detail on the individual livestock in a large herd. She flipped a page, seeing lots more records. Something niggled at her brain.

Daniel stepped closer. "Are you looking for something specific?"

Suddenly the air seemed charged. Her skin tingled as if she expected him to brush against her again. She turned toward the shelves lest he realize she'd gone a little weak in the knees.

Her gaze landed on the music box, and their dance, their nearness, the feel of his hand on her back swarmed in her brain and she could think of nothing else. Heavens, she had to stop thinking about him. She couldn't be falling for the wrong brother.

Only she was, which was all the more reason she had to marry Rafael soon.

"Just looking around," she managed to say. She averted her gaze from the music box.

An odd tripod with a box on it sat in the corner along with several poles linked with chains.

Daniel closed the open books. "That's my father's surveyor's equipment. Back in thirty-five, after the Mexican government took over California, they required landowners to document and mark their land. He liked California so much he decided to stay. So he married my mother and took over running her ranch."

She couldn't quite put a finger on what bothered her about the ledgers. "I very much get the feeling you are trying to hide something, Mr. Werner."

He folded his arms. "And here I was offering to show you anything you wanted to see."

"Anything?" she asked.

"What would you like to see, Miss O'Malley?"

She tried to read the expression in his dark eyes. "I want to see the rest of the house."

"This way, then." He opened the next door, one of a pair off the courtyard, and she discovered it led to a wide hallway. Beyond the open doors at the far end was grass. He opened a second door to Rafael's room.

Odd that it was so much larger than Daniel's, but then it was his ranch.

That seemed far too easy. "Then I want to see Rafael."

He raised his eyebrows. "He'll be back in a few days."

"I can't wait a few days. I need to speak with him. Alone. Today."

He ducked his head.

Her nose stung, and she blinked back possible tears. She'd never been a crier. She wasn't going to start now. She whirled out of the doorway and opened the door opposite. Branding irons, tongs and all manner of equipment hung on the walls, marking it as a storage room. Boxes, barrels and sacks were stacked and piled about, barely leaving room to get through. She didn't see any place where a person could hide.

Daniel's dark eyes followed her.

"So showing me anything doesn't include Rafael," she said.

Daniel's steps faltered.

If Rafael wasn't on a drunken spree and keeping to his bed, why was he avoiding her? "Is your brother disappointed in me?"

"No." Daniel slid his hand over the door frame and looked away. "Not that I know."

"I know I'm not as pretty as Selina or my friend Olivia, but I am thought presentable." She'd never thought of herself as ugly, although perhaps only a notch above plain.

Daniel's eyes met hers. "You're beautiful."

Her cheeks heated as she realized what she'd said. "I'm sorry. I wasn't fishing for compliments, and you don't have to say that."

"If Rafael doesn't think you're pretty, he needs spectacles."

In spite of her confusion, a warm shaft of appreciation slanted across the dark muddle of her mind. "Thank you."

His lips twitched. For a second she wished it were Daniel she was to marry. She shook off the thought. He didn't own the ranch, and she never wanted to risk being poor again. It seemed as though all her life had been a struggle to know where the next meal would come from. Even when she had thought she was secure in her job at the mill, the lack of cotton shipments had closed it, leaving her without a job through no fault of her own. She couldn't marry a man who had nothing in his own name. Not only were there future children to consider, but she hoped that Rafael might be able to employ some of her family members on the ranch or in the house, that one day she might be able to reunite her scattered family.

"Madre's room is next, but she is cooking by now."

"Is your brother having second thoughts about marriage? If he is, you can tell me." She caught Daniel's arm, wanting him to be honest with her, but touching him set off alarm bells. "If something has changed since I set out from Connecticut…" Her voice trailed away.

"Nothing has changed. But really, you should let me show you more of the ranch today."

She should pull her hand back, but the firm feel of his forearm was like a magnet to her palm.

"If you come with me to the vineyard and orchards, this afternoon we'll see if we can spot the herd," said Daniel.

The last thing she should do was spend more time alone with Daniel, but if that was the only way she'd find Rafael, then she had to go with him.

## Chapter Ten

*You asked a great many questions, and I will attempt to answer them in what is likely to be a haphazard fashion. It will likely take a novel or two, so I will answer over the course of several letters. You need not reply to every letter, but if you could manage to write once a fortnight, I will be content.*

Daniel looked at the hand on his arm and resisted the urge to fold his over the top of it. Anna didn't mean anything by it, and the riot of sensation going off in his body was more than inappropriate when she was trying to learn when Rafael would marry her. "He's not avoiding you. It's just that everything has been *loco* around here since the horses came up missing."

Even he'd gone *loco*, telling her they could try and spot Rafael with the herd this afternoon, but he had to get her out of the house or she'd end up following one of them straight to Rafael.

*"Loco?"* her mouth formed the word, but her eyes turned distant.

"Crazy. Plumb crazy. I'm sure in few days…" How long did it take a gunshot wound to heal enough to not appear so fresh that Rafe could marry her? "Rafael will spend more time courting you. He's already frustrated he's spent so much time trying to track the thieves and has nothing to show for it."

She slid her hand off his forearm, and spikes of desire slammed him.

"Couldn't you have gone to check the herd and question the cowboys instead of Rafael?" she asked.

A wave of guilt swept over Daniel. Anna was trying desperately to sort out the seeming rejection by her beau, and he couldn't explain it had nothing to do with her—or everything to do with her, given that she'd shot Rafael. "I could have, except he knew I needed to see to my produce. I tracked yesterday, too."

Her mouth flattened.

He didn't know what to say, so he walked ahead of her and tapped on his mother's bedroom door. When there was no answer, he opened it.

Anna came up beside him and looked in. He tried to imagine how she saw the ornately carved headboard, the brightly colored rugs on the floor. This chamber was the only bedroom with a fireplace, which was only needed on the coldest of winter nights.

Anna's brow knit.

"Seen enough?"

She shook her head and walked into the room. He wanted to grab her and pull her out. He'd seldom been in this room, hadn't wanted to be in there since his father died. The space reminded him too much of the morning his poppy had been stiff and cold and the parent who had loved him was gone.

He'd been half-afraid of Rafael then. Rafe had been bigger, tougher and not always kind in the way of an older brother to a pesky brother five years younger. But that night Rafe had crawled into bed with Daniel and held him as he wept. His brother had shielded him from Madre's rage when he'd spilled or broken things and had loved him when he most needed it. Last night Daniel had sat by Rafe's bed long after everyone else slept, giving him water when he woke and watching over his brother until Rafe told him to go to his own bed before he fell over.

Anna headed toward the large wardrobe and threw back the doors. Inside were dozens of dresses that Madre hadn't fit into in ages. Anna shifted them as if she expected to find something behind them. Good Lord, was she expecting to find Rafael hiding behind their mother's skirts?

"He's not here."

She backed out of the wardrobe and shut it.

He frowned at her. "We should leave. Madre won't like finding us rifling through her things."

"You're not rifling." She looked toward a strongbox under the bedside table. "What's in the little safe?"

"Valuables, I imagine. That is what one puts in a safe. But you'd have to ask Madre."

He couldn't remember being far enough in Madre's room to have even noticed the stout box before or the padlock on it. Rafael kept the money in the safe in the office. And his mother's jewelry—what she wasn't wearing—was scattered across her bureau. Still, it wasn't any of his business, nor Anna's. "But you shouldn't ask, because then she'll wonder why I'm showing you her private quarters. Come on. We're done in here."

She took one last look around and sauntered toward the door.

"Do you want to see the kitchen? Although you've already seen it."

"In the dark. I'd like to see it in the light of day."

"This way, then." He only hoped that if Madre and Juanita were preparing food for Rafael, they wouldn't be obvious.

They entered the kitchen, and Anna looked around.

"Good morning, I have some *chile* and eggs for you," said Madre. She was stirring a lot of eggs in a skillet.

Anna blanched.

"Ma, will you make me some without the chiles?" he asked. "My stomach is upset."

Madre narrowed her eyes, but then he jerked his head toward Anna as he rubbed the spot on his chest where Rafael's wound was. Madre would think she was making them for Rafael but would have to serve some of them to him.

Madre rolled her eyes and muttered, "Fine. I will make special eggs for you. You go wait at the main room."

Anna's visual inspection of the kitchen returned to Madre. "Where is Juanita?"

Daniel stiffened. Was she even now taking food to Rafael? But, no, a basket was on the table. If he didn't miss his guess, it would be filled with food and drink for Rafael.

"She forget to feed the chickens when she gather the eggs. She is a silly girl. Do not worry, Miss O'Malley. I will not let her pour your coffee again. I will tell her she has to eat in the kitchen instead of with us."

"That's not necessary."

Oh, but it was. Here he thought he'd been brilliant loading Rafael in the wagon and taking him down to the hide in the trees along the creek in the early-morning hours. He could fetch him back and return him to his room in the evening, but he might as well rest in the wagon during the day. It wasn't as if Rafael was in any shape to be out of bed, but Anna was onto them and trying to catch them out.

"But I insist," said Madre.

His mother hadn't witnessed Anna looking in every nook and cranny to uncover Rafael. The last thing he wanted was anything more to spark her curiosity. He should have realized her inquisitiveness would be boundless from her letters. She had wanted to know everything.

"Miss O'Malley is coming with me to see the grapes after breakfast." He caught her around the waist and steered her with a hand to her back toward the door. She moved smoothly as if he were guiding her in a dance.

As long as they stayed a few miles away, she wouldn't be able to tell if Rafe was with the vaqueros, but he had to get her out of the house so she wasn't following Juanita or Madre to the trees as they took care of Rafael. "You do ride, don't you?"

Her green eyes bore into his, and she blinked. Her mouth snapped shut as her eyes shot daggers at him. He had her safely to the doorway and moving forward, but he didn't want to let her go.

Daniel's palm still pressed at the base of her spine, and even though he was pushing her through the door of the main room, the feel of his hand soothed her. She wanted to protest that she hadn't been able to look in the larder or the pantry off the kitchen, but she didn't really expect Rafael was hiding there.

Daniel looked down on her. Amusement danced in his eyes. "You might want to change into something more sturdy. I'm sure Rafael could handle the disappointment if we see him."

"Should I change now or wait and see if I make it through breakfast without a stain?"

"After. The eggs will be done soon. Although I bet you're safe." He moved away from her.

The loss of his touch left her feeling as though he'd taken away a beloved heirloom.

He ran his palm along the long table. "My father made this table, the porch and shingled all the roofs from one giant sequoia tree."

The way he caressed the wood made her shiver. But one tree couldn't have produced enough wood to do all that. "Methinks you've kissed the Blarney Stone."

He looked blank.

Her Irish. "Sorry, you're telling tall tales."

"Not tall tales, tall trees." He smiled. "My father took me to see them before he died. Many of them stand more than three hundred feet tall, and it would take twenty men holding hands to reach around them. See, the tabletop is all one piece." He pulled out a chair for her.

She looked at the grain of the wood and couldn't find a seam. Perhaps he was telling the truth. "All right. I don't see a joint."

"You should have Rafael take you to see the giant trees one day."

The only problem was she'd much rather see them with Daniel. How could she have fallen for the wrong brother? She sat and let him push in her chair. "Is it far?"

"Maybe a hundred miles. Took my father four trips with two pairs of oxen to get all the wood home." He went around and seated himself on the opposite side of the table.

Mrs. Werner came in carrying two plates heaped with eggs. She set them down in front of them. "I'll be back with the coffee."

Anna looked down at her eggs laced with tomatoes, onions and green bits of chilis.

Daniel slowly slid his plate across and hooked a finger under the edge of hers and pulled it toward him. "Thought you might want a trade."

The plate in front of her contained none of the green. Her heart flipped over. She looked up to meet his dark eyes.

"Madre forgets that not everyone likes their food spicy." He seemed so very aware of her and what she was doing.

"I'm sure I'll get used to it in time, but thank you."

Still, she wondered at his subterfuge to get his mother to fix eggs without the chilis. And her belief that they weren't hiding Rafael from her faltered. Were they more comfortable tricking each other than asking for what they wanted? And where was Rafael? Was he simply avoiding her or was there a deeper game afoot?

Daniel saddled two horses and led them to the front of the house to wait for Anna.

She didn't come out the front door as he expected. Instead, she came around the side of the house, her straw hat shading her face and a muted green-and-blue plaid gown molding her form down to her waist with only a gentle flair of the skirt below instead of the wide skirts of her other dresses. The air suddenly seemed thin.

He sucked in a deep breath and tried to keep his wits about him. "You just had to check Rafael's room one last time," he said mildly. He waved an arm in the direction of the open front building that was the barn. "Want to check in there before we go?"

Her head tilted to the side, and she studied him for a minute. "If you don't mind, I believe I will."

"Be my guest," he answered.

She wouldn't find Rafe in there, and he supposed that her determination to check the building showed that he hadn't entirely convinced her that they weren't hiding Rafael. He should start trying to learn what she would do if she found out the stagecoach robbers were them. Although how he'd manage that without tipping his hand, he didn't know.

He hitched the horses to the porch and followed after her. Upon entering the structure, he found her on the ladder looking into the loft area. In other parts of the country a loft might be used to store hay, but there was no need for that here. Grazing could be had year-round. She would quickly see that other than a few bags of grain, nothing was up there. He moved to the bottom of the ladder and did his best to avoid looking up the skirts she had lifted in the front, exposing a great deal of white petticoat.

She lifted her foot off the rung and reached down.

"Satisfied?" he asked.

She missed the rung and slid down the ladder. He caught her around the waist and swung her down.

"You startled me."

"My apologies, Miss O'Malley." It must be tricky to climb a ladder with skirt and petticoats.

He didn't want to let go of her, even though he had set her safely on the ground. If she thought her person less appealing clad in a simpler gown, she was mistaken. The lack of ornament only meant his gaze went straight to deciphering what was underneath.

"Oh, call me Anna." She brushed her hands together. "You are to be my brother soon."

*Brother. Damn.* His thoughts were far from brotherly, and he had to stop thinking of her in that way. He turned and walked out of the barn into the sunshine. "Shall we go?" he asked once he thought he could speak. "Anna."

It was a simple no-frills kind of name, but it suited her. And it went better with his name than with Rafael's, which was a *loco* thought he tried to quash.

She stopped halfway between the barn and the house. She turned around. "Where is the wagon?"

"Rafael has it."

She turned around and looked at him, her brows beetled together.

Daniel lurched into an explanation. "He took supplies up to the men. And if he plans on slaughtering one of the animals, he'll need it to haul the meat back."

She stared at him, and he bit his tongue rather than make up more excuses for why Rafael took the wagon. She couldn't know it wasn't normal. And too much explaining would sound fishy.

"Are you ready to mount up?"

She nodded and continued toward him. He just drank in her approach. He should have pretended to adjust a saddle or something.

"What?" she asked as she grew near and his appraisal was obvious.

"Are you always so curious?" He boosted her into the saddle.

"Well, nothing has been as I expected it to be." Her hand braced on his shoulder, and fire singed his veins. *Santa Maria*, he had it bad. He needed Rafael to get well enough to assume his courting role.

She leaned forward and stroked her mount's neck. And even watching her stroke the dumb beast sent a blast of heat through him. He was telling Rafe tonight that he couldn't do it anymore. He couldn't keep standing in for his brother, when in the end she would be Rafe's wife.

"Try this one." Daniel handed her a freshly plucked grape.

Anna bit into it, and spikes shot from her mouth along her jaw, pulling the corners of her mouth back. "Too tart," she answered.

He handed her another. The juices burst in her mouth sweet as sin. "Much better."

He burst one open with his thumb, wiggling apart the plump flesh.

Was he planning on taking the entire day picking single grapes? She cast a glance toward the steadily rising sun. "What are you doing?"

"When most of the seeds turn brown, they're ready," said Daniel.

"I thought you said you needed to water the vines."

"Wanted to check them before I had to walk in mud." He cast a glance at her. "Told you it would be this afternoon before we can try to find the herd."

Anna sighed. Without his help she'd never find Rafael, so she'd have to wait. She'd be better off if she could remember to be grateful, but patience had never been her strong suit.

They walked along the rows of vines and Daniel picked a handful of grapes from different clusters and checked them for ripeness. "If you want, you could go sit in the shade of the orange trees while I work."

She glanced over to where he'd spread a blanket on the ground in the shade. She was too impatient to sit waiting on Daniel, but she couldn't get on the horse and just ride off looking for Rafael. As Daniel had pointed out, the land was vast. Before they'd been gone fifteen minutes the low roll of hills and wooded areas had blocked the house from sight. Getting lost would be frightfully easy. Besides, she had no idea which way to go as they hadn't seen the cattle from the crest of any of the hills they'd passed over on the way to the vineyard and orchard. "That's all right. I'd like to talk."

"Okay." He said it easily, as if he weren't trying to hide anything. But then he'd been easy with her checking all the rooms. Probably because he'd known she wouldn't find anything. "What do you think of California so far?"

Did it matter what she thought of California? The more important question was what did Rafael think of her? She raised her head and looked across the river toward the mountains. "What I've seen is beautiful."

"It's all beautiful." Daniel folded back his sleeves, exposing strong forearms. "Even Death Valley is beautiful in its own way."

"The name doesn't sound pretty." She jerked her head up away from her fascination with his hands with their long tapered fingers and the sinewy strength of his forearms with their coating of fine, dark hairs. Even with the mountains, rolling hills and lush river to look at, she'd rather look at him. How was she going to manage marriage to his brother when Daniel was around?

She'd just have to, she told herself sternly. Just like she'd marched to the mill each morning. Marrying Rafael was what she'd come to do, and she was going to follow through. Even as they rode and Daniel pointed out distant landmarks and the boundary markers at the southern edge of the ranch, her stomach had churned with the knowledge that Rafael was the man who owned it.

Daniel continued his explanation. "Well, a group of forty-niners were foolish enough to try and cut through the valley instead of going the long way around." He strode toward the fence and a tarpaulin that was tied to it. "Only half of them made it out alive. Nothing can live there long. It's too hot and dry."

She trudged along beside him as he pulled on leather gloves, then uncovered a hoe and a shovel.

He took the hoe and hacked at the weeds sprouting around the grapevines.

"What do you do with all these grapes?"

"Mostly sell them. Keep some and make wine."

"You said you might plant other things next season."

"Thinking about melons and lettuce."

As long as he was interested in planting other things. "Have you considered growing potatoes?"

"I'd like to. A lot of easterners crave them. I heard tell of a man in San Francisco who paid a hundred dollars for a potato, but I don't know the first thing about growing them." Daniel turned the dark loamy soil. "No one around here does."

"I do. I could help." She cast around and saw a low ridge running along the ground. "We used to make little mounds like that and plant the potatoes in them." That was what they'd done back in Ireland.

Daniel gave her a half smile. "The mole line? That ground raised up in the fifty-seven earthquake. That was a bad one. The ground shook for a full minute. The house had a lot of damage."

A frisson of unease ran down her spine. Not only was everything not as it seemed here but the very ground could move under their feet. "I've never felt an earthquake."

"You will. But most of them are nothing."

"If you say so." She swallowed hard and rubbed

her arm while staring at the ground that apparently might decide to toss her about at any second.

"I do. I've lived through too many little ones to count, but only the one really bad one." His tone was gentle, almost as if he knew earthquakes scared her and he was trying to soothe her. "The bad ones don't happen all that often, maybe once every fifty to a hundred years. So we've got nothing to worry about."

She nodded, although she wasn't entirely reassured.

Daniel leaned on his hoe, his head tilted to the side. His lips slightly curled. "We don't get snow, tornadoes or hurricanes. Nature must have some means of reminding people she's still in charge."

"I suppose," said Anna.

"So if you want to educate me on how to grow them—" he resumed hacking at the ground "—I'll see about sending back east for potato seeds."

She smiled. He really didn't know anything about potatoes. "You don't use seeds. You just plant the potatoes themselves. You can even start them growing roots, then cut out each eye and plant the chunks. They are the easiest things in the world to grow, as long as you don't have too much water. Then they can get blight."

He'd stopped and was watching her, a grin on his face.

"You knew potatoes don't grow from seeds."

He shrugged. "Just wanted to see if you knew what you were talking about."

She should be annoyed, but she wasn't. It was more like a private joke they were sharing. She smiled back. "I know I should not, but I do. And I would be eternally grateful to have potatoes as long as we can keep some for eating."

"Of course. We'd keep as many as you want." He moved to the ditches and pulled up wooden gates to make the river water divert through the trench in the row he'd just hoed. At first the trickle of water went no more than ten feet. The dry earth greedily soaked it up. But as the dirt darkened from saturation, the water flowed farther and farther.

"I lost some of my vines and the irrigation windmills with the flooding last winter, but I can't get too far from the river. It is too dry for them."

Now that he was relaxed, she should start prodding. She bit her lip and tried to form the right question about Rafael, but nothing came to mind. She bent and pulled a couple of weeds from the soil.

"I didn't bring you out here to work." He leaned on the hoe.

"Won't it go faster if I help?" She straightened and brushed her bare hands. She should have worn her gloves. "Then we can go find Rafael."

Daniel's expression went flat. "No, it won't go faster. We have to wait until the ground is saturated. I can't leave the sluice gates open, or the river will flood the vineyard."

"I just want to get everything settled." She looked toward the mountains. "I thought I would be married by now."

"You still want to marry him?" Daniel swung the hoe at the ground.

She hesitated long enough that Daniel stopped attacking the soil, and his dark eyes searched her face. Was he testing the waters because he felt the attraction between them, too?

Her heart thumped awkwardly in her chest. If she had any hope of reuniting her family, she needed to marry a man of wealth, a man who could employ or support her brothers and sisters until they could get on their feet. Rafael was that man, not his dependent brother.

"That is why I came out here to California." To a place where the ground could shift underneath her. She had to marry Rafael. When she'd arrived, she'd been eager and believed he was the right man for her. "I want to marry the man who wrote to me, but your brother doesn't seem like the same man."

Daniel stared at her for what seemed like forever. Then he spoke. "And you're not exactly what he should have expected."

Her face heated. "Touché."

"Anna." He sighed. "I've already said Rafael

will spend plenty of time with you, but he has to take care of the ranch first."

"Yes, you've said." She dropped her gaze to the dark green foliage of the grapes. That didn't totally explain his avoidance of her, because he hadn't talked to her long enough to know she wasn't exactly as she'd portrayed herself. "I should think that he would be eager to get to know me, but he seems intent on avoiding my company."

"He talked to you last night." Daniel scraped the dirt.

"You and your mother did most of the talking." Rafael had said hardly anything. Even when she'd been peppering him with questions. She frowned at the long row of grapevines. One thing had been clear in their conversation, though. "Why are the trees and vineyards considered yours when they are on your brother's ranch?"

"My father started them. Besides, Rafe said he'd sell me this bottomland where my vineyards and orchards are."

What was he waiting on? "When?"

His expression faltered. "When the United States gives him the title to the land."

Her heart jolted, and her ears buzzed. Had she heard that correctly? "He doesn't have the title to his ranch? He doesn't *own* all this?"

Daniel waved a hand dismissively. "He has the land grant paperwork from Spain, but the government is making Spanish landowners prove their ownership. The next hearing is in a few months. Don't worry. It's just a formality."

She was aware of his gaze following her, but her mind was spinning around the idea that Rafael didn't actually own the ranch in the eyes of the United States. How could it be a mere formality more than a decade after the transfer of California to the United States? "Could they turn down his claim?"

"Anna," he said with a sigh.

But he didn't say no, which meant he could lose the land. She'd risked everything to marry a man who might end up owning nothing.

# Chapter Eleven

*California is the most wonderful place in the entire world. The weather is mild, the mountains are breathtaking and the valley where our ranch is found is rich with gently rolling hills.*

Daniel stared at Anna's horrified expression. Why had he even mentioned the hearings? He should have let Rafael tell her. "They won't take his land away from him."

"But—"

"They won't," Daniel said firmly. Except they could. And Rafe had been worried enough about it that he'd sent for an Anglo bride to strengthen his position in the proceedings. "Don't worry about it."

"Telling me not to worry doesn't help," said Anna. "So all the other Spanish landowners have kept their land, have they?"

Daniel closed his eyes a second and gripped

the hoe tightly. "Do you know your voice gets lyrical sometimes?"

She pursed her mouth. "I'm Irish. It is how we talk." Then her tone flattened. "Could your brother lose the ranch?"

He hit the dirt with the hoe. "He's not going to lose the ranch, but it has been weighing on him. The proceedings are being drawn out so long that many a ranchero has had to sell his land to pay for the lawyers, translators and the surveys. Winning can be a hollow victory. But the paperwork is in good order, and my father did the surveys."

Her skin turned pale, the reddish freckles standing out in harsh relief against her milky skin. Then red crept up from her neck. The play of colors fascinated him, and he lost the thread of what he should say to Anna. He was digging too deep a hole, and it wasn't with the hoe.

Then he had to wonder if he'd told her because he wanted to know if she would renege on her promise to marry Rafael.

"What would happen if he loses?"

Daniel shrugged. "Then we'll stake new claims for land in the valley. Or buy land. The livestock will still be Rafael's, and if I can't get this section, I'll move as many of my vines and trees as I can transplant." Heat crept under his collar. She wasn't asking about him. "Anyone can claim three hundred and sixty acres and homestead it."

She flinched. It would be a drastic reduction

in the size of Rafael's ranch, and he'd have to get rid of hundreds of head of cattle. Her eyes looked very green, like the underside of an oak leaf, and they begged him for answers. "Why would he advertise for a wife when the future of his ranch is uncertain?"

Try as he might, Daniel couldn't form a lie to shield her from the truth. "He thinks having an Anglo wife will help him at the hearings."

A small sound escaped her, something between a gasp and a cry.

He clutched the hoe tighter. He could not gather her in his arms and comfort her. Could not, should not, would not. "Anna, he did pick you."

"Even though I'm Irish, not English?" She shook her head.

"I doubt that matters. Anglo is Anglo."

"Then what is he waiting for?" Her eyes begged for answers he couldn't give her. "Why is he spouting all this nonsense about courting me?"

Her words burned through his gut.

"For goodness' sake, can we please go find him so I can tell him I'm ready to marry him?" She turned her palms up and gestured. "I don't need a courtship. And if I can help him get the title to the ranch…" She swallowed. "Then I have to marry him."

*Dios*, it wasn't as if he wanted to marry her instead of Rafael. She was pushy and demanding.

And the only thing she cared about was being married to the ranch owner. So why did his stomach hurt? "Fine. As soon as I get the gates open, we'll ride to the top of that hill. We should be able to see for miles."

And please let the herd be far enough away that he could convince her not to follow it.

From the top of the hill, the cattle could have been ants for all the size they appeared. A broad swath of them moved north. A lighter-colored horse appeared at the back of the mass. Daniel wasn't certain which one of their vaqueros it was, but it sure as hell wasn't Rafael.

Anna squinted as if trying to identify the men.

"They're quite far away." Daniel's saddle creaked as he leaned forward. His stomach turned at the idea of more lies.

"I don't see the wagon." She raised her finger and moved it up and down, her mouth forming *one, two…* "I only see six men. Isn't that how many cowboys work for your brother?"

"Rafael might not have reached them yet." Daniel rubbed his itching nose with the back of his hand. "Or he might have gone ahead to where they expect to stop for the night. Either way, it would take hours for us to reach them."

"Hours?" She twisted in her saddle. Her mount sidestepped, and she grabbed the horn to steady herself.

Daniel nodded. Her skirt was hitched up, exposing her calves encased in black stockings above her ankle-high boots. Her dress wasn't meant for riding, and he had to think she was likely to get chafed with only her thin drawers between her and the saddle. But he had no business worrying about those parts of her. "Even if we galloped the horses, I'd say it would be more than an hour to reach them, and you don't look all that…comfortable on horseback." He looked up at the sun. "If you're not a regular rider, I can guarantee you'd be saddle sore."

"I haven't been on a horse for years, but I can manage." She grimaced. "How far away are they?"

"Six to seven leagues." He rubbed his nose again and lifted one shoulder. More like three leagues. And Spanish leagues at that. Really, they were on the far northern edge of the ranch, and the ranch was a little less than eight miles long. "We might as well go back down to the orchard and eat our lunch."

She twisted toward him, her green eyes nailing him. "You really think they're around twenty miles away?"

He cleared his throat. "Spanish leagues aren't quite as long as English."

He started his horse down the hillside.

"Well, if it will take me hours, I'd better get going," Anna called.

Alarm skittered down his spine. "I'm not done in the vineyard yet."

"As long as I keep that line of mountains to my right, I should be able to travel pretty much straight to the herd," she continued blithely.

"I can't let you ride across the open country-side alone," he said.

"Why not? You told me it was perfectly safe."

"When you were with me. And I had a shot-gun just in case." Daniel spurred his horse down the hill. How in the hell would he stop her if she decided to take off across the land? "The horse thieves could still be out there."

She cast him a dark look. "I thought you said the stagecoach robbers were in Mexico."

"Probably in Mexico." The sinking feeling in the pit of his stomach wasn't going away.

She'd been silent as they rode up the hill and now was silent again as they rode down, but he was fairly certain he hadn't heard the end of it.

When they reached the edge of the orchard, he dismounted and went to help her down, but she looked past the trees and said, "I can start ahead, and, if you are so worried about me going alone, you can gallop your horse to catch up to me when you're done."

He searched for a way to stop her, but in the meantime he caught the horse's bridle. "Anna—"

"Either Rafael wants to marry me or he doesn't." She stared off into the distance, refusing to meet his eyes. "I want to know now. Even if I have to ride for hours to confront him."

"How could he not want you? You are beautiful and—" The traits he could list about her, such as she was damn inquisitive, overly skeptical and too smart for her own good, weren't things he thought would help the cause. "And spirited—"

"Neither of you see spirited as an asset. I'm not beautiful, and I'm not a lady. And if your brother wants rid of me, then I wish he'd say so."

He hated that Anna was being hurt by their subterfuge, but if he told her the truth and she wanted to turn them in, they were in a world of trouble. "Everything has been thrown on its head because of the robberies. Trust me—it will all work out in the end. Rafe just asked me to take care of you while he sorts things out."

She looked at him again. He could see the yearning to believe in her green eyes, but also the skepticism in the stiff way she held herself. "Why? What has become more important than getting to know his bride or getting married? Especially if he thinks our marriage will help him keep the land. The robbers are long gone, aren't they? It is more like everyone is trying to hide him from me."

Acid burned in his stomach, and the hairs on his arm stood up.

"Even if I have to spend a night outside, I would rather talk to him *today*."

"You cannot mean to camp with a group of men."

Her eyes narrowed. "It wouldn't be the first time I've had to sleep outside, and the weather is so much nicer here."

A mild outrage flitted through him at the idea of her having to sleep without shelter, but the bigger problem of stopping her from realizing Rafael wasn't with the herd dug claws into his back.

"Please let go of the reins," she said icily.

"You can't go."

"Why not?"

"Because Rafael isn't with the herd."

Her gaze swiveled around and pinned him. Her throat worked as she blinked at him as if she didn't know what to think. "Where is he?"

*Hell!* He was going to have to lie more to her. For a second all he wanted was to just tell her the truth, but he couldn't. Not until he had an idea what she would do if she knew her betrothed was the stagecoach robber she'd shot.

"He's out tracking the thieves." He reached up. "Come on, Anna. Let me help you down."

Shaking off his outstretched hands, she dismounted without his help. Once on the ground, she met his gaze squarely and asked in a deadly still voice, "I ask again, why is finding them more important that getting to know me?"

"Because we might know the men." He tensed,

waiting for the earth to shake or lightning to
strike.

"What?" Her jaw dropped.

It almost wasn't a lie. They knew the men. He
held his breath and watched her face as she figured out what he'd said. Her forehead crinkled in
confusion; then her eyes widened and her emi-
nently kissable mouth rounded in an O.

He tensed.

She snapped her mouth shut. Her pale cheeks
bloomed. Her jaw thrust forward, she stepped toward him. Her voice low, she said, "You know
who took your horses and held up the stage?"

"I said we might," he repeated.

"Who?"

"We have our suspicions."

She took another step in his direction. "Who?"

He scraped at the dirt by his feet. "Could have
been some of our hands or former hands or it
could have been some of our Valquez cousins."

"You know for certain, do you?"

"Of course not." He sucked in a deep breath.
Now was the time to sound her out, find out what
she would do if she knew Rafael was the main
robber. "Rafael is trying to find out, but he doesn't
know what to do if he learns…someone he trusted
did this."

"He should turn them in," she said unequivo-
cally.

"So he can watch them hang?"

She swallowed hard.

He pressed his advantage. "After all, we have other horses and nothing was taken from the stage."

"They. Shot. People."

Not the answer he'd hoped for. And he wanted to quibble about the shooting. He certainly hadn't shot anyone. "You said you didn't want to be responsible for the man's death. How would you feel if it were someone you knew? Perhaps someone you were related to?"

"It doesn't matter." Perhaps she was a little less vehement. "And they wouldn't hang unless they were convicted by a judge and jury."

She paced away down the row and then pivoted and returned while he stood holding the horses. "Rafael is trying to find the robbers, is he?"

"Something like that," he muttered.

"And what will he do if he finds he knows them? Turn them in or help them get away?"

"I don't know."

"Has he no honor?" she whispered.

Daniel swallowed hard. "I believe he is tormented by the idea that he might have to turn them in. I don't know if he's made a decision. He might ask why they held up the stage before he decides."

Her brows drew together. "The robber said he was looking for a man who'd cheated him in Santa

Fe. Or at least that is what one of the passengers translated."

"And if that was the sole reason they stopped the stage, would you want them hanged?"

"Daniel, I shot the robber because he was shooting at us. Whatever their reason for holding up the stagecoach, everything changed when shots were exchanged."

"Who fired first?" he challenged.

"It doesn't matter." Her eyes narrowed. "Is he hiding them already?"

"No. Rafe's not hiding anyone." Technically the truth, because they were hiding him. "I don't know what he'll do when he finds them, but I trust him to do the right thing. Either way his decision will weigh heavily on him. But you shouldn't think his neglect has anything to do with you, because it doesn't. Once he has this settled, he'll make you forget that he wasn't much of a suitor when you first arrived." He would, too. Rafe could charm a coyote if he had a mind to.

She closed her eyes as if she'd forgotten why they had started discussing this. "He should turn them in. That man shot a one-armed ex-soldier in his only remaining arm. I don't think that is something that can be forgiven. What I don't understand is all the trickery."

"We were afraid to tell you what we suspected. Believe me—I'd rather be honest." And that was the truth.

Her eyes narrowed again. "Really? Then why did you lie to your mother to get her to fix me eggs without chilis?"

Daniel sucked in a deep breath. "She already thinks you don't like her cooking."

"You could have just said the eggs were for me." Anna ducked her head and folded her arms. Then she lifted her eyes and tilted her head. "Or I suppose I should have asked myself. But I didn't want the food she'd already made to go to waste."

"Don't worry. They won't go to waste." He nodded his head over toward the water where he'd set a pot in the shadowed shallows. "The eggs with chilis are part of our lunch. But you don't have to eat them. There's beans and bread, too."

"Still, why trick her instead of just asking her to make eggs without chilis?"

He walked the horses to where they could graze. "My mother can be *loco* at times. It is better not to get her angry."

"*Loco*, you said this means crazy?" She shivered a little even though the day was approaching hot.

"Yes." Daniel looked off toward the mountains. "As long as you're on her good side, she's not too bad." He'd never been on that side of her very long, but then she never made any secret of how much she'd despised his father. Rafael's father had been the man she wanted, but he'd gotten away. "But what can I say? She's my mother."

Anna gave a short nod. "I'm glad you've finally told me the truth."

She turned and stalked through the trees.

Yes, not so much the truth, but at least she seemed to believe this story. Why wouldn't she? The pieces fit. Rafael could have gotten drunk in frustration, and maybe she believed he'd gone out searching during the night, stayed out all day and all night, which would explain his exhaustion. Daniel let out the breath he'd half been holding.

It was getting harder and harder to continue to lie to her, but he had to keep on. She considered Rafael's actions unforgivable. At least he knew where they stood on that score. She couldn't ever know that Rafe was the one who had stopped the stage. And he hoped he'd abated her relentless curiosity for a few days. By then Rafe had better be well enough to deal with her. The idea of turning her over to his brother ripped at him. When he wasn't hurting her with another lie, he kind of enjoyed her company. Even though she was too inquisitive and pushy.

# Chapter Twelve

*Yes, the land of milk and honey is an appropriate description. The honeybees are thick when the fruit trees are in bloom, and we always have a cow or two available for milk, although I am told other breeds produce richer milk.*

Anna walked around the orange trees, running her fingers through the flat oval leaves. Tiny little green oranges no bigger than grapes dotted the branches. None of the trees were very tall, but much about California was like stepping into another world.

She tried to sort out what Daniel had said to her. It seemed to fit. If Rafael had been searching nonstop since the horses were stolen, it could explain his exhaustion last night. And perhaps he'd been avoiding her because he didn't want to tell her that he could lose the ranch if the government didn't let him keep the title.

Tendrils of dread snaked in the pit of her stomach at the thought of his losing the ranch. If marrying him would help, if the Spanish in California were treated the same way the Irish were back east, she had no choice. She had to marry him.

She cast a glance back toward where Daniel was staking the horses so that they could drink from the river. He looked up and met her eyes, watching her steadily. Her breath caught. It was as if he knew the instant her gaze was upon him. He must be watching her meandering path through the grove. She'd needed a minute to calm down after learning about the deception they'd perpetrated. She understood their fear, but that didn't mean she liked being deceived.

"Daniel," she called. She walked toward him. "What would you do if you found out the robbers were your hands or your cousins?"

He rubbed his chin. "Depends." His gaze slid down her body and then back up.

A wash of heat flowed over her. He'd probably dropped his eyes to gather his thoughts. It wasn't a sensual gesture to turn her thoughts lascivious. But when his brother had given her one of those kinds of looks deliberately, nothing had stirred in her.

"If you got that man good with your shot, I might consider that punishment enough."

And there was the barb in his appraisal. Still, it didn't pack much of a sting. By now he knew what she was and didn't seem to mind. "But I only shot one of them."

"Leave it to Rafael."

She tilted her head, looking at Daniel. At this distance something about him seemed similar to the robber. Her heart gave an irregular thump. What if it had been his cousin?

"Do your cousins look like you?" she asked as she walked nearer.

"Don't know. I haven't seen them in years." He turned around and lifted a saddle from the horse she'd ridden.

Which she supposed was his signal that he didn't want to talk about the holdup any longer. Talking about it any longer wouldn't serve any purpose.

But she knew what she had to do. She had to find a way to get into town and tell the sheriff. It was only right. Daniel wasn't there. He didn't know the carnage the robbers had wrought. Clearly, the brothers were loyal to family and friends, but a crime had been committed.

"Do you think Rafael would mind if I bought some material? Since your mother doesn't let me do anything at the house, I'd like to sew a new dress."

"There's nothing wrong with what you're wear-ing," he said without turning around.

Except she'd owned this gown since she was sixteen, and it had faded considerably since then.

The seams were frayed, and it was too short and too tight. "Well, I wouldn't mind seeing how Selina is getting along."

He jerked at the straps of the second saddle. She watched his shoulders move under his shirt. Something tickled low in her belly.

"We'll have to wait until Rafe gets back. Then I'm sure he won't mind taking you."

Somehow that solution disappointed her, because she'd rather go with Daniel.

"I have letters to mail."

He turned around and looked at her. "Who is using trickery now?"

Her face heated. Drawing her hands behind her, she took a step back. "I'm not."

He removed the second saddle and set it on the ground. Then he stepped toward her. "Anna." His tone contained a warning and a berating combined.

She felt pinned like a misbehaving child, but she'd be damned before she retreated.

He drew off his gloves and took another step toward her at the same time as she stepped forward.

Her breasts brushed his chest and a burst of fireworks went off inside her, stunning her into standing like a statue. His nostrils flared, and he looked down into her eyes as if he'd experienced the same trailing sparks and pings. He sucked in a deep breath and repeated, "Anna."

His tone was softer, soothing, seductive. Her

knees wobbled, and she grabbed his upper arms to steady herself. He felt so strong, his muscles bunching under her fingers. His scent was a mix of the clean salty sweat of labor and something infinitely more earthy, more him, and it fogged her senses until she just wanted to lean in and breathe him in.

He reached around her and pulled her against him, and the sensation rocketed through her. She wanted to push her breasts into him.

His fingers slid along her jaw, tilting her chin up, and he whispered, "Anna," across her lips.

A delicious shiver slipped down her spine. It seemed to her she had been waiting forever for this first kiss. For three thousand miles she had anticipated this, and now it was going to happen.

His lips touched hers, warm and firm. For a second they stayed just like that, their lips clinging to each other's. Then his tongue delved into the juncture, changing the kiss from a sweet thing to a wicked assault on her senses.

She slid her hands up his arms and around his neck, hanging on and straining up on her tiptoes to better join them together.

The kiss swirled on and on. She never wanted it to end. His arm tightened around her, and sensation after sensation rocked through her. Everywhere their bodies were in contact tingled, and the private place between her legs began to ache with need. She shifted closer.

He slid his hand from her jaw to trail down her throat, over her shoulder and down the side of her back until he reached her hip. His fingers pressed into the small of her back, urging her hips to tilt into him.

Her breathing turned ragged, but she didn't want to end the dance of their tongues.

A horse whinnied.

Daniel jerked back. What was he doing?

He groaned. Anna wiggled closer, sending desire coursing through his veins.

He had to stop. She was Rafael's bride, not his.

It took every ounce of willpower he had to push her shoulders back and break the contact between their bodies.

She stared up at him, her green eyes dewy, her parted lips slightly swollen. More than anything, he wanted to pull her back into him or better yet carry her over to the blanket and make her his.

The horse whinnying again shot alarm through him. God forbid anyone had witnessed him kissing his brother's intended. Only a riderless horse pranced along the opposite riverbank. Thank God for the horse's appearance just when he was on the verge of pulling her hips against his erection.

He looked back down at Anna. "I never should have done that."

Her mouth snapped shut, and the light in her eyes faded.

"You should have stopped me," he muttered.

He gave her a little shake. He should have stopped himself. "It can't ever happen again."

She ducked her head, and the ridiculous flowers of her hat filled his vision. "It was just a kiss." Her voice shook.

It had been so much more than "just a kiss." He'd felt her hesitation when he'd deepened the kiss. Not in the way she pressed against him, or wrapped her arms around his neck, but as if she hadn't been quite sure what she was supposed to do. But she'd figured it out damn quick.

Oh, God, she had felt perfect, her response eager in a way that only fueled his passion even more.

He wrapped his arm around her shoulders and squeezed. A brotherly hold. "You didn't do anything wrong. It was just a kiss." Just a dance, just a kiss, they couldn't continue or it would be something that couldn't be mistaken as less than it was.

She pushed away and stared at him. "Why did you do it then?"

What kind of woman needed an explanation of why a man kissed her?

An innocent.

Which only made him feel a thousand times more guilty. If Rafe had been well enough to marry her, Daniel never would have had a chance with her. "I lost my head."

She gave him such a skeptical look, he had a hard time not laughing, but it was not a laughing matter. "And I'm not taking you to town if all you're going to do is run straight to the sheriff and tell him what I told you. We don't know anything yet."

She blinked, then seemed to find herself. "I could walk."

"You could."

He glanced past her toward the horse on the other side of the water, wondering if one of the tethers on the horses he'd staked had broken or the horse had pulled the stake from the ground.

He really looked at the horse, then swallowed hard. It wasn't either of the horses they'd rode here, but one of the ones he'd set loose in the foothills of the Sierras the other night.

His spine stiffened.

Anna swung around following his line of sight. "Oh, my."

How in the hell was he going to explain this one? His steps jerky, he walked toward the river, trying to get his mind off Anna and that explosive kiss and sorting through the dozens of lies he'd told her in the past couple of days.

"Looks like one of our horses is trying to come home. Must be the one that Rafe thought they lost."

"No, it couldn't be. This is the one that the robber with the rope was riding. I recognize the white spot on its nose."

Daniel winced, wishing her memory wasn't so

good. It was indeed his mount of the other day. He stepped to the edge of the water. He clicked to the horse. "Come on, old boy."

The horse splashed into the water and crossed to them. "You're certain it's the same horse?" he asked, although he knew the answer.

His horse nudged him, and he stroked the white blaze.

"Do you think the robbers only borrowed your horses so that their own wouldn't be recognized?"

"Possibly." He pushed his face into the horse's neck as if he were overjoyed to have the horse back, but really to hide his mirth. He had to stop laughing at the wrong time. The day couldn't get any worse.

"We have to go to town now," Anna said.

He bit back his amusement. "No, we don't."

She put her hand on his back, and a shaft of desire stabbed him low and hard.

"We have to tell the sheriff that your horse came back and that…that…"

He twisted to look at her and why she was having difficulty speaking.

She swallowed hard. "That the robbers were your cousins."

"No." How in the hell did she reach that conclusion, other than he'd put it in her head?

"They must have set the horses free after they stopped the stage. And you said it yourself, the ranch is not easily located." She rubbed his back, and her touch was agony although he knew she meant it as comfort. "And the robbers looked a lot like you and your brother."

Tension zinged through him. The irony was too great for him. "Great, I'm going to get my cousins hanged."

Anna hated to be the one to confirm what must be Daniel's worst fear. She stood behind him and rubbed along his ribs trying to offer comfort. Of its own volition her hand stroked longer, reaching his waist. His muscles were taut. The heat of his skin reached through his shirt. Her bones seemed to melt as she remembered being pressed against him.

"Anna," he said in a low voice that sent a shudder racing down her spine.

How would she ever hear him say her name again and not think of that amazing kiss?

"If you don't stop touching me like that, I'm going to do a whole lot more than kiss you."

She froze. Could he feel the prurient interest in her touch? She jerked her hand back. "I'm sorry."

"Just go over to the blanket and give me a minute to think." He sounded strangled as he spoke.

"What is there to think about? You and Rafael must have believed your cousins were responsible from the beginning. We have to tell the sheriff." She wished he would turn around, but he buried his face in the horse's neck.

His shoulders shook.

Was he crying? Dismay swept through her like a raging current leaving her cold, drenched and heavy.

"Daniel," she said softly, stepping toward him. She hesitated to touch him after his warning. In the end the compulsion was too much to resist. She put her hand on his shoulder. "It is not your fault if your cousins did something heinous."

The shaking stopped.

She tried to give him consoling pats, but the warmth of his skin through his shirt had her stroking his shoulders, first with one hand, then with both.

"Do you ever do as you're told?" He spun around, caught her wrists, pulled her arms apart and looked down at her. His eyes were completely clear, his lashes dry.

If he had not been crying, why had his shoulders been shaking?

"I was only trying to console you. I know it must be difficult to think your own flesh and blood behaved so dastardly."

"You have no idea." His mouth twitched as if he was trying to hold back a grin. "And neither do I."

The light in his eyes danced, and he folded his lips inward.

"Were you…laughing at me?"

"You are so serious. Come on, Anna. All we know is that one of the horses managed to find its way back home. Not an uncommon thing with animals. I know of one man who lost his dog after coming to California and six months later he got a letter from his folks back in Missouri saying his dog had shown up at their door."

"But the robbers looked—"

"Like every other man of Spanish decent. Dark hair, dark eyes, dark skin."

"You're not so dark skinned," she said weakly. She'd thought there was something similar about them, but was it just their Spanish blood that made her think that?

"The sheriff already believes the bandits were Mexicans. Did you see their faces well enough to identify them? Did anyone? How long a look at them did you get?"

"It seemed like forever," she whispered.

His eyes flickered, and then the light in them faded as if his amusement had disappeared. "But it was likely only a few seconds, and they were masked."

Her belly knotted as her fingers curled into fists. She sputtered, "But—but you said—"

"There's no proof yet. Let Rafael learn what he can before you go off half-cocked. If he has to, he'll go down to Mexico to visit our cousins and learn if they were away."

Her face hot, she twisted her wrists out of his grasp. She felt unbalanced. A moment ago she had felt so connected to this man; now she was uncertain of him. "I don't understand you."

"Don't you? I would rather not know if the robbers were people we knew. I would not go searching for the truth, but Rafe is different from me." He tilted his head. "He thinks he must find the men responsible, especially if there is a connection to us. Apparently you two are well suited in that regard."

So was he saying she and Rafael were better matched? Or just trying to remind her she was engaged to his brother? A fact she shouldn't have forgotten. Somehow that made the kiss they'd just shared feel tawdry and cheap.

And it didn't seem as if Daniel was suggesting she should end her engagement with Rafael and marry him instead. She wouldn't make the mistake Selina made in thinking when a man kissed you or more he was intent on offering marriage.

She didn't want to marry a penniless younger brother anyway. Except the idea that the kiss meant nothing to him burned holes in her resolution. She needed to remember she was to marry Rafael—whenever he'd finished this business with uncovering the robbers' identities.

Daniel looked over to where Anna sat on the blanket, her back to him. He supposed that was deliberate as if to tell him she could not care less about him. But the way she sat with her knees pulled up and her arms wrapped around her legs made him think that he'd wounded her. Again.

Blackness gnawed at his insides. He swung the hoe at the ground, burying the blade in the stem of a grapevine. Damn, now he was killing his plants.

He threw the hoe, disgusted with himself and the whole situation. If he'd been watching what he was doing instead of watching Anna, he wouldn't be in danger of mortally wounding a plant that took three years to bear fruit, five to produce well.

He washed his hands in the water running through the nearest sluice gate and retrieved the food and bottle of wine he'd brought. Lunch was bound to be awkward because he'd kissed her.

He could think of nothing but kissing her again.

The best thing to do was pretend nothing had happened. He walked up to the edge of the blanket. "Hungry?"

"I suppose I could eat." She sounded normal.

He let out a breath he hadn't realized he'd been holding. Sinking down on the opposite corner of the blanket, he set the sack with their lunch in between them.

"You must have built up an appetite working so hard."

That was it, polite talk about nothing. He shrugged and planted his thumbs on the cork in the wine bottle. "We can see if the fruits of last year's labor turned into vinegar or wine."

She reached up and unpinned her hat and set

it on the blanket beside her. He couldn't help following her every move. In the dappled sunlight, the molten copper of her hair was like new pennies mixed with the gold flakes that came out of the streams up north.

"What?" she asked, patting her head as if expecting to discover a strand had slipped free.

His throat felt thick. He'd forgo lunch in a heartbeat just to kiss her again. "I don't think I've ever seen hair quite that color."

"'Tis fairly common where I'm from."

"Connecticut?" He felt a little slow.

"Actually, Ireland. We came over when I was ten. My family lives in New York, but I answered an advertisement for mill girls in Connecticut. Are you going to tell Rafael what happened?"

There she went again, diving straight into the problem. Did anything frighten her?

The last thing he should do was tell Rafael, unless he wanted to claim her as his own bride. His heart gave an odd jolt. The thought was *loco*.

He wasn't ready to settle down. At twenty-seven, Rafe was barely ready, and he was five years older. And other than wanting to kiss her, she was annoying as heck. He didn't want to *marry* her. He swallowed hard. "I'll tell him if you want me to."

She blinked. Her eyes were unusual, too, a clear light green, not merely some indeterminate shade between gray and brown. "Why would I want you to?"

Everything inside him sagged. She would only want him to if she wanted him to marry her instead of Rafael. "You don't seem to like letting sleeping dogs lie."

Nope, she poked them with a stick, which was why it was hard trying to keep the truth of the stagecoach holdup from her.

She wrapped her arms around her legs again and leaned her chin on her knees. "I never know what you're going to tell him. Won't he be angry?"

Daniel looked down at the cork he was working free. He had no idea what Rafael would think. His brother might be glad to be free of the woman who had shot him. On the other hand, he might care a great deal once he was well enough to marry Anna. "I imagine he'd be a bit put out."

Still, once Rafe was well, he'd likely make Anna trip all over herself to please him, the same way Madre and Juanita did. Even the Indian girl he'd grown up with had fallen for Rafael. She'd been the daughter of the mission-raised Indian woman who cleaned for them most of the years he was growing up. And just as he was working up his courage to steal a kiss from her, he'd discovered her sneaking into Rafael's bedroom at night. She'd been *his* age, *his* playmate, *his* companion—how she must have laughed at his pathetic attempts to hold her hand.

Anna stared off into the distance. "I'm not good at hiding things. I'm not much of a lady."

She dropped an arm and traced a triangular pattern in the blanket with her fingertip.

He imagined that finger on him, learning the angles of his body. His blood grew thick. "I doubt if he cares all that much about you being a lady."

Her eyes jerked to his. "But you said—"

"I lied. I was trying to keep you from discovering that Rafe thought he knew who the robbers were." Somehow that lie seemed to be falling in on itself faster than the others were. "And he was looking for them day and night."

Her eyes narrowed as he stumbled through his explanation. His lies were wrapped in lies, and it was only a matter of time before he tripped over one or tangled them so badly even he couldn't figure out how to unwind them.

He finally freed the cork of the wine bottle. "You want to try this first or do you want me to?"

"I'll try it," she said. "Did you bring glasses?"

"No, sorry. We're sharing the bottle. It isn't as if we haven't..." He stopped. He couldn't just refer to their kiss. "Here." He thrust the bottle in her direction.

She took the wine, and he got busy getting out the napkins and food. He unlatched the wires holding the crock lids with the leftover eggs and the seasoned beans. Then he unwrapped the corn bread and the tortillas.

Anna lifted the bottle and took a sip. Then another. "That's actually pretty good."

He hoped she wasn't just saying that as a way to pass the awkwardness. He held out his hand. She gave him the bottle, and he brought it to his lips, trying not to think that he was putting his lips where hers had just been.

The wine was sweet, and perhaps a bit more potent than he'd expected, but not bad.

Anna frowned at the array of food. "Just how are we supposed to eat that?"

"We roll it in the tortilla to make a burrito. Here, I'll make one for you."

As he rolled the burrito for her, she tightened her grip around her knees. "I still don't understand why Rafael didn't greet me the first night I arrived. It wasn't as if he could have known about the stagecoach robbery at that point, and he couldn't have been awake overlong."

*Hell!* The hole in his lies was as wide and deep as Death Valley and just as treacherous. "Actually, he did know."

She scowled. "How could he have known?"

"I didn't know he knew anything until I got back with you, or until the next morning when he told me why he was going out again." Daniel's heart pounded. He had to make this story work. She wouldn't believe anything he said if he tried another. No, she'd dig the house apart until she uncovered everything. And then she'd turn them in. He held out her burrito.

"He knew my stagecoach was held up before we got here?" she asked, her voice tight with skepticism.

When she didn't take her food, he put it on the napkin in front of her. "He surmised that was what happened. While he was out tracking the horse thieves, he heard the gunfire. By the time he got to a point high enough to see, the stage was headed toward Stockton, and he couldn't see anyone else."

Why on earth had Rafael returned fire? He should have just taken off, and nothing would have happened.

"But wasn't he concerned knowing I was on that stage?" Anna demanded.

"He was, but he thought if he tracked the horse thieves the other way—how they came to the ranch—he'd have a better shot at finding where they came from. So he went back and did that until he lost the trail in the dark. The waiting to learn if you were all right drove him to drinking." A trickle of sweat slid down his spine. She would find out the truth. He rolled his own burrito with fingers turned clumsy. He had to distract her.

"I would have thought he'd be worried enough about me to follow the stage to Stockton."

"I don't know. Maybe he thought the thieves might have taken you and he wanted to try and run them down."

Her lips flattened.

"Anna, you don't have to marry him if you don't want to." Why in the hell had he said that?

Her eyebrows flicked. "That's just it. I want to be married."

But did she want to be married so much she didn't care who her husband was? Or only cared so long as her husband owned the ranch? He should suggest she might want to wait until she made up her mind. He stared at the burrito he was making, trying to form the right words without making an offer himself.

"I really fell in love with the man who wrote me all those letters. Some days I would get a packet of five or six, and it was like Christmas. It made me believe I had a future with a man who so loved his home and his family. I have to find out if Rafael is the man I thought he was."

Daniel dropped half the filling out of his burrito he was fumbling so much. The trouble was, Rafael couldn't have been bothered to write. All the letters had been written by Daniel. But that was another truth that couldn't be exposed.

## Chapter Thirteen

*My social commitments extend into May,
and I couldn't possibly travel before then.
I have friends that will be traveling at that
time, so I would prefer to travel with them
rather than be completely alone.*

Anna walked around the perimeter of the courtyard, her boots clicking on the flagstones of the
walkway. She should go to bed, but she was restless. The day had ended with no sign of Rafael.
At first she'd been relieved she didn't have to
face him after the kiss she'd shared with Daniel,
but the longer he stayed away, the more doubt
needled her.

She wanted to believe Daniel. His story made a
certain amount of sense, but a few things seemed
like square pegs shaved off and forced to fit in
round holes. If she just had some proof…of something.

The more she thought, the more her thoughts

swirled. Even circling the courtyard was starting to take on the semblance of water circling a drain.

She hesitated at Rafael's door. Something was bothering her about his room, something beyond the fact that it was twice as big as Daniel's. She knocked. After several seconds ticked by and she heard nothing, she tried the knob. Once again the door was locked, although she and Daniel had gone through it that morning.

Looking over her shoulder, she didn't see anyone else in the courtyard. Mrs. Werner had retired. Anna had watched her go into her room and the light go out.

Juanita had gone to the kitchen after supper, and Anna hadn't seen her since, but then the girl had been told to give her a wide berth. Daniel had muttered something about seeing to the animals and had left out the front door.

Reaching up, Anna slipped a hairpin from her bun. She bent it open and inserted it in the lock. After jiggling it around, she felt the lock give but not turn. The thin strip of metal twisted instead of pushing the tumbler. She pulled out a second pin and, after a fast look around, added it to her first. The lock clicked just as the door to the main room opened.

She jerked upright.

"Anna, he's not here," said Daniel from across the courtyard.

"That would be why he hasn't answered my

knock then." Stepping in front of the door, she pulled out the bent hairpins and shoved them in her pocket. "Why is his door locked?"

"Maybe to keep nosy people out." Daniel walked across the courtyard, the moon catching blue lights in his hair.

Her stomach fluttered as if she'd swallowed a sparrow. Surely he couldn't have seen that she'd picked the lock. She resisted the urge to put her hands behind her back. "I was just seeing if he'd returned home. I'd like to speak with him."

"I know." Daniel drew to a stop in front of her, his face shadowed under the walkway's covering.

The light coming out of the long room windows was enough to see by, but with his back to it, she couldn't make out his expression. She heaved a deep breath. "But we came through this door this morning."

"Did we?" murmured Daniel. His voice spoke of sin and temptation.

What was wrong with her? She was engaged to Rafael. She at least owed him loyalty until he made an appearance. "Yes, we did," she said primly. "Who would have locked it if Rafael didn't come back?"

"Juanita when she cleaned, perhaps." He stepped closer. His voice lowered. "Does it matter?"

"It just seems…odd."

"What seems odd is that you are not in bed."

"Neither are you," she pointed out.

"The work of a rancher is never done."

"Especially since it all must fall to you while Rafael is off chasing robbers."

Daniel reached toward her and caught a hank of hair that had fallen when she removed the pins. He rubbed it between his fingers. "Even in the moonlight it seems lit from a fire within."

Her breath caught. He was near enough he could surely hear the pounding of her heart. Did he mean to kiss her again?

"If you are so curious, we can go through the other door."

If he had meant to dissuade her by pretending he didn't care if she looked, then he fell short.

"Excellent idea." She strode toward the doors leading to the hallway.

He followed. He opened it for her, and she entered the interior hallway, which was black as pitch. Her heart thundered for a second, but Daniel lit a match.

The tiny flare of light was enough to spur her forward to the other door to Rafael's room. She twisted the handle before Daniel could block her, and he gave her an amused look.

Before he caught the door to hold it open for her, she knew the room would be exactly as it had been that morning. Empty. "Light his lamp, please."

"You can see no one is here."

She swept the room. The shadows in the corners likely weren't hiding anyone, but just as it had this morning, the room bothered her. "If you won't light the lamp, you must not want me to see something."

He sighed loudly, walked across the room, lit another match and bent to light the lamp on the table beside Rafael's low bed.

"See. He isn't hiding robbers or goats or naked women in his room."

"Naked women?" She jerked back so hard the frame of the door bit her shoulder. Of all the things he could have said, that shocked her.

"Sorry, bad joke. I am with men too much." His eyes flickered as he looked at her. There was an element of sheepishness but anger, too.

His actions were just as confusing to her as Rafael's were. Was he with men too much or was he thinking of naked women—or more likely her naked? She was the last woman he'd kissed. Was he thinking of bedding her? A shudder ripped through her.

Then again, the anger she sensed kept her wary. Was it because she was knocking on her fiancé's door instead of his? Did he think she was seeking to join Rafael in his bed?

*Bed.* Her thoughts jerked to Rafael's bed. The bed was much lower than the others in the house, even the bottom bunks of their hands' rooms. That just seemed off.

Her eyes on Daniel, she crossed the room and yanked back the blanket, exposing the bare rope supports of the bed frame.

Alarm flashed across Daniel's face.

"Where is his mattress?" she demanded.

"Not on his bed," Daniel said. His pulse raced. Coming up with another fabrication that explained why the mattress was gone made him feel as if his horse had decided to ride him. Improbable excuses swirled in his head, everything from Rafael had an accident like a little child, to he'd caught it on fire smoking in bed. Oddly they all featured Rafael as an irresponsible or immature figure.

"I can see that," retorted Anna.

God, he was tired of lying to her. And as much as he'd like to make Rafael into a stupid fellow, the man was waiting in the wagon bed until the coast was clear. Only it wasn't. He needed to get Anna out of Rafael's room and into her own bed.

For a second when she left the doorway and stalked toward him, his fantasies had taken over. He'd hoped and wanted her to come to him, tilt her head up for a repeat of the kiss they'd shared that morning.

"All I know, Anna, is it isn't here, and it is late. You and I have mattresses on our beds and we should be in one—them." Lord, did he really just say that? He must be more tired than he realized.

She stared at him for a minute, then gave a slight shake of her head. "He took the wagon and the mattress because he found your cousins and the one I shot is badly hurt."

"Oh, for Pete's sake, Anna." Actually, she was too damn close to the truth. "He probably took it so he didn't have to sleep on the ground. Besides, the wagon is his to take or leave."

She stepped closer, and a swelter of desire nearly knocked him off his feet. He drew in her scent, sweet, sun-kissed and so seductive. Her breasts would touch his chest if he leaned forward just a couple of inches, and the fallen strand of her hair caught the lamplight and promised fire.

"You're lying."

When he had first crossed the courtyard and seen her standing at Rafael's door, he'd thought he'd scare her with a repeat of the kiss, but he'd forgotten she didn't scare so easily. And now he wanted so much more than a kiss. He had a hard time remembering that Rafael and Juanita waited just outside.

He had to get her out of Rafael's room and tucked in her own room, and in a way that would keep her locked inside, which meant he had to make her think it was dangerous for her to be wandering around. But the only thing that he could think of was kissing her.

"You know he found your cousins and is trying to hide them or take them to Mexico." She poked him in the chest.

A riot of sensations exploded in him just from her touch.

"I know no such thing." He caught her hand and pulled her into him. "But I do know this." He stroked the back of his fingers across her soft cheek. "I want to kiss you. I want to take you to my room and make you mine."

Her eyes widened, and she stared up at him, her lips parting.

Damn it, she was going to let him kiss her, maybe more. His blood thickened, and he grew hard and ready. "And if you don't stop me, you won't be fit to marry any man."

Her eyes narrowed as his meaning settled in. "You're just trying to scare me."

*God, yes, and please let it work.*

"You wouldn't hurt me, Daniel Werner."

He leaned close to her ear and whispered, "I wouldn't hurt you, but I'd thoroughly enjoy ruining you." Just as he pressed his lips to the tender flesh behind her ear, she shoved him away.

"Well, it is just too bad you're not the owner of this ranch, and this isn't your room. Because the owner is the man I came out here to California to marry. Not his lying, sneaking, penniless brother."

Her words were like knives. This is what he wanted, except it hurt like hell. "Not quite penniless."

"But lying."

He let the accusation stand. "And I never said a thing about marriage."

She stepped forward, back into reach, and glared up at him. "If any man ruined me, he'd have to marry me, even if I have to hold the rifle on him at my own damn wedding."

Then she grabbed his head and pulled him down for a hard kiss. Just as it started to get interesting, she shoved him back. She stood there panting for a second, looking flushed, ferocious and so very adorable.

All he had to do was grab her and she wouldn't resist, and he wanted to more than anything. But Rafe was not well and was waiting to get settled for the night.

"And that is the last kiss you'll ever have from me," she said, then pivoted and headed for the door.

"Liar," he mocked.

She shivered but left him standing alone.

Anna shut her door and leaned back against it, panting as if she'd run a mile when in truth she'd only run across the courtyard. Daniel's low-voiced taunt echoed through her. What had she been thinking?

She wasn't experienced enough to use kissing as a weapon. Yet, she'd known Daniel's threat was empty. Not that he wouldn't bed her, given half a chance, but he wouldn't do it against her will as he'd tried to imply. No, if he'd been serious about "ruining" her, he would have grabbed her breast or her bottom. He would have pinned her to a wall so she couldn't escape. Instead, he'd run the back of his fingers across her cheek, which was such a sweet, caring gesture she'd almost willingly have allowed him anything.

She'd been angry he hadn't taken the choice away from her. But if Rafael needed an Anglo wife to keep his ranch—she'd do anything to go back in time and stop her parents from giving up their farm in Ireland—how could she fail to help him?

Like almost every other thing, there was just something a little off. He'd hesitated a bit too long, hadn't kissed her when he had to realize she would have allowed it.

More than allowed, encouraged.

She was going to find out why he was intent on getting her back into her own room. Slowly, she cracked her door and peered out. The corridor doors were closed again, but the light still burned in Rafael's room. She could see the faint outline around the window and a swath of light cutting the recessed darkness of the well from under the door she'd unlocked.

Daniel hadn't entered his own room. She would have heard his door since his room was next to hers, so she waited, watching. Yep, she was just a regular Pinkerton detective. She needed a better plan.

First she'd remove her boots and tiptoe across to Rafael's door well and see if it was still unlocked. Then—well, one thing at a time.

Daniel went out the back of the house, where the wagon was waiting. Rafael inched toward the tailgate of the wagon. Juanita held his arm, helping him. Daniel put up his hand, stopping them.

Rafael groaned and dropped back against the mound of bedding behind him. He rasped, staring at Daniel.

Both of them were looking to him to tell them what to do, which was novel. "You need to get better. Fast."

Rafael's chest rose and fell, but he just stared mutely at Daniel.

Yes, with brilliant instruction like that they wouldn't look to him for long. Rafael was probably just as eager to get well as he was to get him well.

"He needs his bed," said Juanita.

"I can't lie to her anymore. She knows something is going on." Daniel ran a hand through his hair. He missed his favorite hat. "You can't go back to your room, or she's bound to discover you in there."

Rafael's brows drew together.

"She's nosy and determined to learn what we're

hiding from her. She's going to keep checking your room until you *return* home." For that matter she'd probably start checking for the wagon, too.

"He sleep my room," said Juanita.

"No!" said Rafael.

"Shh," Daniel and Juanita said in tandem.

Daniel considered the idea, then discarded it. They would have to move Rafe through the court-yard to put him in Juanita's room, and she'd have no place to sleep.

Rafael put a hand to his chest and leaned his head back. He didn't seem to be improving.

"We'll put you in the storage room. She won't suspect you are in there."

"No…space," rasped out Rafael.

He could pull out the crates for the grapes, say-ing he was getting them ready because they would be ripe soon. Then if Miss Nosy caught him or saw the crates, the explanation would make sense. "Come on—you can wait in the breezeway while I make room."

"Need my…bed," said Rafael.

"No. You need to not have Anna find you be-fore you can carry on a conversation." He pulled his brother and his bedding toward the tailgate. He wasn't going to argue with Rafe, and his brother wouldn't be able to dash for his room when he couldn't walk without help. "Then, as soon as you can, you need to start courting her."

"No!" Juanita's dark eyes glistened in the

moonlight as she shook her head back and forth. "You marry her." She was looking straight at Daniel.

Daniel's stomach dropped. How had Juanita gotten that idea? He resumed pulling his brother off the edge of the wagon. "I'm not marrying her—Rafe is."

"But you kiss her."

For a second they just looked at each other in silence.

Rafael clamped a hand around his wrist. "You cur."

"What did you think was going to happen when I have to spend all day with her?" Daniel slung Rafe's arm over his shoulder.

"Didn't think…you'd…steal…" Rafael wheezed. "Should beat…you."

Daniel pulled his wrist out of his brother's grasp. "Yes, you do that. I'll wait while you catch your breath."

Only it didn't seem like Rafe could catch his breath.

Daniel tugged his brother off the wagon, while Juanita helped steady him. "And then I'll beat the hell out of you for putting us in this fix."

Rafael glared.

"Besides, it is a way to stop her from asking a million questions. And you know she'll want you when you're well." Women always did. "Juanita, get the door, and check that Anna isn't in the passage before I haul him in there."

The maid scurried off, and Daniel took a step toward the door.

"Don't…touch…her…'gain," huffed Rafael.

"For Pete's sake, you couldn't be bothered with her for months and now you're angry I kissed her? You even said you were fine with her being damaged goods as the reason she couldn't find a fellow back east to marry her." Only Anna wasn't damaged goods. She was an innocent. The way she reacted to his quip about naked women was as revealing as the way she'd hesitated the first time he'd kissed her. "Besides, she's promised to use *my rifle* on me if I should attempt more."

"Aren't…doing…it…right…then," said Rafael.

"Shut up." He was doing it plenty right. "She just wants to marry a property owner." Which Daniel would be, if Rafael would ever sell him the land he'd promised. Not that he wanted to marry Anna.

Juanita appeared in the doorway and beckoned them forward.

In a low voice, Daniel told his brother, "The newest story is you and I think it is our cousins who held up the stage, and you're trying to get to them before anyone else does."

He filled Rafe in on all the ins and outs that went with that particular lie as he hobbled him into the breezeway and lowered him to sit leaning against the wall. Juanita went past them and then returned with the blankets and pillows and arranged them around Rafael.

"So invent…cousins," said Rafael. "Martinez… cousins."

Juanita gasped.

"I already said Valquez cousins. Why would you want to shift blame to your father's family?"

Rafe shrugged. "Why not?"

"I'm not going to get some poor men named Martinez hanged," Daniel told his brother in a low voice. "And make no mistake—Anna will go to the sheriff with names if she has them. Why would you shoot a one-armed man?"

Juanita's dark eyes shifted to Rafael.

"Didn't…realize." He looked down. "'Til… after."

Daniel shook his head and opened the storage room. Using the spill of light coming out of Rafael's room, he started pulling out the crates he used for fruits and shifting things around to make room for Rafael.

He'd just put the fourth crate on the stack when the click of a door was like a gunshot. Every muscle went tight as he whipped around. He knew before he made it into Rafe's room that it was going to be Anna.

# Chapter Fourteen

*I am disappointed your social commitments
will not allow you to leave until spring, but
I will await your instruction as to when you
might travel.*

Daniel appeared in the other doorway before
Anna had taken two steps away from the door
she'd picked open earlier.

"What are you doing?" he demanded.

So much for her secret sleuth abilities. She'd
tried to shut the door gently, but the catch had
made a loud click. She put her shoulders back as
if she had every right to be in her future husband's
room—after midnight. "I heard noises. I thought
Rafael might be back."

"I'm getting out the crates for the grape harvest."

She leaned to see around him. Wooden slats of
crates were stacked in the hallway. "At this time
of night?"

Daniel rubbed his hand across his eye and forehead. "The lamp was lit, and it needs to be done." He dropped his hand and looked exhausted. "No use in putting it off."

A spurt of anger that Rafael would leave too much work for Daniel to do alone burst in her. She'd expected Rafael to be sneaking back into his room, not finding Daniel working.

"He shouldn't leave all the work to you."

"He doesn't, Anna." He opened his mouth as if to say more. Then closed it. He casually leaned against the door frame, blocking her vision of the hallway.

Was he working, or was it just another subterfuge?

The bottom of her belly felt hollow. In spite of Rafael riding up and having dinner with them, she couldn't shake her belief that he'd been hiding in the house that first day. And there was just something havey-cavey about Daniel pulling out crates at this time of night.

"When do you sleep?" she asked.

"When I can." His mouth twitched, and his eyelids lowered for half a second.

A shudder rolled down her spine.

"I could pull out the crates for you," she offered. "Until I get some sewing to occupy my time, I don't have much to keep me busy."

"You're not sneaking into Rafe's room because

you are looking for an occupation." He scowled as he walked toward her.

Half wanting to retreat, she put her hands behind her back and reached for the door handle. "I wasn't sneaking."

"Because you always enter a man's room without knocking." Daniel took another menacing step toward her.

"Actually, I do. I have very bad manners, I guess," she said. The image of him sprawled across his bed yesterday morning intruded into her thoughts. "I didn't knock on your door, either."

Her insides were turning into mush. Her resolve to catch them at whatever they were hiding slid under an awareness of Daniel. The way his kiss had tasted, his earthy scent, the hardness of his chest against the softness of hers.

He stopped and scrutinized her, which almost left her…disappointed. Surely not. No, she was here to determine if he was hiding Rafael.

The minute Daniel relaxed and the ghost of a smile crossed his lips, she darted around him and raced to the hallway. He reached to catch her, but she had enough experience evading older siblings to make him miss.

"Anna, it's not what you think," he said, right behind her. He caught her arm.

She stared at a stack of wooden crates in front of the storage room. Across from her the door stood open, but it looked much the same as it had that afternoon. A burlap bag leaned against some barrels, and she didn't remember it being there earlier, but Daniel could have moved it to get at the crates. As before she didn't really see a place for a grown man to hide.

She twisted free of Daniel and ran to the end of the hallway and pushed open the doors. She looked left and right. Nothing was there but grass.

If Rafael were back, he'd be in his room, wouldn't he? Why would he run and hide? She let out a long sigh with something short of relief. She still didn't know what was going on, but finding Rafael would have been disappointing.

She turned around, and Daniel was pressing his palms to his temples and had his eyes closed.

Her neck tightened. What was he afraid she'd discover?

"Is he here?" she demanded.

His eyes popped open. Daniel closed the distance between them in two strides, but he didn't stop until she was pinned against the wall. His body pressed against hers, and he caught her face in his hands. "Would I do this if my brother were here?"

He brushed his lips across hers. She could shove him back. She should shove him back. Instead, her arms wound around his shoulders. And she came apart. Her resolution to not kiss or be kissed by him hadn't lasted an hour.

She whimpered, and her lips clung to his. His

fingers slid into her hair, and pins pinged on the tile floor.

He pulled back, searching her face.

"I was so certain I'd find...something," she whispered.

His forehead crinkled. "What is it you think you're going to find, baby?"

"I don't know. I just know things aren't right." Did he even realize what he'd called her?

His dark eyes searched hers. "You're right. Things aren't right."

He kissed her again, and she tingled all over, especially where they touched. The pads of his fingers traced down her neck, and her heart pounded. Her bare toes curled into the cool floor.

But before she could ask what he meant he was kissing her deeply. Her bones turned soft, and she clung to him.

In every other way, she was so confused, but Daniel's hold was so right. His touch was a combination of reverent and demanding, and his fingers splayed against her ribs, while his other hand threaded in her hair, teasing it down.

His hardness pressed into her belly, and his kisses grew more insistent. He wanted her. He wasn't ignoring her or hiding from her. If she let him take her, he would decide her future for her.

A need for more than his kiss built in her. She strained to lift higher, so the hardness would press against the ache low in her. She wanted him to slide his hand up and cup her breast. His thumb brushed the underside, and shivers ran down her spine. He closed his hand around that part of her, and she pushed into him as he gently kneaded. Then his thumb brushed across her nipple, and a sharp ribbon of pleasure shot from his hand to her private parts.

She moaned into his mouth.

He growled and cupped her bottom, lifting her up. She wrapped her legs around his thighs, fairly wanting to climb him and become part of him. Letting him support her weight, she rubbed the back of his calf with her instep.

With a low groan, he rocked into her, and a starburst of sensation clouded her thoughts. Yet he seemed to be holding back. She slid her hands around to his shoulders and down his arms until she could reach around his waist.

He eased away, and she tried to pull him back into her.

"Anna, we have to stop," he whispered.

Words seemed like foreign things for a minute as she stared at him, not comprehending.

He leaned his forehead into hers. His breathing was ragged. "We have to stop while we still can."

Holding her with one arm under her, he brushed his fingers across her cheek. Then he peeled her away from him and pushed her shoulders back against the wall. "I have to take you back to your room now."

Her feet protested the cool tiles as if they were a sudden jolt back into reality. "Oh," was all she could manage.

His mouth twitched as if she amused him, but he wouldn't laugh at her. Then his eyebrows drew together and he canted his head. "Are you barefoot?"

"Uh-huh."

He bent and scooped her up, one arm under her knees and the other around her back. The night was not so cool that carrying her was necessary because of her bare feet. It must mean he wanted her in a bed not a tiled hallway. Anticipation wound around her as new pings of excitement danced through her body. She laid her head against his shoulder and put her arms around his neck.

A short minute later, he set her down outside her room and took a step back. Did he not mean to carry her inside?

Need thrummed in her body. She took a step toward him. "Are you coming inside?"

His nostrils flared, and his gaze dropped to her lips. "Do you really want me to ruin you?"

Connecting ruin to something that felt so right didn't make sense. It was as if his kisses had rendered her stupid. A part of her screamed yes. She didn't want to stop, but she couldn't be foolish. "I don't know."

She put her hand on his chest, feeling his harsh

breathing, the tension under her fingers, as if her touch affected him as deeply as his touch affected her. "I've never felt like this. I don't want it to end."

"Anna, I want you more than you can know." He cupped her cheeks and brushed his lips across hers. Then he pushed her back and turned her to face her door, so she couldn't reach him. "But you have to know what you want."

Never had she felt so needy, as if she couldn't go on if he didn't finish what they'd started. But he seemed almost blasé about it.

How could she know what she wanted if the person she'd come to marry hadn't been around for her? But Daniel had. Her mind swirled.

She wanted Daniel with an ache that went bone deep. "What would it mean if..." She searched for the right words, to ask the question he hadn't.

"It would mean you couldn't marry Rafael."

A cold spike lanced through her arousal. Would it mean more than that? Perhaps Daniel needed prompting. "I want to be married."

"I know," he answered softly. "To a man—"

"Yes."

"—of means."

"To a man who can take care of me." She waited. Hadn't she made her position clear earlier? That if she was going to sleep with a man, she expected him to marry her. Was that why he was balking?

As the seconds ticked by the proposal never came. He hadn't spoken once of caring or love, only wanting. She clenched her eyes shut. She was just another foolish woman mistaking a man's desire for more than it was. For a woman it was all woven together, the strands inseparable, but not so for a man.

"Go to bed, Anna. I have to go put out the lamp and make sure no animals can get into the storage room. We left the back doors open."

She cast one look over her shoulder at him, but he was looking toward the doors to the passageway.

Coldness seeped through her, finally numbing her desire. She turned the knob and stepped inside her room. She wouldn't make that mistake again.

Daniel stared at the door, wishing more than anything he could follow Anna inside, make love to her until exhaustion set in, but he had to go figure out where Juanita had gone and if Anna had seen the wagon. He suspected Rafe was disguised as a lumpy sack of cornmeal.

His fists clenched, he ran across the courtyard and into the breezeway. He secured the doors, then retrieved the lamp from Rafe's room.

He carried it into the storage room. "You can come out now."

The burlap sack didn't move, but Rafe's wheezing echoed in the silent room. He set the lamp down and reached for the sack. He pulled it up, and yellow bits covered Rafael's hair and back. Juanita appeared in the doorway. She dropped down to her knees beside Rafe and brushed the cornmeal from his hair.

"Can't...breathe." Rafael scrabbled at the barrel, while Juanita pulled the sacks she'd tossed over his legs away.

All the time Daniel had been kissing Anna—more than kissing—he'd expected to feel Rafael's hand on his collar, yanking him away. Instead, his brother was in earshot, barely breathing.

His chest slammed as if a horse had kicked him square center, dispelling the last lingering haze of desire. How could he have been lusting over his brother's bride when his brother was in here fighting for his life?

Rafe slapped Juanita's fussing hands away, twisted and grabbed Daniel's arm. "Bastard."

It wasn't an epithet Rafe used often, seeing as how it could be said of him without malice.

Daniel's insides twisted.

Juanita rolled back to her heels and looked uncertainly between them.

"Well, the minstrels I hired to distract Anna didn't show." He'd had to do something or she would have started tearing apart the house looking for Rafael, or he would have had to lie to her again. Kissing her had seemed liked the best option. Didn't hurt that he wanted to kiss her every time he looked at her. Still, he hadn't needed to go as far as he did. And if he hadn't known Rafe was nearby, he might not have been able to stop. Anna went to his head faster than whiskey.

"Juanita, would you go get those blankets and pillows?"

She nodded and popped to her feet.

The second she left the room, Rafe hooked his fingers in Daniel's collar at the throat and yanked him down. "Least wait…'til…dead."

Rafe's hand dropped, and he labored to breathe.

Daniel's throat tightened. "I'm going to get a doctor."

Rafael shook his head. "Then…have to…say… cousin…shot me." He spun his finger by his ear.

He was right that the explanation was *loco*, and if too many people heard it, the whole story would fall apart. Hell, Anna didn't even believe it all the way. "I'm not going to let you die. People will think I killed you because you wouldn't sell me the land you promised me."

For a second Rafe's eyes crinkled.

Relief poured through Daniel. It must have just been the thick burlap sack that had been impeding his brother's air and now that it wasn't over his head, he was at least no worse.

"I'm going to go help Juanita with the mattress. I'll be right back."

Rafael nodded. "Close…th' door."

Daniel went out the back of the house and

looked for the wagon. It was no longer standing where he'd parked it.

Juanita rounded the corner, her arms full of bedding.

"Where is the wagon?"

She rocked her head toward the front of the house.

The quiet girl was smarter than he thought. *"Gracias."*

Juanita shook her head and went through the back door and slipped. She wobbled, her back arching and her arms coming up, but she didn't fall. She twisted, looking at the tiles as she continued on.

Hairpins. She'd slipped on one of Anna's hairpins. And he was going to have to gather the damn things up and get them back to her, or she'd come searching for them. The trouble was if she opened her door to take them, he didn't think he'd be able to resist her. He knew if she asked for the moon, he'd promise it to her—or marriage, which would be a hell of a thing. A woman shouldn't be engaged to two brothers. Not that he was anywhere close to being ready to take a wife.

Anna picked up the folded paper with her name on it. It had been slipped under her door sometime in the night. The writing was familiar; she'd seen it dozens of times. Before she came her heart had soared with each letter she'd received from Rafael, but she dreaded opening this one.

Had Rafael come back in the night? He must have to have written her this note.

She unfolded the paper, and her hairpins dropped out. Her breath snagged as the memory of Daniel threading his fingers through her hair flooded her mind.

Squinting at the note, she read the one line.

*Much as I hate that you will use these to restrain your beautiful hair, thought you might miss them.*
*Daniel*

Her hand went to her hair. But then she knew he liked it. Funny, she'd always envied Olivia's pale blond locks and Selina's rich dark tresses. Her hair had always seemed like just another thing that marked her as Irish, like her freckled nose, and not in a good way. But Daniel made her feel beautiful, and her anger with him eased just a bit.

She flipped it over and looked at her name. Goodness, the brothers had very similar hands. As isolated as their ranch was, they had likely been taught to form their letters the same way by the same teacher.

The relief that went through her as she realized Rafael wasn't back didn't make sense. Or perhaps she didn't know what she would do with him. She was, after all, still engaged to Rafael. And Daniel had ignored her hints. Still, she gathered the pins and quickly dressed.

She wouldn't lose her head like she had last night. She couldn't.

A knock on her door had her rushing toward it. She threw the door back, her heart nearly in her throat.

Juanita stood there, her eyes downcast. "Visitor for you."

*A visitor.* She didn't know of anyone locally but Selina. She took a deep breath, trying to still the butterflies that had begun in her stomach. She would be excited to see Selina, but she wondered what could have brought her to the ranch so soon. She jabbed the last of her hairpins in her bun, hoping it would hold. "Is it my friend?"

"Mr. Sheriff and a man."

Her heart fell like a stone. Who would the sheriff have brought with him? She started to ask Juanita but realized the futility of it. Could it be a suspect they wanted her to identify? "Is Rafael back?"

Juanita raised her dark eyes and looked daggers at her. "No." As if it were somehow her fault that Rafael had gone out hunting down the robbers.

## Chapter Fifteen

*My immediate family consists of my widowed mother and my brother. Both of whom are eager to meet you.*

When she walked into the main room, all eyes turned to her. In the midst of several people who were all a blur, Daniel stood with his arms folded, talking to the sheriff. For a second he was the only one she saw as his eyes landed on her and softened.

His mouth had been on hers; his hands had been on her body. Heat traveled down through her.

A chair screeched. Her attention jerked to the rest of the room's occupants.

"Hello again," said the artist who'd been on the stagecoach with her. He stood by the table. Mrs. Werner poured a cup of coffee.

"You two know each other?" asked Daniel.

"We arrived in Stockton together," she said. "How are you doing, Mr. Crump? Hello, Sheriff."

Daniel's eyes darted toward the artist. He tilted his head slightly, and a look of puzzlement crossed his face.

"I'm doing well, Miss O'Malley," Mr. Crump said. "The sheriff here has hired me to do a rendering of the two thieves who attacked the stage." He pushed toward her a drawing of a masked man and a second man without a face. "Everyone saw the thief in front, but you are the only one who got a good look at the second man."

The sheriff stepped toward her. "The stage company is offering a two-hundred-dollar reward for the two men. An accurate drawing on the wanted poster will help."

"Do you think it is a good likeness?" asked Mr. Crump.

She examined the drawing. His eyes were the only features of his face that were identifiable, and she thought they might have been spaced differently from how Mr. Crump had them. He looked so eager she hated to say anything. Besides, how likely was it that a man could be identified from his eyes alone? "It is similar, but I didn't see him for long."

"Now, what do you remember about the other man?" Mr. Crump flipped open his sketch pad.

She had been so focused on the man she'd shot that she'd scarcely given the second man much thought. Or remembered the moment when time had seemed to stand still and their gazes had met.

"Why don't you sit down, Miss O'Malley," said the sheriff. He pulled out a chair for her next to Mr. Crump's.

Oddly reluctant to describe the second man, she took the offered seat. "I mostly remember he had dark eyes, I think."

"Don't you remember?" asked Mr. Crump.

Mrs. Werner and Daniel watched her with interest. "He had that cape up over his nose and his hat drawn low. I think he had dark hair, but I don't remember actually seeing his hair."

"Do we really know more than the men were of Spanish descent?" asked Daniel.

"Well, just tell me if the eyes were similar in shape to the other fellow's," said Mr. Crump. "A person's eyes can tell a lot about him."

She looked in her mind's eye and began describing. Mr. Crump asked her a lot of questions. Across the room the sheriff questioned Daniel about Rafael. She listened, intent on his answer.

"He is backtracking where they came from," Daniel answered. "I should tell you one of the horses I reported stolen came back."

"Miss O'Malley," said the artist, jarring her back to his sketches. He pushed his sketchbook under her nose. "Like this?"

Keeping half an ear on Daniel's description of the horse's return, she frowned at the pencil sketch. "A little deeper set, I think."

Mr. Crump bit his lip as he shaded more.

"Would you say he was the same complexion as his companion?"

"No, lighter." She shook her head as she stared at the pencil drawing. Recognition hovered just on the edge of her brain, but she wasn't certain if she was relaying the second robber's looks or eyes she had more recently stared into. She cast an uneasy glance toward Daniel.

His gaze met hers as if he was waiting to catch her look. He glanced at the sketch. A faint pucker appeared between his eyes.

"Were his eyebrows thicker or thinner?" Mr. Crump pestered.

"I'm sure I don't know."

Mr. Crump persisted, and she finally said impatiently, "Thicker, much thicker."

Daniel arched his perfect eyebrows as if to question her short answer. When she looked back at the sketch, the eyes no longer reminded her of Daniel's, but she couldn't really remember the robber's, either.

Juanita slipped in the door and looked at the drawing of the first robber. "Oh."

Everyone looked at her.

She narrowed her eyes, looked at Anna and said, "It look like Martinez."

"Martinez, the former owner of this rancho?" asked the sheriff.

Daniel jerked as if someone had kicked him. His tanned skin turned chalky.

Mrs. Werner rushed to the table and grabbed the sketch. "No! It does not look like him."

She turned to Juanita and spoke sharply in Spanish to her.

"Stop it," said Anna. "Yelling at her won't help."

What was wrong with Daniel? She tried to meet his eyes, but he was staring narrow-eyed at his mother.

"Well, it wouldn't be Mr. Martinez," said the sheriff. "He'd be in his sixties now, but could he have had a son?"

Daniel barked a laugh, then cut it off with a cough. No one answered.

Daniel looked ill. If he feared his cousins were about to be exposed as the robbers, feeling sick would be expected. His tension was palpable. He tightened his arms across his chest and rocked on his feet while watching his mother.

Mrs. Werner slapped the drawing on the table and thrust out her chin. "It does not look like any Martinez I know."

"Have you seen any of the Martinez family members lately, ma'am?" asked the sheriff.

Anna stared at Juanita, who had gone pale and was shaking. She stood up and went around the table and put her arm around the girl. She questioned her gently, "Do you know this man in the drawing?"

Daniel asked her a question in her native language.

Juanita spoke a few words in Spanish, then curled to hide her face in Anna's shoulder.

"She says there are quite a few Martinezes related to the man who used to own the ranch, but he never married."

The sheriff nodded. "That was what I thought."

Anna rubbed Juanita's back. "It's all right. You're being very brave."

"Juanita would know the Martinez family best," Daniel said. "She's at least met them in Mexico."

Juanita slipped out of Anna's hug and gathered breakfast dishes off the table.

"Why aren't you out tracking with your brother, Danny?" asked the sheriff. "You seem good at it, too."

Daniel hesitated a minute, then said, "The grapes will be ripe any day now. I can't risk missing their peak."

The sheriff nodded. "Do you have enough, Mr. Crump?"

"I believe so." The artist surreptitiously slid the controversial drawing into the pages of his sketchbook and closed it. "Thank you, Miss O'Malley."

The sheriff smiled at Anna. "Have you had occasion to fire that rifle, Miss O'Malley?"

"No, but I keep it by my bed just in case."

The sheriff cast a sharp look at Daniel.

Mrs. Werner whipped her head around and stared at Anna. The tension in the room was as thick as stew. Questions swirled in Anna's brain.

"Danny, tell your brother I want to talk to him as soon as he's back." The sheriff tipped his hat to them. "Ladies."

She considered running out after the sheriff, but really she had nothing to add. She didn't know what had upset Daniel so much. He'd suspected his cousins before Juanita recognized them.

Anna's thoughts tumbled. She must have misunderstood the sheriff—because the old owner couldn't still be alive. Not if Mrs. Werner owned the ranch. Martinez had to be Mrs. Werner's maiden name. But of course it must have been. Valquez must be the surname of her first husband. The prior owner must have been Mrs. Werner's father or perhaps an uncle.

Still, they had confirmation that the robbers were their cousins, just as Daniel had told her. And now the sheriff knew.

The door shut, and Mrs. Werner and Juanita began a rapid argument in Spanish. She heard Rafael's name, then the word *loco*, but it was one of the few Spanish words she could identify and the rest became a spatter of gibberish. She lost interest in trying to follow the conversation.

Daniel stood stock-still, his head down, seemingly finding the floor powerfully interesting. She walked toward him, wanting to tell him it would be all right, even if it wouldn't be.

As if he had to call himself back from a long way away, he lifted his gaze and narrowed it on the two shouting women. "Stop. What's done is done."

"So now the sheriff knows it is your cousins Rafael is following?" she asked him.

He said wearily. "The Martinezes are not *my* cousins."

"But—" How could she have thought she'd seen a resemblance between the robbers and him—or was it just that there was a similarity between the men because of their Spanish descent? "Martinez wasn't your mother's maiden name?"

"Valquez."

Mrs. Werner turned toward Daniel and raised her voice again. She shook a finger at him. His expression was flat except Anna thought anger flashed in his eyes.

He held up his hand. "Madre, was this ranch *owned* by José Martinez?"

She went still, and her face darkened. "Not this one. He own other ranch."

The light drained out of Daniel's eyes. "What other ranch?"

Anna didn't understand the significance of the question, but she knew Daniel was deeply disappointed. She took a step toward him and reached to touch his hand.

Suddenly Mrs. Werner was glaring at her. "You have a rifle?" she asked in a chillingly low voice. "How you have a rifle?"

"The sheriff gave me the rifle the robber dropped."

Mrs. Werner's hands balled into fists, and she jutted her chin forward. "Why he do this? Why he give a rifle to a girl?"

"Because I shot the robber."

Mrs. Werner came at her like a charging bull.

Anna's heart slammed against her rib cage, and she brought up her fists. She wouldn't back down. She'd done nothing wrong. It certainly wasn't her fault if her future in-laws had criminals in their family.

Daniel stepped in front of his charging mother and caught her shoulders. She tried to bowl him over, and he pushed back, holding her in place. He asked in Spanish if she wanted Anna to know that she'd shot Rafael.

Mrs. Werner swung and shoved at him, cuffing him on the side of the head. "I kill her." She descended into a mixture of Spanish and swear words. "This is all your fault."

"Of course it is." At least that much remained the same, but everything he'd believed for years was false. And he almost didn't know which way was up. He felt sick to his stomach, and Madre wasn't helping.

He wrapped his arms around her and pulled her back. Her flaying elbow caught him in the ribs. He *oofed*, then tightened his hold.

"Damn *puta*!" shouted Mrs. Werner.

"Anna, go outside," he said.

"I can take her," Anna said fiercely.

"Anna!" He bit back the wry laugh that threatened to erupt at the idea of her and his mother who outweighed Anna by probably a hundred pounds, going at it. All his mother would have to do was sit on Anna.

He didn't have time to make certain Anna followed his dictate as he wrestled his mother into a chair. She kicked and clawed. He was trying very hard not to hurt her, but she was like a crazed cornered animal.

"Stop it, Ma. Or I'll tie you to the chair until you calm down." He slid around to the back, where he held her down out of range of her heels and fists.

"She tried to kill my—"

Daniel slapped a hand over her mouth, cutting off her words. Madre screamed against his fingers.

Juanita sidled up beside him. "She go outside."

He whispered in his mother's ear, "She doesn't have any idea she shot Rafael, Ma. As long as she doesn't know, she can't turn us in."

"Do not let her know," pleaded Juanita. "Keep Rafael safe."

"Yes, you weren't a lot of help telling the sheriff the robbers are related to us," Daniel muttered.

"But Rafael say—"

"Rafael is stupid." Daniel switched to Spanish, because he wouldn't be surprised to find Anna with her ear pressed to the door. If his brother hadn't been stupid enough to hold up the stage in the first place, then none of this would be a problem now and so he told them.

Juanita's dark eyes filled with moisture. "I should not have say they look like Martinez."

"It's all right. I know you were trying to help. Now, why don't you go fix some breakfast for Miss O'Malley? I don't think she's eaten."

"I do eggs, no chiles," she said and scrambled for the door.

"We're just lucky she hasn't recognized us. And if she figures it out from your tantrum, Madre, you can't blame me."

He'd seen the sketch. It looked like the eyes that stared back at him from his shaving mirror. But then Anna had veered away from what looked like him into other traits that didn't. He didn't know if she had deliberately altered the details or if she simply didn't remember that moment when he'd stared into her eyes. A moment he didn't think he could ever forget.

His world had started spinning out of control

at that moment, and it only seemed to spin faster and faster.

"I'm trying to keep Rafe's neck out of a noose, not put it in one, and you are making that damn hard." Half prepared for more blame, he lifted his hand away from his mother's mouth.

She whimpered and went limp.

When she didn't shout or try to bolt, he loosened his grip around her and the chair. "Now I'm going to have to go learn what Miss O'Malley has figured out."

His mother clasped his arm. "I will do anything to save Rafael. Tell me what to do."

"Don't do anything," Daniel said, but he doubted she'd listen to him now when she never had before.

"But you will want him dead now that you know."

"God, Ma. I don't want him dead. He's my brother. I don't know what I'd do without him." It felt as if an ox were sitting on him, and he couldn't hold his shoulders back. He rubbed the bridge of his nose. "You should go to your room. I'll tell Miss O'Malley you felt unwell."

"I want to talk to my son."

"You are talking to your son," he shot back. He knew she meant she wanted to talk to her favored son, but his patience with her was gone.

Her lower lip quivered. "I want to talk to my Rafael."

Of course she did, but not before he talked to him first and found out what Rafael knew and how long he'd known it.

## Chapter Sixteen

*My family has owned this ranch since last century, when it was granted by the Spanish Crown to my mother's family. When my family first settled here, there were few people outside of the missionaries and natives, but I'm afraid the secret is out and everyone knows of the beauty of my state now.*

The front door opened, and Daniel came out. Her pulse raced just looking at him.

He walked to the edge of the porch and said, "Juanita is fixing breakfast."

"Will she spit in it?" Anna asked as she returned to the porch. She was amazed he was thinking about something so mundane and ordinary as her breakfast when so much had happened this morning. His consideration lit something warm and soft inside her.

The edge of his mouth curled up. "She's a safer bet than my mother right now."

His dark eyes searched hers with a question in them.

"I'm sorry." Anna stopped in front of him.

"What do you have to be sorry for?" The corners of his eyes crinkled as he looked down at her.

"I shot your cousin." *That your mother is crazy.* She took a deep breath. "And I'm sorry for whatever upset you."

He could be upset because of his mother, but she thought it had started before that. "What was it the sheriff said that has you worried?"

The hint of amusement disappeared. His expression fell as he looked off into the distance toward the mountains. "Nothing important."

"Didn't seem unimportant," she countered. Interesting that he hadn't immediately leaped to voice concern over his cousins—or cousins he'd just disavowed—or his mother's fit.

He looked so careworn, she wanted to hug him, but he folded his arms.

"Won't you tell me?"

He returned his attention to her. "If you must know, my mother has been lying to me my entire life, but it's not important and it doesn't change things. Shouldn't have been a surprise to me."

But it had been a shock. She was certain his disappointment had been tied to the question he had asked about the ranch. She'd been trying to understand how everything fit together. "Who is this José Martinez?"

Daniel stiffened. "You need to ask Rafe that."

"I can't ask Rafe that because he isn't here to ask." Her stomach knotted. When he was back, she needed to have a serious conversation with him about their future. But Daniel was here and knew the answer. And she wasn't even sure if she wanted to know because of Rafael, but she wanted to know why it affected Daniel so strongly. "I'm asking you."

He sighed. "It's not my place to tell you."

But his nonanswer told her something. The details of the earlier conversation clicked together, shifting and coming more into focus. Like watching a train pulling into the station back in Connecticut. At first all you could see was an indistinct black-and-gray thing; then as it grew closer you could see it was an engine with smoke billowing out the top.

Daniel stepped off the porch, putting them on the same level, although he was still taller than her. His eyes went to her hair and then came back to her face. "What do you think about the portraits for the wanted poster?"

Uneasiness settled in her belly. Now she was the one who wanted to avoid answering. She shrugged. "I don't know how well a person could be recognized by just their eyes."

"But they're good likenesses?" Daniel's eyes narrowed. He seemed to be waiting for something.

Her stomach grew hollow. Just as it had in the

moment when she hadn't been certain she was describing the robber's eyes or Daniel's eyes. She looked down. "Close enough."

She didn't really want to talk about the robbery because with it always came with that moment when the robber had realized she'd shot him. Knowing she'd done the right thing, that she'd saved the people she traveled with, didn't mitigate her feeling that shooting a man was a horrible thing to do. "I want to understand your family."

"No. You do not," he said. "You'd never want to be a part of it, and Madre would never forgive me."

His mother, not his brother?

The other moment from the holdup when she'd caught the attention of the robber with the lasso intruded into her thoughts. Somehow it was as if her life had split in two at that moment. A before and after. The before and after should have been the moment she'd pulled the trigger, but it seemed earlier as if not only her life had changed but she'd changed, too, when her gaze locked with the robber with the lasso. "I don't like talking about the holdup."

"I don't like talking about my family," he countered.

But Daniel had given her one too many clues. He'd said the Martinezes weren't his cousins, but Rafael claimed them. And he'd said that his mother's maiden name was Valquez. The name Rafael used as his middle name, and he'd taken the surname of Daniel's father as his last name, which made her think he didn't have one. "José Martinez is Rafael's father, isn't he?"

"Ma, give him room to breathe," Daniel said from the doorway of the storage room.

The room was cramped enough with Rafael's bedding wedged in between some barrels and the wall. There wasn't even room for him to lie flat, although he seemed to breathe easier half reclined.

Now with Madre kneeling by Rafael and clasping his hand, the room was even more cramped.

"I don't know how much time I'll have," said Daniel.

Juanita had promised to ring the dinner bell if Anna left the main room. She was going to try to occupy her with breakfast and then questions. But how long she could keep inquisitive Anna busy remained to be seen.

He'd wanted to talk to Rafael before their mother got to him. He wanted to know how much Rafe knew and tell him that Anna knew too much, which was as much his fault as anything. He hadn't meant to say anything, but then he'd gone and opened his mouth about Madre lying to him his entire life.

Oh, he'd known that José Martinez was Rafael's father. And he'd known Mr. Martinez had refused to marry his mother even though he'd gotten her pregnant. Rafe had told him that years ago, but he hadn't known Rafe's father had *owned* their ranch. No, he'd been told that Rafe's father was just one of the many vaqueros who'd worked the range. That Martinez was the former owner put a new light on things.

"She knows who your father is."

Madre turned, and her eyebrows flattened. "Why you tell her this?"

"I didn't. She put it together from what the sheriff said and what she already knew." The trouble was he had no idea how much more she had put together. She hadn't wanted to talk about the robberies or the thieves. He didn't know if she'd deliberately given wrong details to the artist.

Rafael shook his hand free from Madre's two-handed clasp. "I planned to tell her…before we got hitched."

"She's smart, and she won't stop digging until she has answers that satisfy her." Hell, the only way he knew to stop her questions was to kiss her, and he couldn't keep doing that. Although desire shimmered under the surface every time he so much as looked at her. He shook off the unbidden response. "It is only a matter of time before she puts together it was us, not imaginary cousins. She was close to realizing when she was with the artist."

"No, no, she cannot know this." Their mother tried to take Rafe's hand again.

"Ma, give us a minute alone," said Rafael.

"We cannot let her find out," she urged. "We will have to get rid of her before she knows. Before she tells."

He remembered what she'd said about getting rid of the horses. "For Pete's sake, Ma, the next thing you'll be telling me is to take her up into the mountains and put her out of our misery."

His mother stared at him.

Cold spread through him, freezing the blood in his veins. She couldn't think he was serious. "That was a joke, Ma."

"Don't joke about that," said Rafael. He cast an uneasy look at his mother. "I'll marry her… Then she can't testify…against me."

"I don't—"

"Ma, get me coffee." Rafael shot a quelling look in his direction. "And food."

Hell, he'd remembered Anna hadn't eaten, but he'd plumb forgotten Rafael hadn't had a chance to eat.

Daniel helped her to her feet, but then she pushed him away and scurried toward the court-yard.

"That'll buy us…few minutes."

Daniel turned back to his brother. "You're talking better."

"Easier sitting down." Rafael rubbed his chest. "Still hurts to breathe."

"I should have gotten you out of here this morning." But he'd overslept. After so many nights in a row with only a couple of hours' sleep, he hadn't stirred out from bed until well after dawn. Fortunately, Anna hadn't been up at that point, but just as he was getting ready to go rouse Rafael and get him out, the sheriff had arrived. "But you are going to have to talk to Anna soon."

"Not yet."

"Soon." Not only did Anna need to have a chance to make up her mind; he needed her to transfer her affection to his brother before he was in too deep.

"Hell, such a mess." Rafael rubbed a hand across his forehead. "You'll just have…to keep Anna…busy."

"Really, Rafe? I only know of one way to keep her from asking questions. Didn't think you wanted me doing that." His neck grew warm, and he glared at his brother. "And you can't marry her to keep her from testifying against you. It only means she can't be *compelled* to testify against you. Nothing will stop her if she wants to." Not much would stop Anna.

"I know." Rafael struggled to sit up more. "Marry her 'cause she wants to."

Daniel's stomach burned at the thought. She might very well prefer his brother once she got to know him.

They were wasting time arguing about Anna. He didn't know how long he'd have, and he had to ask Rafe what he'd come to ask him. "How long have you known?"

Rafael's eyes widened; then he looked away. "That my father sold the ranch...to your father?"

Daniel folded his arms.

"Since I saw the bill of sale and then your father's *supposed* will at the last hearing. The one Ma had filed when I was sixteen." Rafael plucked at the bedding. "It had to be forged, but I didn't know before that the land was never Ma's."

The last hearing had been three years ago. Rafael had come back worried, but Daniel hadn't suspected anything like this. His chest squeezed. "Why didn't you tell me?"

"Because Ma will kill me, then you."

"Ma won't kill us." Every muscle he had tightened. But she'd steal the land that was rightfully his. Madre clearly thought the ranch should belong to Rafael. Until today he'd never questioned that. Madre was here long before his father had arrived, and it hadn't occurred to him that *his* father had *purchased* the ranch from the prior owner. It made more sense to think Madre inherited it, and his father had married her and run the ranch. But she didn't inherit from the man who wouldn't even give her or his son his name.

A new horrible suspicion formed in his mind, and jolted his spine. Rafael had been so reckless in the past couple of years. And the nonsense about his will. "Have you been trying to get yourself killed?"

Rafael refused to meet his eyes. "The ranch should be yours."

"I don't care who owns the ranch." Fire singed his stomach. "I can't imagine trying to run it without you. Damn it, Rafe, we can split the ranch or you can keep it and sell me the bottoms for my farming. I don't care, but stop trying to get yourself killed."

"I may have succeeded this time."

Daniel's stomach turned. "No."

"You said Anna won't stop." He heaved a breath. "The hands…will be back…soon. Can't hide…the truth…forever." Rafael leaned back and closed his eyes, exhaustion apparent in the pain lines beside his mouth and on his forehead. "Do me…a favor."

"What?" asked Daniel

"Get the lawyer."

"Why? No! Forget the land. It doesn't matter. We can figure that out later. You just need to get well."

"Want to ask him…what will happen…if I go to Mexico."

Was his brother going to become a fugitive? A whole new wave of shock made his legs shake. "But—but what about Anna?"

"Take her with me." Rafael waved his hand.

Daniel felt as if a frog had gotten loose in his chest and was hopping every which way.

Madre returned with the coffee and a plate heaped with steak, eggs and cornbread. "I go get the priest. You come home tonight. You marry her tomorrow."

"Can't stand yet, Ma." Rafael set the cup on the floor beside him. "Give me a week."

*What the hell?* Anna would belong to Rafael in a week. No more kissing her, no more touching her, never seeing that fiery mane of hers across his pillow. It was as if he'd lost a vital part of himself.

"You hitch the buggy for me, Daniel," said Madre. "I'm going to get the priest."

The dinner bell rang. "Come on, Ma. We've got to go."

"Danny, send a note...Juanita."

"What is he talking about?" asked Madre.

"Just some ranch business that needs to be done." He pushed her out the storeroom and shut the door. "He wants you to take Juanita to town with you. She can run a couple of errands while you make arrangements with the priest."

He steered his mother toward the back of the house, picked up an armful of crates and carried them toward the courtyard. Couldn't have Anna wondering what he was doing in the breezeway.

Anna wondered at Juanita's sudden chumminess. Had trying to comfort the girl when she revealed she recognized the man in the drawing helped? In any case, she needed to think about what she'd just learned, and think about her uneasiness when it came to the drawings of the two robbers. And of course, she planned to check Rafael's room again.

More than anything it had been Juanita's question about marriage that had spurred her to end the conversation. Daniel emerged from the hallway across the courtyard, a stack of crates in his arms.

"Have you seen Juanita?" He walked toward her.

"I left her on the porch. She was showing me the bell." Which was odd, because Anna hadn't asked to see it. But Juanita had insisted before she went she had to see it.

"Ma is going to town. I want Juanita to go with her." Daniel stopped a few feet from her and shifted uneasily. "I know you want to go into town, but you shouldn't go with my mother today."

Anna rolled her eyes, but she agreed.

Had Daniel engineered an errand for his mother to separate them? Anna's main reason for wanting to go to town was to talk to the sheriff, and since he'd come here and knew the Werners suspected their cousins, she had nothing to say. With everyone else out of the house, she and Daniel would be alone. Her thoughts shimmered down an unseemly path.

He started forward. "If you want, Juanita can

mail any letters you have. I'll have a load of grapes to take to town in the next day or two. You are more than welcome to come with me then."

She fell in step beside him. "Won't you need the wagon?"

"Yes." Daniel looked blank.

"Doesn't Rafael *have* the wagon?"

"Hell." His mouth flattened. "If he isn't back tomorrow, I'll have to go get it."

Since his arms were full, she reached to open the door for him. "Why is your mother going to town?"

"She wants to see the priest."

"Confession, perhaps."

He smiled, and it was like the sun breaking through the clouds on a gloomy day. "One can only hope."

Juanita stood uncertainly in the middle of the room.

Daniel lapsed into Spanish. Then he turned to Anna. "I will head to the vineyard after I get Ma off. Do you want to come with me?"

She hesitated. That was where Daniel had first kissed her. Being alone with him was a bad idea. It would lead to other things, and she didn't intend to allow those other things until he promised marriage. Heat stole over her face. "I think I will stay here in case Rafael comes back. I want to talk to him right away."

His dark eyes searched hers. He gave a short, tight nod. "Suit yourself."

"I'll go get my letters." Besides, if everyone was gone, she could hunt around and get the answers no one would give her. She had a right to know what this family was so intent on hiding from her. Especially if it was to be her family, too.

## Chapter Seventeen

*My family dined with the governor and his wife. The table was set with the whitest damask linen, china plates so fine light shone through them and silver so shiny the spoons could be used as mirrors. They brought in fresh lobster from Maine and made a most delicious sauce to go with it. That was the first course. The second course was...*

Daniel stayed out late gathering the ripe clusters from the vines and throwing dirt clods at the birds stealing grapes. He was tired, and his back hurt. Normally, he would have had Juanita, Rafael and a few of the hands to help him, but this year he was on his own. The work wasn't hard so much as it involved a lot of bending and stooping.

He'd shed his clothes and washed off in the river before returning to the house.

He almost hoped Anna had discovered Rafael

hiding like a rat, but when he drove the loaded wagon up to the house—another inconsistency in the stories they'd woven—he found Madre and Juanita in the main room.

"Where's Anna?"

"After supper, Miss O'Malley go walk in circles," said Madre. "Why you leave her alone?"

"I thought she'd come with me when I asked her to go to the vineyard." He shrugged. "Couldn't force her to go when she said no. That would have been suspicious."

"You should have stayed here." Madre leaned back in her chair.

"I had work to do." He didn't even bother to mention he needed to harvest his grapes. Madre wouldn't care—she'd berate him if the grapes went bad on the vine. But she wasn't berating him now, which must mean Anna hadn't discovered Rafael.

His shoulders sagged. He wanted her to discover the wagon. He wanted her to discover Rafael. He wanted her to refuse to marry his brother. Hell, he just wanted a supper plate held back for him.

"The priest will come in five days."

"Short week," he muttered. Daniel's gut burned as it had all day. "I'm going to get something to eat."

He headed for the kitchen, hoping he didn't

have to fix a meal from scratch. The courtyard was dusky, as the sun had dipped below the roofline. Anna walked along the flagstones along the perimeter. Her steps clicked rapidly, and her movements were tight, agitated.

Still, he liked watching her and only regretted there was not enough sun to light the fire in her hair.

"Daniel," she called.

He closed his eyes. He shouldn't encourage her. She wasn't his. He should be discouraging her. He gave a brief wave and turned toward the kitchen.

She stepped swiftly to meet him at the door. "I'm glad you're home. I need to talk to you."

"Not now."

Her eyes opened wide, and her mouth rounded in an O for just a second before her features fell.

Then he felt like a heel. "Never mind, what is it?"

If she talked about her upcoming wedding or Rafael, he might punch a wall.

"Have you had supper?" she asked.

"No. That would be why I am headed into the kitchen."

"Would you like me to fix you something?" she asked cautiously.

He sighed. "I'd like that, but I'm perfectly capable of getting my own food." He'd been doing it for years.

"I would be happy to cook for you," she said.

"If I let you talk."

"I can confine myself to discussing food," she said.

"That might be a first," he replied.

Her eyes glittered, but she folded her arms and lifted her chin. "Well, you can go to the main room, and I'll bring it to you when it's ready."

He didn't want to go back in where his mother was. Plus, knowing Madre, she'd take offense at another woman in her kitchen cooking. "Just no questions, Anna." He wasn't up to lying to her anymore. "Okay?"

"I might have to ask you how you want your food."

"Cooked." He pulled open the kitchen door and held it for her. "Thank you."

Her lips twitched. "Don't thank me yet. It might not be like your mother would make."

"That wouldn't be a bad thing. I have eaten a meal or two in town."

"I explored the kitchen earlier, and I made a bit of starter dough. I'll make some rolls from it."

"Okay."

She urged him to sit as she bustled around the kitchen. First slapping a bit of dough on the table and adding flour, milk and butter, then kneading it. She retrieved what was left of a haunch of beef from the larder, and she told him to sit back down when he rose to help her. She cut off a good-sized steak and started frying it in a skillet. When she finally finished, she was flushed and a strand of hair had slipped down to drift in front of her face.

He almost didn't notice his stomach growling as he watched her, because she set off another kind of hunger in him.

She set down a plate with a roasted tomato, a juicy steak and a couple of small rolls. "The rolls won't be as light as I hoped. The dough just wasn't ready yet."

"Smells heavenly." He picked up the knife and fork she'd set before him and tucked in.

After working all day, he was hungry enough to think burned beans would taste good. But in no time at all he was scraping the plate with the last of his roll. She had moved to washing the dishes and was surprisingly quiet.

"I could get used to your cooking. Easily. That was just what I needed."

Her gaze flicked to his cleaned plate, and the ghost of a smile crossed her face.

Now that he'd forced her into silence, he missed the barrage of questions, missed the way she looked at him as if he had answers. He only hated that his answers had been lies.

"Come on. You can leave the rest for Juanita to finish. Let's go into the courtyard, where it is cooler."

She dried her hands and tucked the loose strand

of hair behind her ear. He held open the door for her, and they stepped out into the twilight.

He sighed. He supposed she wanted to talk about Rafael. Again. Seemed as if they were always talking about Rafael. "I assume Madre told you she arranged for the priest to come in five days."

Anna turned and bit her lip. "How can she know Rafael will be back in five days?"

"Good question. You should ask her."

"I did. She just told me not to worry." Anna's forehead furrowed. "I don't think I'll be ready to marry Rafael then."

An odd little hope flared to light. "When do you think you'll be ready?"

Anna ducked her head to the side and folded her arms. "Maybe never."

"Didn't you arrive prepared to marry him?" he asked.

"I did," she said softly.

They walked along in silence for a while until they reached her door. He should bid her goodnight and go to his room. Then after she settled, he could sneak out to check on Rafael. But instead he stopped walking.

She turned to look out at the empty courtyard. "The thing is, he could have told me where he was going or what he was doing or left me a note."

A shaft of remorse that he hadn't thought to

pass off a note to her stabbed him. But that would have only helped Rafe's cause.

"Nothing he's done since I arrived shows he holds me in any esteem. Leaving, not telling me anything, when he spoke to the rest of you." She lifted her chin. "I want to do what I can to help him keep the ranch, but he hasn't spared me any thought."

He should remind her that she had been sleeping when Rafael supposedly left, but he couldn't find the energy to force out the lie. Okay, not entirely a lie, because he'd taken Rafael out before dawn to be certain she wouldn't see him.

"It may be that I did not deserve consideration given my deception, but he couldn't have known about that then," she continued. "If he lost all respect for me when he learned I shot the stagecoach robber, we won't have the basis for a good marriage."

"You're going to have to make up your mind what you want, Anna."

"I don't have a family that can afford to take me back. The mill is closed, so I don't have a job to return to. I keep thinking he paid for me to come out here, and I owe him."

His gut tightened. Did she think she was obligated to marry Rafael because of the cost of her travel? "You don't have to marry him, Anna."

She turned and studied him. "I may not have

a lot of choice. I want to be married to a man of means."

This new pensive Anna concerned him. "You shouldn't be left alone all day ever again."

She looked down. "I'm just confused. I would like to talk to Rafael long enough to know if we would rub along well, but…" She shook her head and pressed her lips together.

"But what?"

Her cheeks darkened. "He seemed handsome enough, but I don't ever think of him."

Did that mean she thought of him? His ears perked up, waiting, hoping for her to say more.

"Then I think of those letters he wrote me, and I think I want to be with him."

Oh, hell. He felt the truth bubbling up, and he couldn't hold it back. "Anna." He waited until her gaze was focused on him. "I wrote those letters."

Her forehead puckered.

He didn't know if he expected anger or disappointment, but he watched her with his breath held. Her eyes turned faraway, and then she nodded. "That makes sense."

"How does that make sense?" burst out of him.

"Because the writing on the note with the hairpins made me think Rafael had written it. And because what you wrote seems like you. Daniel, it was you—"

He kissed her then. She'd come to marry him, not Rafael. Of course, there was still her expectation of marrying the owner of the ranch, but she couldn't know he was anything more than a younger brother who liked to grow things and hoped to have his own small stretch of land one day.

Her lips clung to his, and she wrapped her arms around his shoulders. Desire flung his sanity and caution to the side, and he pulled her tight against him and deepened the kiss.

She strained up on her toes and made the sweetest little mew as his tongue tangled with hers. He pushed into her until she was against her door and still he wanted closer. He wanted her so badly. The black fire that had been burning in him all day burst into bright, colorful flames. Scorching hot flames of need.

His arm around her back, he pulled her tighter against him, tight enough to feel her breasts pressing against his chest. She arched into him. Yet he needed closer. Her leg wrapped around his, and he wanted to pull her up, as he'd had her last night, but this time Rafael wasn't a few feet away. This time he wasn't certain he could stop if she didn't stop him.

This time he wanted nothing between them, no clothes between his hands and her skin, nothing between his privates and hers, no misunderstanding or shades of his brother. He drew his head back and she went with him, clinging, sucking on his lip, until he had to wrest his face to the side.

For a second only their heavy breathing filled the air.

"Am I doing something wrong?" she whispered.

He turned and drank in the uncertainty in her liquid green eyes. He brushed his lips across hers, slowly, gently, fighting the passion that would have him ripping her clothes open.

"Oh, Anna," he whispered against her sweet lips. "If we continue this, you can't marry Rafael."

Her lower lashes came up, and he watched her eyes, fascinated by the fierce determination he found there.

"If we continue, I will use the rifle on you if that is what it takes to make me your wife."

Well, marrying her would be one way to reclaim ownership of his rifle. "You won't have to shoot me to get me in front of the priest."

His heart galloped at the idea he was committing to a woman who'd never be afraid to go toe to toe with him, but at least she didn't try to work guilt or obligation against him.

He would owe her a proper proposal in due time. He'd do it right on bended knee, with all the right words and declarations, but right now they were beyond that. He reached for the doorknob and turned it, leading them both into her room.

He spun away from her, threw the bolt and closed the curtains to the courtyard. His blood thrummed hotly through his veins. He wanted things right for her. He found a match and lit the lamp. Then he worked at getting his boots off.

"Oh, do we need the light?" Her voice had a slight tremor.

"How else can I see you?"

"You want to see me?" she squeaked.

He dropped a boot to the floor, and she jumped.

He'd half expected her to shed her dress, let down her hair and climb into bed, but Anna was an innocent. She stood in the middle of the room, looking pointedly away from the bed and rubbing her arm.

He caught her hand and pulled her against his chest. "I want to see your magnificent hair." He tilted up her chin. "I want to look into your beautiful eyes. And how can I kiss each freckle on your nose if I can't see them?"

"I don't expect you to kiss my freckles," she said sounding a little more normal and skeptical like his Anna.

He caught her face in his hands and looked down into her eyes. "And here I was hoping for some strategically placed ones."

Her eyes widened, and she turned bright red.

If he played this right, he'd have her inventing freckles to kiss. He wanted her to enjoy the experience as much as possible. He never wanted her to look back and think she might have enjoyed it more with Rafe.

A shudder of concern snaked through him,

tempering the burning need and turning it to a softer thing. A part of him that was more concerned with her pleasure than his own. Odd. This need to take care of her, to put her needs first, must be what love was.

He kissed the end of her nose. "You're so beautiful, baby. Why wouldn't I want to see you? But if you don't want to look at me, you'll just have to close your eyes."

He kissed her long and slow and backed her toward the bed.

Her gasp and clutching at his arms signified when they'd reached it. He kissed her until she went soft against him.

Then he eased back. "Okay, don't panic. I'm going to take off my other boot."

"You'll have to teach me what to do," she murmured.

"It's a mutual thing, Anna."

Her eyes widened.

"You'll have to teach me what you like." He wrestled off his second boot.

She flushed again. "I feel like I should be doing something."

A wave of tenderness swept through him. He guided her to sit on the bed. "Yep. Letting down your hair while I take off your shoes."

He dropped to his knees and reached for her laces.

She put her trembling hands in her lap and

wrung them together. "And then we get un-dressed?"

Always the questions. "Not until you're ready." He tugged at the knots and leaned forward to kiss her hand. "But I'd very much like to lie down with you."

The first laces undone, he stuck his finger in, tugging them loose, and then slipped off her boot.

He gave her an escape if she wanted it. "You don't have to do anything you don't want to do. If you want me to leave, I will."

"I don't want you to leave," she murmured.

The words were a balm to his soul. Heat pulsed through his veins; yet he knew he had to keep his lust lassoed until she was ready. But there was more than desire. There was more than need. There was a rightness to this bigger than himself as if he'd somehow known when he first saw her photograph. He didn't just want to make love to her. He wanted to hold her through the night and to wake up with her at his side in the morning.

She threaded her fingers in his hair, and he turned and pressed his lips to the inside of her wrist.

Her stiff intake of breath let him know she liked it. He didn't know how long he could man-age soft and tender, but for her he'd try.

"When will I know if I'm ready?"

"We'll figure it out, baby."

# Chapter Eighteen

*The calf refused to cross the water. He stood on the far side and bawled. All the men tried to coax him across. Finally I climbed off my horse, picked up the calf and carried him to the other side. However, in crossing the river the fool animal was either scared witless or enjoyed the water because the minute I set him down on the bank, he ran back across to where he started and commenced bawling again.*

Anna shook with need as Daniel stretched out on his side and pulled her down beside him. He was not as urgent as he'd been out in the courtyard, or even last night, and she couldn't shake the feeling she was doing something wrong. That she'd done something to cool his ardor. But at the same time she was desperate to feel more. She wanted to run her hands over every part of him, but with his withdrawal she was afraid to. She didn't know exactly how this should go, and she didn't want him to think her too bold or too Irish or too eager.

But she wanted him with a power that made her shake. While he was gone during the day, she'd been counting the seconds until he returned. The world seemed dim without him there.

Something happened when he was close, as if the air turned to a magic potion she could get drunk upon. She wanted to be closer to him as if somehow she could crawl inside him and become part of him and he part of her. He was the one who had written the letters that made her long to become a wife to a man with such a kind soul, a man who saw beauty and humor in his world. She just wanted to be a part of that. And it was if she'd come home to him.

He caught her hand and put it on his chest. "Do you feel how hard my heart is beating?"

"Mine feels like it is trying to leap out of my chest," she answered. The steady tattoo under her fingertips excited her even more. "It is like that for you, too?"

"Of course it is." He stared into her eyes.

She was unable to look away. Parts of her ached for him. What was he waiting for?

He twined a finger in her hair. "Anna, I don't want to hurt you, so if I am, you must say so."

"You won't hurt me." That much she knew.

She also knew that Daniel was more methodical and reasoned than she was. When they married, he would probably force her to think things out, while she would urge him to act sooner than he would otherwise. It would be a good trade. They would fit together like two puzzle pieces making a better whole.

"I hope not much," he said before tilting her chin up to kiss her again.

He started slow, his lips just tantalizingly brushing hers, then more until their heavy breaths melded and her body tingled. He had merely been holding her, but he rolled her to her back and slowly slid his hand over her ribs, then over her breast. Explosions went off inside her, and she arched into his hand. He rubbed his fingers across her nipple, and sparks shot from his touch to low within her.

She slid her hands across his back, relishing the solid muscle and wondering if she was evoking any of the same sensations in him that he was coaxing from her.

But she must be. His breathing turned harsh, too. He jerked away and pulled his shirt over his head and slung it across the room. He pushed the buttons of his undergarment through their holes. The lamplight bathed his bronze skin in a soft glow and painted wild shadows on the wall.

"Touch me, Anna. I'm burning for you."

The invitation bubbled through her. She placed her hand on his chest and began an eager exploration. His skin was hot to the touch, and the pace of his heart was just as fast as earlier. And he felt so good. His skin was taut over hard muscles. His nostrils flared as she touched him boldly, running her hand over his stomach and down to brush the male parts of him before rubbing his thigh and hip.

He groaned and joined their mouths. The kiss was deeper, longer, and her body tingled from head to toe. He eased his knee between her legs. She opened to him, and he settled his hips between her thighs. That hard male part of him nudged her. A shiver of anticipation went down her spine and seemed to land in her secret place.

Her hips rolled in a circle, and she strained to rub against his hardness. She wrapped her legs around his, pushing even closer, toward the explosive need that flooded her with warmth and wanting.

"That's it, baby," he murmured against her lips.

She grabbed his hand and put it against her breast.

He laughed low and caressed her flesh until she was nothing but a mass of sensation. She wanted more. Now. What was he waiting for?

"Please, I'm ready," she mumbled and then moaned.

He unbuttoned her dress and then lifted her skirts, bunching them around her waist. She just wanted out of them. She wanted his skin against hers.

"Damn, you have on a lot of clothes," he muttered.

"So do you," she whispered. "Too many."

His eyes crinkled as he unfastened his trousers and shoved them and his summer-weight underwear off. He guided her up to a sitting position, and for a second all she saw was a flurry of white as he tossed her petticoats and dress over her head. He unhooked her corset, running his fingers over her freed flesh. Her drawers followed and landed on the heap of their clothing.

She grabbed the sides of her chemise to rip it open, and his hands landed on top of hers and stopped her. She whimpered in protest. He worked free the small buttons of her chemise.

Once they were bare as newborn babes, he settled her back against the bed. Holding her tight, he rolled her underneath him. He kissed her deeply, groaning. Everywhere his skin touched hers, she tingled. A white-hot need burned in her core.

She gripped his backside, trying to draw him closer to put pressure on that part of her. "What are you waiting for?"

He pulled back and looked down into her hot face. All parts of her were burning.

Brushing back her hair from her face, he squinted at her, then pressed a gentle kiss on her lips. His eyes were so dark, she was lost in them. "You, beautiful."

Streams of need were flowing through her and gathering in her private place. The stream raged into a river, and she twisted, trying to push against him.

He looked at her and breathed out heavily. Then he tucked his head into her neck as he moved into her. A burst of pain clouded her pleasure. She tried to squirm away, but he held her close.

His lips brushed her ear, and he whispered, "Easy."

The word contained an odd mix of tenderness and impatience. A rush of sensation flowed through her and gave more heat to that place. She went soft against him.

He pushed harder. Her body gave way as he penetrated her. At first it was strange, but then it was as if she and he were two pieces designed to fit together. Warmth swept through her. They were joined, and it felt so right, so meant to be.

He was breathing hard, but he lifted his head up and stared down into her eyes. His eyes were so dark, she couldn't tell where his pupils began. His fingers gentle, he stroked her cheek. "Are you all right?"

She was filled with a joy she'd never known before. He was so kind and sweet, so handsome and strong. She nodded. She was. The pain had been just a momentary burst. "Do you always stop at this point?"

His lips curled. "Not usually. You're special."

Then he stared down at her a long time. "I meant to take longer."

"Is it over?" she cried. It couldn't be over, she felt so undone.

"No. Not by a long shot." He rocked his hips.

She brushed her hands over his back. His skin was hot and damp, and he shuddered.

He kept looking into her eyes, and heat crept over her face as a new warmth curled around the riot of sensation in her body.

"I've wanted you from the first minute I saw you," he whispered.

"I knew that was not a brotherly hold at the stage office." She slid her leg up the back of his thigh, relishing the feel of the roughness of his hairs against the smoother skin of her leg.

"Then, too," he said. He thrust into her again, and his breath hitched.

Her thoughts clouded.

Then he kissed her again, urgently, insistently, deeply, and the storm blew past too fast to be noticed. His hips moved faster, and she tensed, her body singing and straining toward him, toward the intensity of sensation where their bodies were locked together.

He caressed her breasts, grasping and rubbing

across her nipples, sending shooting spikes down her body.

Then he stopped kissing her, groaned and scrunched his face as he pumped hard into her. She tightened her hold on him, certain this must be the moment of complete pleasure.

His breathing turned ragged, and the tension left him. His weight pressed her down into the bed. Had he experienced that rapture and she had not? Was that how it was supposed to work?

"Daniel?" She was glad he had found pleasure, warm that she could do that for him, except her body was so alive. She twisted her hips, trying to get him to rock into her more. "Is it over?"

"Not yet…baby." He kissed her again, slower and surer. Then his lips slipped to her neck.

"Daniel." She felt frantic, as if he had run ahead of her and she couldn't catch up and she didn't even know the destination.

He pulled out, and she sobbed in frustration. She reached down to his backside and tried to rejoin them.

"Shh, Anna, we're not done."

"But—"

"I see some freckles I really need to kiss." His breathing eased into a steadier, slower rhythm.

He very much seemed done, and she wanted to sob in frustration again. They'd been so much a part of each other and now it was as if they were not and she wasn't ready for it to end.

His mouth moved down her throat and across her collarbone. He caught her hands and pulled them up above her head. He slid his palms down the inside of her arms, over her breasts and down her sides.

"This freckle," he said. Then he caught her nipple in his mouth.

Liquid gold poured through her veins and to her mound and the part of her that was empty.

"Those aren't freckles," she tried to say sternly. But it came out too breathless to sound at all like a reprimand.

"Mmm," he hummed and flicked with his tongue.

She arched and moaned.

She hadn't known it would feel so good to have him play with her breasts. He flicked the other nipple with his index finger. She watched his hand on her, his dark hair skimming along her pale skin.

He continued sucking and nipping until she was twisting, holding his head to her breast. She only missed that hard part of him thrusting in her.

After leaving her breast, he repeated his actions on the other, then slipped down and kissed her quivering belly.

"By gum, you're a redhead down here, too." His fingers threaded into the hair covering her mound.

She smacked him on the shoulder as he sucked

on the inside of her hip bone. "What are...you doing?"

"I'm sure I saw a freckle down here."

His intent became obvious as he slid lower. "No!"

Then he pressed his lips to the part of her where every sensation called home. She nearly rocketed off the bed, but he had his arms across her thighs, holding her pinned.

"Good..." Words were too shattered to form, let alone say.

He flicked with his tongue, and her thoughts exploded. She tried to form words, form an objection, but the pleasure was so intense she could do nothing but writhe back and forth, moaning, nearly screaming, as he continued to tease that part of her. She lost control of her body as she strained toward and fought the power of what he was doing.

He found a rhythm that made her legs quiver and sensations built to a place she didn't think she could stand. Then she shattered. Every part of her was throbbing in a pleasure so deep it was like nothing she'd ever thought could happen.

Daniel slid up her body and thrust into her, feeling the last throbs of her release.

She moaned.

Her passion was more than he'd hoped for, almost more than he could handle as he had lost it too quickly, like a green boy, the first time. He rocked into her.

She mewed and draped a limp arm across his shoulders. Her calf slid against the back of his as he made love to her, thrusting slowly this time. Stroking her lovingly instead of grabbing at her. Kissing her freckled nose, each eyelid, and a freckle on her forehead.

He was being greedy, but she enchanted him with her wild cries and the way she made love with every part of her body: her mouth, her busy hands rubbing, exploring, her legs twining around his legs or around his waist, her hips twisting.

He moved into her as deep as he could go.

She gasped and tightened her arms around him.

He hesitated, wanting to be certain it was a good gasp. Her heels dug into his backside, pulling him tight against her, providing the motion when he didn't.

Wanting to savor her, he kissed the corner of her mouth, but already his control was slipping. He tried to hold back, but the fire and need raged in him until all he could do was give in to the building pleasure. At the same time, he knew it had never been like this. He'd never felt this whole as if she was the part of him he'd been missing his entire life.

Just as he was unable to hold back any longer, she cried out and twisted, her body pulsing around him. Her second orgasm pushed him to a peak higher than the first time.

Totally drained, he collapsed on top of her, and this time he didn't move. He could sleep for a thousand years.

"Daniel." She pushed at his shoulder.

He groaned. He was probably crushing her.

She pushed harder. "Daniel!"

He didn't want to separate from her, so he rolled, taking her with him. She sprawled on top of him, and the weight of her, the touch of her satiny skin, the slide of her hair—amazingly cool in contrast to its fiery color—all were perfect. And his. All his.

"What if they heard me?" she whispered.

Now she was whispering? "The walls are thick. I doubt anyone heard you."

He stroked her hair.

"But what if they did?" she said to his neck.

What if Rafael had heard? It would be better if the news came from him. But she wasn't thinking about Rafael. She could only be referring to his mother and Juanita. His mother's room was across the courtyard, so he doubted she'd heard anything, and Juanita wouldn't say anything. She'd be glad Anna was with him instead of Rafael.

"Then they will think I am a very lucky man." Or they would think Rafael was. "Although you are fairly loud."

She gulped and tensed. Then she was shifting

around and reaching down the bed. He held on to her hips lest she uncouple them. He was strangely reluctant to let her loose.

"Where are the covers?" she muttered.

"I tossed them onto the floor." He patted her cool bottom. "If you're cold, I'll warm you."

She stopped wriggling for a minute. "I'm just so naked."

He laughed.

She wrenched away and leaned off the side of the bed.

"I like you naked," he said. "I'm planning on spending a lot of time with you naked."

She snagged a petticoat and pulled it up on the bed. He yanked it out of her hands and sent it sailing across the room. It only went slightly out of reach before fluttering down.

He went to nudge up her chin for a kiss, but she kept her head ducked down. Had he failed her in some way? Unless she was a damn good actress, he'd satisfied her at least once—perhaps he'd been mistaken the second time. "Anna, what's wrong?"

She shifted off him and moved to sit on the side of the bed, the knots of her spine peeking through the tangled length of her hair. "We need to talk, and I can't have a discussion without clothing."

In his experience not much good ever came after *we need to talk*. The afterglow of pleasure dimmed a little. "There is nothing we need to talk about now." Perhaps she needed reassurances.

"We're in this together now. Anything else can wait until morning."

"But I have to tell you something."

His heart thumped oddly. What could she possibly have to tell him? He didn't doubt her innocence. He didn't doubt her pleasure. Was she still hiding something about her past? He couldn't think of anything that would make a difference. "It won't change anything. You're mine now."

She swiveled and looked at him. Hell, the avowal surprised him.

Her eyes were bright, and the edges of her mouth curled in a tremulous smile. Then she ducked her eyes as her creamy skin fired. Tenderness washed over him at her awkwardness in the wake of their lovemaking. He suspected he really did love her, because he'd never been so amused and concerned at the same time. But he'd make that declaration with all the pomp and ceremony it deserved.

He sat up. "Fine, I'll get your nightgown, but only because if you stay naked, I might not be able to resist making love to you again. And I don't want you sore."

"Was it really making love?" she asked a little breathlessly.

"That's what it felt like to me."

He swung his legs over the side of the bed and looked around for the covers he'd tossed. They lay at the foot of the bed on the floor. Her nightgown hung on a hook on the far wall. He stood and padded across the space.

Her fingers curled into the mattress, but she didn't avert her head. That was his bold Anna. Instead, her gaze shot to his face as soon as he turned around. Then, as if she couldn't help herself, her eyes dipped lower. Her jaw dropped, making him want to roar with pride.

He handed her the nightgown and gathered the tossed sheets and blanket from the floor.

She hastily pulled on the worn cotton gown, and he sat next to her.

"Don't you want to get dressed?" she asked.

"No." If he got dressed, he'd start feeling like he should check on Rafe. He pulled the sheet across his lap as a concession to her modesty. "What is it you want to tell me?"

"Well, show you." She popped off the bed and paced across to her trunk and opened it. She pulled out a sheaf of yellowed papers. "The thing is, while everyone was gone today, I was snooping around."

His gut tightened. He didn't think he was going to like where this was going. "What, in Rafe's room?"

Her eyes shifted, and she chewed on her bottom lip. "Actually, in that strongbox in your mother's room. Things just didn't seem to make sense, and it didn't look like it had been opened in a long time."

"What did you do? Break the lock?"

Her shoulders lifted and never went down. "The key was in her wardrobe. I know I shouldn't have, but I looked inside and on the bottom were these papers. And some were in Spanish, so I brought them into my room to try and read." She watched him carefully.

"And?" A white-hot burn ignited inside him. He half knew what she was going to say.

"I found the bill of sale for the ranch from José Martinez to August Werner, and I found your father's will. That was in English. The land is supposed to be yours, Daniel. The ranch is supposed to be yours. Your father bought it and left it to you, his only son, not to your mother and not to your brother."

He stared at her, his gorge rising in his throat. Everything should be crashing down around him, but there was only silence. After all, only his hopes and dreams had fallen.

Anna knew the ranch should be his before she had sex with him. And here he thought she'd picked him, knowing he only intended to purchase a small bit of land. Apparently, she didn't give a damn which brother she was with as long as it was the brother who owned the ranch.

# Chapter Nineteen

*One of the mares dropped a foal this morning. He was a determined fellow and was on his feet less than five minutes after his birth. His mother's efforts to clean him had him wobbling and hopping about until he let out a loud neigh, and his mother allowed that this child would always have dirt behind his ears.*

Anna didn't think Daniel grasped the significance of what she'd said. He didn't have to *buy* his vineyards and orchards from his brother. He was the rightful owner of the ranch.

"No," he said.

His voice was cold and angry, but then to learn you'd been cheated of what was rightfully yours for years was bound to stir up resentments.

She took a step toward him. "Yes, it all should be yours—or almost all." His father had allotted a small portion for Rafael to use.

He stood, and suddenly she felt small.

"The ranch is Rafael's and is registered in his name. A bunch of old papers isn't going to change that."

"But I don't think you understand."

"I understand perfectly."

"Just take some time and look at the papers." She stepped forward and held them out.

"I should burn them," he said.

"No!" She stared at him. "You can't."

He grabbed the papers out of her hands and tossed them on the bed behind him. He took a step closer. She shrank back. Her heart was pounding, and her mouth was dry. Why was he angry with her? The question froze on her lips as he scooped up his trousers from the floor and stepped into them.

Now he was getting dressed?

"You shouldn't have been snooping. And understand this, Anna O'Malley, I wouldn't want the ranch without my brother here. It is his ranch and his cattle, and any agreement we have is between him and me."

"Did you even know?"

"I knew," he said in a low voice.

She stared at him, trying to understand what he was saying. Her mind spun and stuck in a loop of confusion. Why would he not want what was his? She sorted through what she had learned.

The strongbox had contained other things: a

lock of fine hair folded in a paper with Rafael's name on it, a picture drawn by a child, a card for Mrs. Werner with Rafael's signature. But nothing from Daniel. She hadn't thought much of that at the time other than Mrs. Werner must have stopped using the strongbox and her mementos from Daniel were stored elsewhere. But she hadn't found anything else in her room or in the office.

Clearly, Rafael was the favored son. But so much so that Daniel didn't feel he could claim what was his? What kind of family stole from the rightful heir?

Daniel snatched the rest of his clothes from the floor and picked up his boots. Was he leaving her room? A minute ago he had acted as if he never wanted to leave.

"I'm sorry," she whispered.

"Yes, me, too." He grabbed the papers and walked out the door without looking at her. He paused in the doorway, his back to her. "Only a fool would marry a nosy, meddlesome fortune seeker like you, and I'm not a fool. Nor is my brother."

His words were knives slicing her open. She gasped.

What had she done? She shook all over, the room suddenly feeling like an icehouse. She'd thought he'd be hurt, maybe sad or even angry with his mother and brother, but she'd never thought he'd be angry with her.

\* \* \*

Rafael blinked open his eyes. "'Bout time you showed up."

Daniel resisted the urge to snap at his brother. It wasn't Rafael's fault Anna was a fortune seeker. Hell, he'd said she was from the beginning. Almost every Anglo who came to California was a fortune seeker. Some were willing to work for it, whereas Anna just wanted to marry it. He folded his arms across his chest.

Rafael struggled to sit up. "Heard my bride walking around the courtyard earlier."

"She's not your bride any longer," Daniel said curtly.

"Wh-what?"

"You heard me."

"She isn't going to want to marry you," Rafael snarled.

Daniel didn't respond. He'd wanted to hurt her, so he'd lashed out, but he'd regretted the words almost the minute he had said them. He wasn't certain what would happen or how he'd feel in the morning. Still, she wasn't having sex with him and then marrying his brother. That much he wouldn't tolerate. If she was that full of smarm, she didn't deserve to have either of them. And he sure as hell wasn't going to want to see her every day.

Rafael's face twisted. "What did you do?"

Daniel sighed. "She wanted to marry me."

"You told her about your father."

"No." He hadn't needed to. She'd found out on her own. "But I doubt you want my leavings."

Rafael sucked in a deep breath and his eyes glittered. "You bastard. She was mine."

"She was never yours," said Daniel.

Rafael pushed to his feet and wobbled.

Which was too bad, because Daniel would have loved to punch him for getting him in this mess.

"I can't believe you stole her from me," Rafael said.

"I told you it was a bad idea for me to spend so much time with her." Daniel's chest burned. "But if you hadn't got yourself shot, she might still be yours."

"Was that her in the office earlier poking around? I thought it was you, but Juanita said you were out all day. Did she find out how much money you're making with your fruit?"

God, how bad could it get? Had she tried to inspect their books, learn how much they made, how much he sold his fruits for?

"No. She couldn't have looked at them. I locked the ledgers in the safe." He'd done that shortly after he'd shown her around the house. The way she kept looking at them had concerned him. If only he had paid closer attention to his intuition.

And she couldn't have gotten in the safe. Only he and Rafe knew the combination, and it wasn't written down anywhere.

Now the papers she'd liberated from his mother's strongbox were secured in the safe, too.

He'd spent the past hour reading and rereading the will, the surveys, the bill of sale and the original land grant from a representative of Spain. The words had just been blurs on the page. His thoughts were much more on Anna. Her gasping, her twisting, her coming for him.

Rafael leaned his palms against the lid of a barrel and bent forward. "If you compromised her, then you have to marry her."

"Don't go all noble on me now," said Daniel. "She knew what she was doing." The knot in his gut loosened. But he wasn't going to show Rafael how deeply her money-grubbing nature hurt. "And she's tough. She can take care of herself."

Rafael rubbed his chest. "I know."

What Daniel needed to know was what she would do now. Would she stick with her scheme to marry him and try and convince him to claim the ranch? Or would she try to go back with Rafael?

"You're standing and talking better. You're going to pretend to have come home tonight. And remember when you talk to her, you couldn't possibly have had this conversation with me."

"So I get to be told twice that she doesn't want me? That will be novel." Rafael cast a wry glance his way. "Or maybe she'll change her mind when she talks to me."

"If that's going to happen, I'd rather know now." Daniel tried to make it sound like a joke, but it wasn't. "But you're still not going to marry her."

Rafael took a shaky step. "I'm not sure I can carry off being uninjured."

"Go back to your room. I'll get your stuff. You can tell her you've been up for three days straight and are exhausted. Besides, the lawyer will come tomorrow, and I'm not sneaking you around to see him."

"When I get better, we're going to have this out," said Rafael.

Was that scheming woman going to destroy his relationship with his brother? Rafe had been the only one he could count on, the only one he thought cared about him since his father had died. "You can get another bride. Only the next time you need to write your own damn letters. And tell her you're poor as a church mouse, but you're a hard worker. Maybe that way you won't get saddled with a woman who is only after the ranch."

Rafael stared at him. "So you're going to claim the entire ranch," he said tightly.

How the hell had Rafael gotten that out of what he said?

Daniel swiped up the bedding from the floor. Wouldn't hurt his brother to think that for a while. He'd show him the will tomorrow and that his father had wanted Rafael to have a hundred head of cattle or the cash equivalent and the use of a couple thousand acres of the north pasture—the Spanish land grant hadn't allowed the land to be split. No doubt if he'd lived long enough for US laws to apply, he'd have wanted Rafael to have the land permanently.

"Are you going to kick me off your land, too? Ma will be so angry."

"Damn it, Rafe. This is your home. I'm not getting rid of you." Unless he decided to marry Anna, after all.

Daniel shook off that thought. No, that scheming little hussy was not more important to him than his brother was.

Anna hadn't slept, and when she'd finally worked up the courage to go to Daniel's room, he wasn't there. She was sick with worry that she'd messed up everything, even her chance for a respectable marriage.

Daniel had let her believe he would marry her. He'd said they were together, that he wanted to make love to her again, but he hadn't actually declared himself or asked her to marry him. For all her bravado, she couldn't imagine holding a rifle on a man to get him to the altar.

A sob welled up from deep inside her, but she stuffed her fist in her mouth to keep it from escaping.

She'd known that giving herself to him before marriage was a mistake, and she'd gone in eyes wide-open. He'd even warned her it would change everything.

She managed to get herself dressed and entered the main room quietly. She waited for the looks of shame to come her way. Instead, Mrs. Werner was bustling around the table, her arms laden with platters of eggs, tortillas and thin strips of steak. Juanita set plates on the table. Five plates.

Mrs. Werner beamed at her, just as the door to the courtyard opened. "See, I tell you my Rafael will be home before the priest comes. You will be married soon."

Daniel walked through the door, and his eyes narrowed on her. She could see Rafael behind him, but she watched Daniel for an objection or a correction. He must have heard what his mother said, but he didn't say anything. Merely pressed his lips together.

A shaft of pain seared through her. She swallowed hard and lowered her gaze to her empty plate, fighting the sting in her eyes.

Rafael took his seat with a small grunt.

"Are you not glad to see your future husband?" asked Mrs. Werner.

Anna raised her gaze to Daniel and said, "Yes."

He ignored her.

Her face burned.

Juanita poured coffee into her cup.

Was he just going to pretend nothing had happened? Had he decided he didn't want her and was just going to abandon her to Rafael?

Mrs. Werner gave her an odd look.

Anna turned to Rafael. "Did you find the robbers?"

He twitched, and his hand went to his chest. "No. Tracked 'em to the border."

"And you didn't follow them across?"

He put up his hand. "Don't you worry about it."

"Don't worry about it? I've been worried— We've all been worried for days."

"He tell us later," Mrs. Werner said blithely.

Anna frowned. Mrs. Werner didn't sound as if she'd been worried, and she beamed at Rafael.

Rafael gave her a heavy-lidded smile. "Have you been worried about me, Anna?"

She wanted to scream. She opened her mouth to say she'd been worried about the robbers getting away. Daniel kicked her under the table.

She stared at him. Why hadn't he said anything? Her mouth worked, and she lowered her head.

"I'm here now, sweet. Everything will be all right." Rafael patted her hand.

She jerked her hand back into her lap and then looked him in the eye. "I thought you knew where your cousins live in Mexico."

"We don't know it was our cousins," said Rafael.

He hadn't been here. He didn't know about the drawing for the wanted poster.

"Yes, we do. Juanita identified the drawing of the shooter."

"Let's not talk about that at the table," Rafael suggested. "I'm sorry I wasn't here. I hope my brother was keeping you entertained."

*Entertained?*

The brothers exchanged a look. She looked at Daniel again, and he glared back at her.

Was that all it was to him? Bile rose in her mouth, and she shoved back from the table and raced outside to the front porch.

A few minutes later she heard the door. Her heart leaped into her throat.

She turned, and it was Rafael. For a second she was numb. Her hopes plummeted like rain from the sky. Torrents of rain, but the sun shone and it was only inside her. She'd ruined everything with Daniel. He'd meant what he'd said when he left her room last night.

"I don't think I've ever seen a more disappointed look on a woman's face," said Rafael.

"I'm sorry. I can't marry you."

"You wound me, sweetheart," he said on a low note and stepped closer. "Wouldn't you like to get to know me before deciding that?"

Her throat grew too thick inside to talk. She shook her head.

He paused a minute, then gave her a wistful look. "Not even if my brother won't?"

She had no idea what she'd do, but she couldn't

stay here if Daniel didn't love her and wouldn't marry her. She hadn't come three thousand miles to become a mistress. She'd have to go into service, if not in Stockton then in San Francisco. Ironic, she'd come all this way to escape being a maid like her mother and sisters, and she would become one anyway. She shook her head again, and moisture welled in her eyes. She tried to blink it back, but one fat tear rolled down her face.

He stepped closer. The air didn't charge the way it did when Daniel stepped close. "Hey."

She swiped at her cheek.

"So you went and fell in love with my brother," Rafael said.

She nodded.

"I'm not used to losing to him. Don't know that I like it." He rubbed her shoulder. "Sure you don't want to marry me?"

"Mr. Werner, I can't."

He put his hand on her other shoulder. "You know, I didn't really expect you to come to me pure."

Her face burned, and her body vibrated with shock. Daniel must have wasted no time in boasting to his brother. "Do you know what…?" She couldn't finish the question.

He gave her an easy smile. "Figured there must be a reason a pretty girl like you with a rich father couldn't get a decent fellow back in Connecticut."

"Oh, no!" Her lies, and he'd assumed she wasn't

an innocent. Right now she was too hurt to be angry, but she was going to have to read him the riot act later… Except there wouldn't be a later. "I have to go. I'll get work."

"You're trembling." He pulled her into a hug. "It's all right, sweetheart."

It wasn't all right. It would never be all right.

Sobs she'd kept down for hours bubbled like a pot of water in a rolling boil. Rafael's arms slid around her shoulders, and he eased her against him. She bounced her fist on his chest and he grunted.

He moved her hands up to his shoulders and then rocked her, murmuring soothing words and promises for his brother that she knew Daniel had no intention of keeping.

# Chapter Twenty

*So many of the men around here are going off to fight. They look so smart in their blue uniforms, but just the other day we received news of a neighbor who fell in battle.*

Daniel stood at the window, watching his brother charm Anna. A sick burn in his gut ate at his insides. In no time at all, Rafael had Anna in an embrace. He looked over Anna's head to the window as if to say, *What the hell?*

No female had ever preferred him over his brother. Not his mother, not Juanita, not the former maid's daughter and certainly not Anna. He'd known he'd lose her the minute Rafe talked to her, really talked to her.

He had seen enough. He wheeled on his heel and went through the house and out the back. He didn't stop walking until he was in his vineyard. Hell, he had grapes to pick.

Except he found himself flinging clusters of

grapes into the crates, which was no way to treat the fruit.

He dropped to the ground and put his head in his hands. Hell, his brother always won, so he didn't even fight. He'd learned to joke and laugh at the irony. And there was no bigger irony than he should own the ranch, but his illegitimate half brother was going to end up with the girl he loved, with the ranch, with everything. He didn't feel like laughing.

The idea of Rafael having her burned like acid.

He grabbed at the nearest grapevine and ripped the thing from the soil. He could wrangle the cattle, too. Hell, he did it all the time. He could rope and brand and geld as well as his brother; he just preferred the fruit. He wanted both for the ranch, cattle and produce.

And could he really be mad at Anna for trying to better her lot through marriage? It wasn't as if she could go pan for gold or go digging for oil. That was man's work. A woman's only option to improve her station was to marry. So should he blame her?

She had looked stricken at the breakfast table. And she hadn't been looking at his brother as if she wanted to be with him. Nor did she seem adverse to hard work. In fact, she seemed impatient with the lack of it.

No, he could decide what would happen with

the ranch, and if he had to claim it to get her, he would. Rafael would just have to deal with it.

He picked himself up, dusted himself off and headed back to the house. He'd tell Rafael to go to hell and claim Anna as his bride.

The buggy in front of the house let him know the lawyer had arrived. His boots hit the porch, and the front door swung open. A hope that for once someone was waiting on him, that Anna was waiting for him grew in his acid-eaten heart.

Madre stomped out. Her face was red, and she shook a finger at him. "Where have you been?"

"This is the first time you've ever been waiting for me to come home, Ma." Disappointment pulled him down.

She lapsed into Spanish and vitriol exploded out of her mouth. How could he have ruined his brother's life, how could he have stolen his brother's bride, how could he have let her shoot him and how could he be so ungrateful?

"Stop it. Stop talking!"

"Do not speak to me this way, Daniel Werner."

"Or what, Ma?" He walked past her into the empty main room. "You'll lie to me some more about my father? You will not speak to me like this any longer, or you will not have a home with me."

She sputtered, and he ignored her. He would have to deal with her and all the lies she'd perpetuated for years, but he'd address that later. Right now, he just wanted to straighten things out with

Anna. "I'm going to marry Miss O'Malley, and you're not going to stop me. Rafael isn't going to stop me. Where is she?"

Madre grabbed his arm and started pleading. "You have to let Rafael marry her so she cannot testify against him."

"No, Ma. She doesn't know anyway." Unless something had changed. "Where is Rafael?"

"He take the lawyer to the office."

Daniel shook loose of his mother and walked into the courtyard. Anna wasn't making her usual rounds of the perimeter. Was she with Rafael?

He stopped at her door and knocked.

"Yes."

Her voice seemed thin. But he didn't wait for permission to push open the door.

She was kneeling in front of her trunk, placing her brush and comb in the tray. She cast a glance over her shoulder, then quickly averted her face.

So much for a warm welcome. He wiped his damp palms on his trousers and launched into what he'd come to say. "You're not marrying my brother." His chest tightened as he waited for her response. "I won't let you."

"No. I'm not."

He let out the breath he was holding. "Good answer."

He moved closer to her.

Her room was as neat as a pin, unlike the wild place it had been last night. Her bed was made.

The picture of her and her two friends was no longer on the bedside table. None of her clothes hung from the hooks, and her hat was on top of her valise, which was on the floor beside the trunk.

"The lawyer said he would drive me into town after he and your brother conclude their business." Her voice wavered, but she wouldn't look at him. "Your brother agreed to loan me some money until I find work."

She was leaving? Yes, of course she was. He hadn't let her think she had any choice. "Anna."

"Mr. Werner, I find this difficult enough."

"Won't you look at me?" he asked gently, but his heart was beating madly. If she left, he'd never convince her to come back. Once she was in Stockton, she'd realize there were dozens of men who'd marry her in a heartbeat. What chance would he have then?

She shook her head.

"You're not leaving." She couldn't discount what happened last night—before he'd lost his mind.

"Yes, I am. There is no reason for me to stay."

Rafe had made getting her in his arms look so easy, but Daniel was like a just-born colt, wobbly and uncertain, trying desperately to get his feet underneath him. "Not even if I want you to stay?"

"No."

The dinner bell rang, jangling his every last nerve. *Not now.*

Why wouldn't she look at him? How was he supposed to propose when she wouldn't turn around? Her incessant questions were conspicuously absent.

"Not even if I grow potatoes for you?" Apparently, he was the one with questions.

She didn't answer. Perhaps she cared enough about potatoes to stay. Yes, brilliant proposal, most men offered rings or flowers, and he offered potatoes. But if it worked, he wasn't going to knock it. He took a step toward her.

"It's time for dinner." She darted toward the door.

He caught her around the waist and hauled her back against him.

"Don't," she warned in a low voice. Her body was tense. And she shoved at his arm.

"Should I write you a letter then? Or just tell you I am a fool?"

"I don't like you very much right now, Mr. Werner. And do you intend to make us late for the table?"

That was his Anna. He opened his mouth to declare himself and propose. Only this wasn't the way it was supposed to be done, holding her so she couldn't escape and her refusing to look at him.

The heavy tread of two men walking stopped him. If his proposal was to be this awkward, he'd rather not have witnesses. He spun her so he was between the door and her; then he backed slowly until he could shut the door.

"We need to talk." He loosened his hold.

"We're done talking. You're a cruel beast." She stepped away, wiped at her face, then turned around.

Her eyelashes were spiky with moisture, and her nose was red. His heart flipped over.

"Okay, I need to talk, you need to listen and then we need to kiss." Assuming she said yes. Of course she'd say yes. She'd come out here to marry the ranch owner, and if that was what it took, he'd tell her he'd get the ranch in his name. He wasn't stopping until she said yes.

"I hate you," she said.

"I love you," he countered.

She jerked away as if he'd slapped her.

"Not the reaction I wanted."

She sat on the bed. "Why didn't you say that last night? And what does it mean anyway?"

He crossed the room and took her hands. "Anna, it means I love you." He lowered himself to one knee. "I want you to be my wife."

Her lower lip trembled, and she looked away. She wasn't going to cry more, was she? He kissed her hands. "I thought that you'd want to hear it when I asked you to marry me. Men say things they don't mean when they're…"

She pinned him with her green gaze and arched an eyebrow. "Have you?"

"No. Of course not!" *Madre de Dios*, this conversation was not going as it was supposed to.

A knock on the door made him wince.

"Miss O'Malley, you come," called Juanita. "Senora Werner do not serve food until you are arrived."

"We have to go." She rose and made for the door until he tugged on the hands he still held, jerking her back and making her stoop a little.

"Are you going to give me an answer? I just proposed to you."

"I don't believe you asked me. You just told me I'm going to marry you."

"Oh, for Pete's sake, Anna. Please, marry me. If you want to take your time before saying yes, then fine. You can tell me yes after we eat if you must." He knew he was making a hash out of it, but between Juanita knocking and her crying, he didn't know how to rope this beast and get it under control.

Juanita knocked again. "Senorita."

He marched over to the door and flung it open, intending to say, "We'll be there in a minute." But Anna slipped around him and, short of grabbing her and pulling her back in front of Juanita, he had no choice but to follow her.

Anna tucked her lips around her teeth, holding back her smile. Of course she'd say yes, but Daniel owed her an apology. He'd ripped her heart out last night; he deserved a dose of the anxiety he'd put her through.

And she really didn't think it was fair of him to trap her into listening to his blundering effort at asking her to marry him.

Although, there was something endearing about his not being smooth at it. She'd wanted to brush his hair back and kiss his forehead.

She'd been half-afraid when he closed the door that he intended a repeat of last night's events and was half-disappointed when he didn't.

Daniel grabbed the door she'd opened and held it for her. Juanita slipped back into the kitchen.

The mood that hovered in the main room was like being smacked. Mrs. Werner's glare hit her like a wall. This for being just a few minutes late? She hadn't found the family to be that punctual before.

"I go get the food now," said Mrs. Werner. "You sit."

Rafael was already at the head of the table, but his eyes had a faraway flat look to them, and the corners of his mouth pulled down. He'd been kind to her earlier, and her anger at his abandonment when she first arrived had become just disappointment. On his right one chair away sat the lawyer. Anna took the seat between them, just so she would not be next to Daniel.

"Have you finished packing, Miss O'Malley?" said the lawyer. "Mr. Werner and I have concluded our business, and I will return to town as soon as I've eaten."

"She's not leaving," Daniel said. He stood by the door, his arms folded.

"My bags are packed and ready."

Daniel looked at her, looked at his brother and then crossed the room. He pulled out the chair opposite hers, and it kept going back until it was five feet from the table. He moved behind his brother's chair and picked it up by the seat and put him down in the vacated spot. He placed the chair he'd pulled away at the head of the table and sat in it, putting him right at her side.

Her heart kicked up a notch.

"I may need to discuss business with you also, sir." Ignoring her, Daniel spoke to the lawyer.

"You could have asked me to move," gritted out Rafael.

"I would have if I thought you would," Daniel said calmly.

His face darkening, Rafael half rose out of his chair. "Damn you."

"Don't I recall you making a fuss about unpleasantness not appropriate at the table just at breakfast?" asked Daniel. His words were pleasant, but the look he leveled at his brother was steely.

"When I'm..." Rafael's voice trailed off, and he sat back down hard. Collapsed really. *Odd*.

"That's what I thought," said Daniel.

Juanita came through the door with several steaming bowls on a tray with Mrs. Werner behind her with a plate of cornbread.

Juanita set bowls down in front of people, but she bypassed Anna.

Mrs. Werner frowned at Juanita. "Give Miss O'Malley her stew," she said.

Juanita returned to Anna's side and lifted a steaming bowl from her tray. The girl trembled, causing the brown surface in the bowl to ripple. She set it on the edge of the table, and Anna reached to push it back.

Juanita slammed her hand down on the edge of the bowl, flipping it and the contents into Anna's lap.

Mrs. Werner shrieked.

"Damn!" Anna jerked back and stood.

The bowl clattered to the floor; the brown stew dripped down her skirt, leaving a big blotch where her lap had been.

Daniel jerked out of his chair, sending it toppling backward. "Are you all right?"

Next to Anna's chair, Juanita trembled. The hot stew dripped off her hand. Something was very wrong with the girl.

And she'd thought that she and Juanita

were getting along. "Did you burn yourself?" asked Anna.

Mrs. Werner jerked Juanita around and slapped her.

Anna threw her arm across the girl's chest and angled herself between Juanita and Mrs. Werner. "Stop it."

She stopped short of saying it was an accident. Very clearly, it hadn't been, but something was wrong.

Juanita started speaking slowly and then faster and faster, but it was all in Spanish.

Daniel half rose out of his chair, his face going pale.

Rafael buried his face in his hands.

The lawyer gaped. "What is she saying?" Anna asked.

Juanita gripped Anna's waist, pulling her back and undoubtedly causing more stains. She pointed at Mrs. Werner. "She say give this bowl to the señorita, it have no chiles, but she dish from same pot. I see her hide the powder in her pocket when she think I look not. When we go to town she buy the powder for the rats. I say we have no rats. She buy anyway. She poison you."

Alarm knifed through Anna.

Mrs. Werner screamed at Juanita, "You are lying, little *puta*."

But as ice water poured through Anna's veins, she didn't think Juanita was lying at all.

# Chapter Twenty-One

*Included in this letter are all the details of your travel. I am awaiting your arrival with great anticipation.*

All Daniel could think was that he'd nearly lost Anna, and she'd never marry him now. His heart was in his throat at how close she'd come to eating the stew. But he had to get control of this situation. He put his hands on his mother's shoulders. "Madre, you need to sit down."

Mrs. Werner shrugged him off, but Rafael caught her arm and led her to his chair. For now she was letting him, but Daniel didn't trust her cooperation. He needed to get Anna out of his mother's sight.

"Why would she try to poison me?" demanded Anna. Her eyes were wide.

"I not poison you, *pssh*," Mrs. Werner said. "Juanita is *loco* girl."

"Don't touch that bowl," said the lawyer.

"There are tests that can be done on what is left in there to see if it is poisoned."

"Maybe Juanita jealous and she try to fix the blame on me. Why would I poison my Rafael's bride?" said the older woman.

Anna seemed transfixed by Mrs. Werner. Then she swung her gaze away from his mother and onto him. "Is it because I found the land deed and your father's will?"

Mrs. Werner shot out of the chair and had one knee on the table. Rafael grabbed her and yanked her down. Then he clasped his chest and coughed.

She began spewing in Spanish about Anna ruining everything.

"Shut up," said Rafael.

Daniel pressed down on his mother's shoulders, holding her in the chair. "Juanita, get Anna to her room and help her get cleaned up."

"No," said Anna.

"Please, baby, you agitate her."

"I *agitate* her?" Anna turned fierce and shoved away from Juanita.

The girl looked helpless as she tried to catch Anna again.

"Miss O'Malley, she just tried to kill you. Would you go barricade yourself in your room with that rifle you have until we get her arrested?" said Rafael.

"You want her shoot another one of us. Maybe she shoot us all." Mrs. Werner twisted and thrashed.

Rafael collapsed into a chair, looking wan. He covered his nose and mouth with his hand.

Anna stared at him, her own mouth falling open. Then she looked at Daniel, her eyes huge in her white face. Even her lips seemed to bleed of color. She put her hand up in the air sideways, like an artist might to block out what he didn't want to see.

He didn't look away, but he knew she'd finally recognized him from the robbery. Daniel's heart sank to the floor.

"It was you. And you." She took another step backward as her expression crumpled. "Not your damn cousins."

"Anna."

She backed to the door and, with her hand behind her, wrenched it open. "You lied to me. Everything you've ever said has been a lie."

"Not everything."

Then she turned and ran out the front, taking his heart and soul with her.

"Good riddance," said Mrs. Werner.

He turned, ready to rip her limb from limb. She was about as good a mother as a fish that fed on its own babies.

Rafael stepped between them, looking exhausted. "Juanita, go get a rope from the storeroom." He patted Daniel's shoulder and then turned toward the lawyer. "Would you fetch the sheriff for us?"

"As a witness to the crime, I can't be her lawyer."

Juanita skidded back into the room with a long coil of rope.

Mrs. Werner tried to get out of the chair, but Rafael held her down while Juanita looped the rope around the older woman and the chair.

Mrs. Werner screamed and rocked the chair.

"She's gone too far this time, Rafe," Daniel told him as a slow rage built in him.

Rafael shook his head. "No, she went too far when she poisoned your father. This time she just got caught."

Daniel's ears rung as he shook all over.

"I'll handle this, Daniel," said Rafe. "Like I should have years ago. You just go get your bride."

Anna stumbled through the grass, tears making it hard for her to pick out her path. Oh, God, she'd fallen in love with a stagecoach robber.

He'd deceived her, made her feel bad for lying in her letters, all the while they'd been the banditos. She'd known they were hiding something. Now all the pieces seemed to slide seamlessly into place, and she wondered that she hadn't realized sooner.

But she'd believed Daniel. A new wash of pain flowed through her.

Rafael was the man she'd shot, and Daniel had been the one who lassoed the outrider.

They must have been concealing Rafael while he healed. In fact, the first time she'd talked to him, he'd seemed weak, breathless. She'd thought him drunk, but it must have been the injury. Then next time he hadn't been much better. The extra bowl for lunch must have been his that one day. She'd known. She just never found the proof, and then Daniel's story about the cousins had seemed so plausible.

But she'd had so many clues. The way Rafael had smelled like blood, the locked door to his room...

"Anna!"

Daniel's voice went through her and made her shudder. She picked up her skirts and ran faster.

"Anna, wait." His voice was closer.

She looked over her shoulder. He was only a couple hundred feet behind her and closing fast.

"You can't outrun me to Stockton."

Was she headed toward Stockton? She hadn't thought beyond getting out of that madhouse. "Go away."

"Anna, please."

Her side knit with a stabbing pain. She pressed against it and ran a few paces before she dropped to a walk.

"I need to talk to you," Daniel said.

"Leave. Me. Alone."

He settled into a walk beside her. For a few minutes they just went along in silence, until she felt stupid. "What?"

"Stockton is that way," he said, pointing.

"I don't believe you. You'd lie sooner than you'd tell the truth." She didn't look in his direction, but he seemed to fill all corners of her vision.

His dark hair caught the sun in flashes of blue. His long legs shortened their stride to match hers. His long-fingered hands curled and unfurled as if he wanted to grab her but wouldn't.

"When you hit the San Joaquin River, you'll need to follow it north to hit town."

"Fine, you can go back now. I'm sure I'll find it eventually."

"Anna, I'm sorry. I never wanted to lie to you."

She didn't answer. His apology was too little, too late.

They continued along stride for stride.

"Don't you want to know why?" he asked.

"It doesn't matter," she said.

Three steps later, he started explaining anyway. "Rafael stole my gun out of my scabbard. I was following him to get him to give it back when he said he just wanted to see you. I wasn't going to be part of stopping the stage, but when the outrider shot at him, I had to do something. He's my brother. I couldn't just let him be gunned down. No matter how much he deserved it."

So that was why Rafael had been looking at her so peculiarly.

"If I had known what he was going to do, I would have lassoed him and hog-tied him."

She didn't want an explanation to soften her anger. "You lied to me again and again."

"What was I supposed to do, Anna? He's my brother, and I didn't want to see him hanged for a robbery that wasn't really a robbery. And because he shot back when they shot at him."

The outrider *had* shot first. Anna continued walking. She didn't want to soften toward Daniel. She wasn't ready to forgive his deceiving her. "Don't you have some grapes to pick?"

"I don't care if they rot—just please come back with me. It wasn't a lie when I said I loved you. It wasn't a lie when I said I wanted to marry you."

"Oh, sure, and then your mother kills me and you don't have to mean it anymore."

He gasped and stopped walking.

He had warned her his mother was *loco*. But she shouldn't have said what she said. He seemed genuine in what he felt about her.

Anna continued on. When she'd gone ten feet and he hadn't resumed his place by her side, she turned and looked at him. He looked as bleak as a man could look. He'd folded his arms and just watched her.

A sliver of heat cut through the cold, bottomless well of pain she seemed to be trapped in. She remembered his hands on her body, his mouth on her lips, their legs twined together.

She didn't want to think about that now. She turned around and resumed walking. The rolling valley stretched out in front of her, miles and miles of empty grassland. She had nowhere in particular to go. Her pace slowed until she just trudged forward.

Did he mean to let her go so easily?

Then his footfalls were right behind her. "Anna, I'm tired of trying to persuade you to stay." He swept her up in his arms and turned around. "You're coming back to the house with me. You'll need to be there when the sheriff comes. Then, if you really don't want to stay, you can leave with him."

His jaw jutted forward as he strode back the way they'd walked.

"You're going to get tired of carrying me."

"I'll never get tired of carrying you." He walked a few steps and said, "Answering your incessant questions, maybe, but holding you close—never." He pulled her tighter against his chest.

"I wouldn't have had to ask so many questions if you hadn't been lying to me." She put her arms around his neck, because folding them in front of her seemed rather silly.

"Well, it is damn hard work lying to you, so I prefer to avoid it in the future."

"You can put me down. I can walk."

"Wasn't a doubt in my mind that you *could* walk," he said and continued on. "But I'm not of a mind to let go of you, and you have not always been Miss Honesty yourself. You might mean to trick me into letting you down and then running off."

"You said yourself I can't outrun you."

"Yes, but I'd rather not spend all afternoon chasing you." He stopped and shifted her. He looked down into her eyes. "I'd much rather kiss you."

She shook her head. "I haven't forgiven you."

His eyes narrowed. "I do think your freckles are darker all of a sudden."

She put her hands over her nose. She hadn't worn her hat. Likely her freckles had popped and her fair skin was burning.

"Perhaps I should stop and kiss them," he said with a lowering of his lashes.

"Don't you dare," she said.

He sighed and resumed walking.

They continued along for a while. They surely were at least a mile from the house. Daniel's breathing deepened, but he walked steadily without showing any signs of growing weary.

All right, she was curious about some things. "Last night when you said you wanted me from the first moment you saw me, were you talking about when you were holding up the stage?"

"Yes. When I first saw you and the sun lit up

your hair, I had a hard time looking away," he said. "You were the only one who saw me. The only one who turned around to look."

She sensed there was more to what he was saying, that he was always in his brother's shadow. Her heart broke for him with the way his mother had treated him, obviously putting Rafael first in all things, even stealing his inheritance from him and giving it to his brother.

"How long have you known about your father's will?"

He smiled ruefully. "I didn't know about it until you showed me. I knew the ownership of the ranch was not what I'd been told for years, but only since yesterday morning." His eyes narrowed, and his jaw tightened. "Ma always told us the ranch was hers. We believed her."

"But your father bought it before he married her."

"In hindsight, I'm fairly certain the only reason she married my father was because he owned the ranch," Daniel said tightly. "She hated him, but he was a good man."

"I don't doubt it." He got his strength of character from someplace.

Daniel's lips flattened. "Rafe didn't know everything, either, but he learned things weren't as they should be when he went to court. He's been trying to get himself killed since then so he could set things right."

All right, so Daniel had been caught between a rock and a hard place. It didn't mean she had to forgive him for all the deceiving he'd done.

"I know with a crazy mother and the ranch ownership in question, I'm not a great catch, but, Anna, I love you, even though I didn't want to fall in love with you. Please, marry me."

"All right, I'll marry you, but I'm still mad at you."

He smiled and spun around in a circle. "Try to forgive me before the priest is scheduled to come."

After a bit of time, he sobered. "I know it will be hard for the next few months. I don't know how this will work out with that woman, but if I have my say, she'll go to prison for trying to kill you." He closed his eyes for a second and swallowed. "It could get mighty uncomfortable."

"What aren't you telling me?" she demanded.

"Rafe thinks she killed my father."

"My God. I really don't like your brother."

"Don't blame him. He wasn't that old when my father died, and he must have been terrified of her." Daniel frowned. "Rafe was consulting with the lawyer to figure out what he should do about the holdup. I don't know how my role will be viewed, either."

"Really don't like him," she repeated.

Daniel tilted his head. "For not liking him, you looked mighty comfortable with him earlier."

"It wasn't the same. I don't look at him and

wonder what it would be like if he kissed me. My heart doesn't beat faster when he catches my eye. I don't miss him when he's not around. He's not you, and I love you, Daniel Werner. Only you. When you drove up to the stage office in Stockton, you seemed familiar to me, as if I'd known you all my life."

"You probably recognized me from the holdup."

She shook her head. "I don't think so. I think my heart recognized you were the one I was meant to be with."

His mouth twitched.

"What?" she demanded.

"You don't want to know."

She scowled at him, disappointment that he wouldn't share what he was thinking soured her pleasure. He probably thought her silly for her thoughts.

He sighed. "Oh, Anna, I felt it, too, but my interpretation of what was happening was much more base. I wanted you with your hair down and nothing else covering you."

Her face heated.

"Which was not a good way to be thinking about my future sister-in-law. But whatever it was, I'm certain we are supposed to be together." Then he kissed her.

# *Epilogue*

*By order of the General Land Office, the patent for the land known as the Werner Ranch, formerly the land grant issued by Spain to one Pedro Martinez, inherited by his son, José Martinez, and sold to August Werner, is confirmed in the name of the sole and lawful heir, Daniel Werner.*

*Sacramento, California, mid-July 1863*

Daniel's heart pounded as Rafael was led into the courtroom. His brother looked thinner than he should, and Daniel felt traitorous that he wasn't standing beside him with his own complicity in the stagecoach holdup.

But as Anna was the only one who'd seen him and she'd declined to testify against him, the prosecutor had decided it wasn't worthwhile to charge him. Besides, his worst act—lassoing the out-rider—had been to prevent the man from shooting his brother. A jury was unlikely to convict him on that act alone.

"How do you plead?" asked the judge.

Daniel knew what was coming, but he couldn't help but tense.

Anna slipped her hand into Daniel's, and the gesture helped ease his nervousness.

His lawyer beside him, Rafael spoke firmly, "Guilty, Your Honor."

The judge's face was impassive as he pronounced, "I hereby sentence you to fifteen years."

Daniel gasped and started to stand. Horror ran through him in cold rivulets. "That's not—"

"Shh! Wait." Anna jerked him back down to the hard wooden pew, then patted his arm. Hard to believe she was the one counseling patience. He almost laughed at the idea he'd tempered her quicksilver nature.

But this sentence wasn't what they'd agreed upon. All the discussions with the lawyers, the statements taken from all the shot men saying they bore the robber no malice and had not suffered any lasting injuries weren't supposed to end like this. He'd been working like a fiend to see that Rafael wasn't locked up forever, because he hadn't trusted Rafe to make the best decisions for himself.

The judge continued, "The sentence to be deferred on condition that you serve in the United

States Army for the next five years. This condition is acceptable to you, Mr. Werner?"

Anna wiggled her fingers, letting Daniel know he was practically breaking them he was squeezing so hard.

"Sorry." He eased his grip but didn't let go.

He didn't know what he would have done without her the past year. She'd been by his side as the false will was exposed and his father's real will was authenticated and the ranch was granted to him. It was determined that his mother had traced most of the will and had just flipped her two sons' names in order to give Rafael the ranch.

Daniel didn't mind learning his mother had been nothing more than a housemaid for the Martinez family, one who'd tried to trap José Martinez into marriage by getting pregnant with Rafael, but he'd minded very much when he learned that she'd lied to him all his life about owning the ranch herself. Worse yet, she'd killed his father, terrified Rafael and tried to poison Anna. He could never forgive his mother for that.

Rafael moved to sign enlistment papers with a recruitment officer who would take him back east to serve.

What if this was the wrong decision for Rafael? After all, if he was still trying to get himself killed, letting him join the army to fight in the war dividing the country may have been the worst thing.

"Will he get himself killed, do you think?" whispered Daniel.

"No, and the war can't go on much longer." Anna leaned into him to reassure him. The news had reached them of one of the bloodiest battles of the war at Gettysburg, but it was one that might have turned the tide. "Let's go get your brother. I'd like to be home before dark."

She popped up and darted forward. For a second he just watched his wife move. She never liked to be still long, except perhaps in the moments following making love when she could chase the world away with a kiss and a smile.

He hadn't exactly been prepared to run the ranch without Rafael's help, but Anna had written to her family and enlisted their help. Her brothers Patrick and Sean were running the ranch in their absence. Her sister Elizabeth was watching their baby boy. More family members were on their way, and her good friend Olivia and her husband, Jack, had stayed with them most of the summer. Jack had been an immense help as he learned as much as he could about ranching.

They would be leaving soon and taking the hundred head of cattle they'd bought from him, driving them back to Colorado before the weather turned.

Anna stretched up on her tiptoes, whispering in Rafael's ear as she hugged him. At one time he would have feared that he'd lose her to Rafael, but he knew that in spite of her efforts to bring Rafael home-cooked food at least once a month that she never looked at his brother that way. The special glow in her eyes was reserved for him and was what he looked forward to every evening when he returned home after working with the cattle or with his crops.

Her love had never ceased to amaze him. The fear of disappointing her made him work that much harder, even when he'd thought there was no way he could manage it all. He loved her so much more than he had a year ago, and he'd loved her enough then that he would have done anything to keep her.

Rafael frowned at Anna, then cast an uncertain look past her. Daniel shook hands with the prosecutor and Rafael's lawyer before joining them.

"You must come," Anna said. "Don't you wish to see your nephew before you go? And we have a fiesta planned." She turned to the man in the blue uniform. "You must come, too."

Daniel wasn't certain that a fiesta when Rafael was released was in good taste. But it was a celebration that could encompass many events—the christening of their son, sending Olivia and Jack Trudeau off with a fond memory and welcoming Anna's friend Selina back from her long trip. He hadn't dared ask if John Bench would be there, too. He had enough troubles of his own without delving too deeply into the tribulations of Anna's friends.

Rafael shook his head. He seemed far too subdued, as if the year in prison awaiting trial had taken something out of him.

Anna smiled at the officer and set to work persuading him that a trip to Werner Ranch wasn't out of his way. The young man didn't have a chance of resisting. When Anna was determined, not much could stop her.

"Was this your idea?" Rafael asked.

Daniel shook his head. "Not just mine. Anna wants you to know there are no hard feelings."

"It's not my home any longer." Rafael's head dipped. "And I need to report for duty."

Daniel's throat tightened.

"Nonsense. The ranch will always be your home, too." Anna came up beside Daniel and threaded her arm in his as if she'd known he needed her. "And when you are ready, we'll figure out which part of the ranch land is to be yours. That is what Daniel's father wanted. That is what we want. You're family."

Rafael's eyes flickered, but there was more to that statement than he knew or could possibly understand.

Daniel had never known what a real family was like. Anna was teaching him what it was to have the unconditional love of family by sharing her family with him. He and Rafael had always been a unit, but until the O'Malleys started showing up, he'd never known what it was like to have family to count on, family to laugh with, sing with and work with. They were people who were happy to see him when he came in at night and never made him feel as if they wished he wasn't there. They trusted his judgment and consulted him, which still felt a little awkward.

Daniel reached out and caught his brother's arm. "Come home with us. Juanita would like to see you. And God knows how much I've missed you. I know you can't stay, but at least come for a night."

"Have you heard from Madre?" Rafael asked in a whisper, as if he couldn't help himself.

Daniel shook his head. "I know she made it to relatives in Mexico, but she didn't stay there. They think she might have gone to Bolivia."

At first, he'd been angry that she'd escaped justice when she took off, but then he'd just been glad none of them had to testify against her. The farther away Madre went, the better he felt.

Anna pressed against his side. "I won't take no for an answer." She nodded toward the recruitment officer. "And your commanding officer has agreed to come, too."

Rafael glanced over his shoulder at the uniformed man.

"Private Werner, come with me to retrieve your

things," the officer said. "We can meet your family outside."

"Think I've just received my first order," said Rafael.

"Step lively, then. We'll see you in a bit," Daniel said. He led Anna through the doors and out of the courthouse.

"I will be glad to sleep tonight in our own bed," Anna said.

Her words conjured wicked images of her naked, tangled in the sheets, her fiery hair spilling across the pillow, even though she probably hadn't meant it that way. Still, he sucked in a deep breath.

Her eyelids flickered lower over her green eyes, and her pink lips curled at the edges. "That, too. But I'm afraid the party may last well into the night."

"We could sneak away for an hour or two."

She shook her head. "No, you should spend as much time with Rafael as you can. Who knows when we will see him again?"

"What did you say to him?" Certainly whatever she'd said had startled Rafael and made him frown.

Her head tilted to the side, and she reached up a finger to his nose. "I'd rather not say."

He could press her, and she would tell him. They had agreed to be totally honest with each other. But he trusted her. He caught her hand and pressed a kiss to her fingers. "Very well, love."

Lowering her hand, he tucked it back into the crook of his arm. "Jack will likely want to ask Rafe ranching questions while he can."

"I doubt there is anything he could ask that you have not already told him."

Daniel snorted. "I don't know how I'm going to manage the next five years without him. He is the best rancher I know."

"Oh, I doubt that," said Anna. "I can certainly think of another of equal or higher caliber."

Daniel frowned and cast through her opinions of other ranchers they knew. "Who?"

She cuffed him on the shoulder. "*You.* Can you not see how the vaqueros look up to you, other ranchers consult *you* and the ranch has not suffered in Rafael's absence?" She pulled out her gloves from her reticule and drew them on. "You and I are too much alike in that we don't see our own value. When I came here, I thought no one would love me if I allowed them to see the real me, but you disliked the person I pretended to be in my letters and it was as if I could never hide who I really was from you."

"And I loved you anyway." He smiled. "I am damn lucky to have you, Anna Werner. I can't image how I would have made it through the past year without you believing in me."

"Believing, is it? I should not trust what I see, should I?"

"Well, I have to make the ranch work, because that is why you married me," he teased.

She grew pensive instead of responding with laughter. "I would have married you even if you only had a single grape seed to your name, because you would make it work. You are stronger than you know, Daniel."

"And you are more beautiful than you know. Both inside and out." What woman would turn her good fortune into a way to collect and mend her scattered family the way she had? What woman would insist her convicted brother-in-law come home? What woman would marry a man whose mother had tried to kill her? Or, for that matter, defend a group of passengers against a man she thought was intent on murder? "And fierce. In a good way."

Her skin pinked, and she looked past him. "I'm serious."

"So am I." She'd talked about him being strong before. Strong enough to weather losing his father at such a young age, strong enough to work like a man twice his age when he was twelve and thirteen, the way Rafael had had to take on the ranch at that age, and strong enough to live with a lunatic mother who made no secret of her preference for her other son for all those years. Although in the end, perhaps Mrs. Werner's desertion was harder on Rafe.

Maybe it was time they both started believing in themselves. "With you by my side, Anna, my love, I can do anything."

She blinked at him, and her faith in him showed in her clear green eyes. "And here I was thinking I had too many freckles."

He swallowed hard at the sudden rush of heat that swept through his veins. No one passing would have any inkling what she meant, but he knew. They had both invented freckles for him to kiss. "You do love me, then."

"I do." Then her lips spread into a wide grin.

\* \* \* \* \*

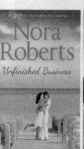 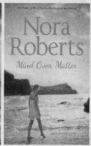 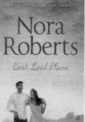 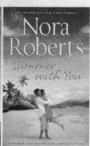

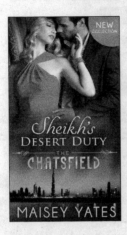

# MILLS & BOON®

## & HISTORICAL

**AWAKEN THE ROMANCE OF THE PAST**

---

## A sneak peek at next month's titles...

### In stores from 1st May 2015:

- **A Lady for Lord Randall** – Sarah Mallory
- **The Husband Season** – Mary Nichols
- **The Rake to Reveal Her** – Julia Justiss
- **A Dance with Danger** – Jeannie Lin
- **Lucy Lane and the Lieutenant** – Helen Dickson
- **A Fortune for the Outlaw's Daughter** – Lauri Robinson

---

Available at WHSmith, Tesco, Asda, Eason, Amazon and Apple

*Just can't wait?*
Buy our books online a month before they hit the shops!
**visit www.millsandboon.co.uk**

**These books are also available in eBook format!**